Irena Karafilly's epic novel interweaves the life of the remarkable Calliope Adham with the events that besiege a village on the Greek island of Lesbos over more than 30 years. Enthralling. — *Herald Sun Melbourne*

Historically interesting, wistfully haunting, and emotively powerful. — *West Australian*

The Captive Sun is a tapestry that is lavish without being grandiose, haunting without being repetitive, and meticulous without being convoluted ... a highly accomplished, thoroughly researched, and compelling read. — *Neos Kosmos*

The Captive Sun has so much to recommend it. The research is impressive, the writing masterful, the plot line intricate and challenging; what Karafilly has delivered is a brilliant character-driven work. It's one of the best novels I've read this year ... I loved this book. — *Write Note Reviews*

This fascinating story about one woman's struggle against social and political tyranny evokes great empathy with the Greek people. Enthralling. — *Weekend Gold Coast Bulletin* and *Townsville Bulletin*

Irena Karafilly has captured the sun against a whitewashed wall, the confusion of love, the healing power of time, while educating us on the price Greece has had to pay. — *Sunday Canberra Times*

This is not only a richly human report of the devastation of Alzheimer's—hideous, poignant and ruefully funny; it is also an acknowledgement of how tangled and endlessly changing our memories of family turn out to be, long, long before the compromises of senility set in.
—ROSELLEN BROWN

* * *

Ashes and Miracles is a brilliant, beautifully written, deeply moving book. —JOSEF SKVORECKY

Ashes and Miracles is a sparkling and profound portrait of 1990s Poland. It is all here—the weariness, the hopes, the paradoxes, the layers of hatred and suffering, the unavoidable glare of history—all the elements struggling for harmony in a post-Communist world. Karafilly has a sharp eye and has used her considerable research with imagination. —PHILIP MARSDEN

... part memoir, part history, part social commentary ... *Ashes and Miracles* is a truly remarkable achievement.
—ROBERT WEAVER, CBC

Karafilly's Poland is a fascinating, unexpected place. She brings to her journey a passionate engagement, a keen eye, and a commitment to letting the people she meets come wonderfully alive. —CHARLES FORAN

Ashes and Miracles is an engaging and reflective journey; a moving personal quest and a deft untangling of a country's historical and ethnic skeins. —RONALD WRIGHT

Ashes and Miracles is a splendid book. I particularly admired the way the author's descriptions of her encounters with Poles in many walks of life were seamlessly blended with glimpses of Poland's troubled history and vivid depictions of cities and countryside. It's all done with great elegance. —WILLIAM WEINTRAUB

Combining elements of both travelogue and autobiography, *Ashes and Miracles* seamlessly bridges the boundary between belles lettres and documentary ... (A) subtle, sophisticated, and beautifully crafted book.
—ELAINE KALMAN NAVES

* * *

Karafilly ... seems to be present, psychologically, everywhere in that world. She becomes not only the tourist seeking a week of sun and cheap romance on the island, but the gnarled fisherman struggling to make a life there; not only the privileged, alienated outsider, but the restless, dissatisfied insider; not only the female, but the male. Her empathetic range is impressively broad ... Karafilly's debut in *Night Cries* offers much pleasure, and makes one look forward eagerly to her next. —ROY MACSKIMMING

THE HOUSE
on
SELKIRK AVENUE

For Lee Kalant,
with very best wishes.

Irena

4. 2. 17

Essential Prose Series 140

Guernica Editions Inc. acknowledges the support of the Canada Council for the Arts and the Ontario Arts Council. The Ontario Arts Council is an agency of the Government of Ontario.

We acknowledge the financial support of the Government of Canada.

THE HOUSE
on
SELKIRK AVENUE

irena karafilly

GUERNICA
EDITIONS
TORONTO • BUFFALO • LANCASTER (U.K.)
2017

Michael Mirolla, general editor
David Moratto: interior design
Cover design: Ranya Karafilly
Cover photo: Bettina Güber
Author photo: Monique Dykstra
Guernica Editions Inc.
1569 Heritage Way, Oakville, (ON), Canada L6M 2Z7
2250 Military Road, Tonawanda, N.Y. 14150-6000 U.S.A.
www.guernicaeditions.com

Distributors:
University of Toronto Press Distribution,
5201 Dufferin Street, Toronto (ON), Canada M3H 5T8
Gazelle Book Services, White Cross Mills,
High Town, Lancaster LA1 4XS U.K.

First edition.
Printed in Canada.

Legal Deposit—First Quarter
Library of Congress Catalog Card Number: 2016952739
Library and Archives Canada Cataloguing in Publication
Karafilly, Irena, author
The House on Selkirk Avenue / Irena Karafilly. -- First edition.

(Essential prose series ; 140)
Issued in print and electronic formats.
ISBN 978-1-77183-230-4 (paperback).--ISBN 978-1-77183-231-1 (epub).
--ISBN 978-1-77183-232-8 (mobi)

I. Title. II. Series: Essential prose series ; 140

PS8571.A72H68 2017   C813'.54   C2016-905963-4   C2016-905964-2

For Norman Kalant

AUTHOR'S NOTE

Selkirk Avenue is an actual street in downtown Montreal, and the historical chapters dealing with the October Crisis are based on well-documented events. The rest of the story, however, is pure fiction. With the exception of Pauline Julien and other public figures, all the characters in the novel are the product of my imagination. Any resemblance between them and persons living or dead is purely coincidental. Although Montreal streets today all bear French signs, I have chosen to use the street names my anglophone protagonist would have been likely to use during her stays in the city.

PROLOGUE

THE MEMORY IS as vivid, as indelible, as any print in her travel portfolios. She has several of them but no images of the long train ride through the Alps, or the unexpectedly short sojourn in the French capital. A week earlier, her camera had been stolen at a crowded party in Urbino. Hence, no visual record; not a single snapshot. And yet, all these years later, Kate's mind still hoards the texture and smell of the night train's upholstery; the way the light seemed to get swept out of the afternoon sky soon after the train had left Milan's railway station.

She was on her way to Paris, to stay with her mother's American school friends. It was mid-September. At some point in the evening, she had bought herself a ham sandwich and was still eating it when a young soldier entered the compartment and settled across from her. He said *Bonsoir* and Kate, too, said *Bonsoir*, and then the whistle blew; the night train was on its way again. There was a dim light in the compartment but eventually it went off. The soldier crossed his legs. In the dark he seemed to be looking straight at Kate but not a word was spoken. Perhaps she imagined it?

She turned and stared out the window, wondering what she would do with her life once her continental stint was over. It was what she was supposed to have figured out, gallivanting with her knapsack through Europe for much of the summer. She had a degree in English and Music, but was no closer to knowing what to do with herself in October than she had been in July. She'd been travelling with another Montreal girl, but Eva had flown back home two days earlier.

So Kate was on her way to the 16th arrondissement, to polish up her French and maybe go back to Canada to work as a diplomatic interpreter. She spoke three languages, but this was her father's idea. Did she want to work as an interpreter? She didn't know. Did she even want to go back home? She didn't know. There was a medical intern who had asked her to marry him, but she wasn't ready to think about it. She'd promised to give Brad Thuringer an answer when she came back from Europe, but still didn't know what the answer would be.

It was beginning to rain. The soldier was very still, but awake as well. The darkness made Kate feel sweetly secure and safe — the way she used to feel in her childhood, after her mother had come to tuck her in and kiss her good night. The soldier lit a cigarette and sat smoking in silence. The burning tip of his cigarette darted about like a restless insect. It glowed red in the thickening dark, with the rain whispering at the windows. The train chugged along, on and on through the murky mountains, the dripping countryside.

After a while, Kate slept. When she woke, it was five in the morning. They were going past a hamlet and, through the open window, there came a sudden breeze, invading the compartment with its seasonal message: the scent of fallen leaves, of stacked hay, of imminent dawn. A shiver ran through Kate's bones. The soldier stirred and lit another cigarette, as if to let her know that he, too, was awake. As they approached the station, a platform light fell on his khaki-clad body and, for the briefest moment, Kate had a mental vision of a very old man sitting by the fire, his hands on his knees. She must have smiled a little at the thought. They smiled at each other: two young strangers who had spent the night together without exchanging a word. That seemed wonderful for some reason.

He asked Kate's name then. Speaking French, he asked whether anyone had ever told her that she looked like Audrey Hepburn. Kate answered yes, though she had grey eyes whereas Hepburn's seemed to be dark brown. The comparison made her blush and drop her gaze. She liked the look of the soldier's hands. They made her think of a famous sculpture by Rodin. How calmly, how serenely, his long fingers rested there, on his wool-clad knees! The night was almost over. There was a sudden ache in Kate's chest.

"My name is Thierry," the soldier said softly. It was a name Kate had never heard and liked. But what's in a name? Surely no name can, in itself, explain what she ended up doing before the sun was up. Kate Abbitson! An ordinary, rather sheltered, Canadian girl, still trying to get over the love of her life, fucking a laconic stranger in a French train compartment while rain lashed at the windows, and the train rocked and rocked in the vanishing night. *Guillaume, Guillaume, Guillaume ...*

She never saw the soldier again. He disembarked at the next station, kissing her goodbye but not stopping to ask for contact details. Perhaps he was engaged, or even married? Perhaps, in the light of dawn, he too was ashamed?

Kate's middle-aged self is certainly pained by the memory, the banal facts of female biology. Not for the first time, she wishes she could tell her twenty-six-year-old son the truth about his biological father but, years ago, she promised to put the past behind her once and for all. And no one could accuse her of not trying hard enough. Having exchanged marriage vows, she carefully wrapped up her whispering memories and stowed them away in a dim, private place.

And there they remained all these years, barely audible.

Until yesterday.

PART I

I think it is all a matter of love: the more you love a memory, the stronger and stranger it is.

—VLADIMIR NABOKOV

ONE

I

Iᴛ sᴛᴀʀᴛs ᴏᴜᴛ to be a perfectly ordinary day; a mild, erratically windy morning on which the fall sky seems undecided between sun and rain and the shrinking hours hint at nothing beyond the usual small blessings and vexations. Wearing robe and slippers, Kate has stepped out onto the balcony to pick up a drying bra, but something in the air prompts her to linger under the canvas awning, gazing down at the leaf-strewn lawn, the empty McGill Ghetto street.

It is still early and the morning is blissfully hushed, scented with must and rain-soaked earth, and a heady whiff of dying chrysanthemums. Not for the first time, Kate thinks it intriguing that autumn should generate this powerful sense of fresh beginnings, this aura of sweet expectancy. It may be an annual occurrence, yet there is something oddly stirring about it, this seasonal communion between inner and outer weather.

Montreal is Kate's hometown, but this is her first time back in nearly a decade. Her daughter has just enrolled at McGill University and Kate has come from Edmonton to help her shop, decorate, make the transition to independence just a little smoother. It is early September. Megan is about to run off to her morning class, but at the last moment pauses at the window to check out the weather.

"Hey, Mom, can I borrow your umbrella?" She tosses the question as she zips her knapsack, but then looks up sharply, arrested by Kate's silence. "Please, Mom!" she says, hands clasped in theatrical appeal. "P-l-e-a-s-e!" She is seventeen years old. She looks like an imploring cocker spaniel.

"Will you bring it back?"

"Yes!" Megan rolls her eyes. She reaches into the fruit bowl, heaves her knapsack, then flutters off, waving, her mouth full of apple and earnest promises. "Have a good day, Mom!"

"You too, sweetheart." Kate closes the front door with a long exhalation. Her daughter refuses to keep an umbrella, but has no compunctions about using others' whenever it rains. It was because of all the lost umbrellas that Kate finally bought herself a raincoat just before they left Edmonton; a chic, hooded European import.

It ends up raining all morning and Kate decides this would be a perfect day to visit the Museum of Fine Arts, easily within walking distance. Halfway through lunch, though, the rain abruptly stops and, once out in the rain-sweetened air, she no longer feels like being cooped up indoors. Her camera slung from her shoulder, she strolls along Sherbrooke Street, pausing to gaze at art gallery windows, clothing boutiques, Oriental rug displays. Outside the Ritz Carleton Hotel, an aging panhandler tries to talk the doorman into letting him use the hotel's facilities. The doorman is a uniformed giant with a square-jawed face in search of an expression. He orders the panhandler to scram, but the puny vagrant is still there, still badgering, when a white limousine slithers to a stop outside the hotel's entrance.

A professional photographer is never entirely off the job. The doorman picks up the panhandler, grabbing him by the scruff of the neck as one might a kitten. *Click.* He deposits him on the corner and gives a quick but decisive shove before dashing back to assist the new arrival. *Click, click, click.* If you have a camera, a photograph is just a click away; a good photograph a dozen clicks away, but a great one easily over a hundred.

It is a damp afternoon but still mild, with barely an intimation of winter in the air. An old black umbrella lies abandoned in the gutter, wind-twisted and vaguely reproachful. Kate slows down and raises her camera. There is the gratifying scent of her own wool and leather, of fresh coffee and buttery croissants baked at the Van Houtte.

As she strolls on, something new begins to stir in Kate Thuringer's heart. This is the first time in months that she has been alone, at leisure, free to go wherever she wants, do whatever strikes her fancy. Quite suddenly, she feels almost happy. It's easy to understand autumn's melancholy, but how do you explain the sweetness?

She keeps on strolling, stopping only once to photograph a pair of twins in matching red rain boots, splashing through a large, muddy puddle. All the interesting shops end at Guy and the reasonable thing to do would be to stop and head back east on the other side of Sherbrooke. There is an optometrist's shop just across the street. What she should do is go in and pick a pair of reading glasses. That's what a sensible woman would do on a free afternoon.

But Kate crosses the street and continues west. Not far, just another block, then up hilly St. Matthew Street. It is windier here. A private-school boy is running down to catch a bus, his striped tie flapping. A dog barks. A few damp leaves come whirling onto the sidewalk. Kate has made no conscious decision to visit Selkirk Avenue, but this is where her feet seem to be taking her.

And then, there it is: a street she remembers as keenly as anything in her nearly five decades on earth. A street she has managed to avoid for over a quarter of a century but now finds herself drawn to with the same perverse compulsion that occasionally makes the tip of her tongue seek out an aching molar.

Selkirk is a short cul-de-sac walled off from the grassy grounds of an adjacent Catholic seminary. It has a row of Victorian greystones, with bay windows in front and fire escapes in the back. When she last saw the street, the greystones were occupied by students and artists and budding journalists. They have all been converted into upscale condos.

Kate slows down, snapping another photo, wondering who lives behind the shiny maroon door. Man? Woman? Couple? If only she could find a magic key that would make her shrink. Let her enter: silent, invisible.

A few minutes go by. Dawdling across the street, Kate watches a postman drop a pack of mail into a large wooden box. He stops to shift his bulging bag, flashes a toothy smile in her direction, then turns and disappears up Côte-des-Neiges Road.

A banal Friday afternoon, but, like a common thief, Kate glances over her shoulder, then crosses the street and raises the lid on the black mailbox. A quick peek is all it takes. Bills, letters, a theatre brochure, all bearing the same name. Antonia S. Offe.

Very gently, Kate lowers the lid. If only she were bold enough to ring the door bell and introduce herself.

The thought is accompanied by a small, inner chuckle. She is, when all is said and done, a fairly conventional woman. All the same, she stands gazing up at the second-floor window; a large bay window that was once so drafty you couldn't go near it all winter. But the windows have all been restored and painted, the once-shabby street quaintly gentrified.

Kate tries to suppress her sudden resentment. She is dimly aware of the crows clamouring over the grey seminary wall, the honking of car horns. A bus comes trundling down Côte-des-Neiges Road, followed by a wailing ambulance. And then, for a moment or two, there is silence. It is only then that she hears someone playing the piano; something poignant and vaguely familiar, which she cannot quite name. She is still trying to identify the piece when a woman appears in the upper window, stopping just long enough to glance at the street, as if to check out the weather. An elderly woman with a cloud of stylish, pewter-coloured hair.

She quickly vanishes but then, almost at once, re-appears in the window, peering down at the street below. Kate guesses the stranger must have belatedly registered her own lurking presence. She may look perfectly respectable in her new fall outfit, but let's face it: a city like Montreal must have its share of well-dressed yet unbalanced women.

There is, in any case, no reason to linger. The piano is still playing as she crosses Côte-des-Neiges Road, stopping for coffee at a familiar convenience store-cum-snack-bar. A middle-aged woman may not look her age, but on a damp day her bones know the truth. The *dépanneur* is now owned by a Korean family but still smells of apples and brewing coffee, bubble gum and freshly baked baguettes. It is a smell that hurts.

Kate goes to the counter and orders a cup of coffee, listening to Céline Dion wail in the background. A couple of customers are bantering with the waitress, braying with occasional laughter. Kate takes out her agenda and starts a shopping list, resisting the impulse to re-read a personal letter stashed away in the depths of her shoulder bag; a fading missive in a blue envelope that unexpectedly surfaced in Megan's new apartment, along with two old Youth Orchestra photographs.

The coffee is hot and strong but offers minimal solace.

At length, Kate slides off the stool and tosses the Styrofoam cup into the waste bin. There is a basket of apples by the entrance, a stack of newspapers in both French and English. She had planned to go into Le Faubourg, buy a few items for dinner, but something about the scent of those freshly-picked Macintosh apples stops her in her tracks.

It takes her all of two minutes to turn around in hopes of finding a packet of letter envelopes. She finds them at the very back of the store, then returns to the counter to write a short note. She slides one of the envelopes out of the packet and inserts the note, silencing an inner voice mocking her foolish impulse. She seals the white envelope and scribbles the stranger's name with her purple felt pen.

Antonia S. Offe.

Not that she really expects anything to come of it.

II

There is something odd about the woman's face. One of her eyes, the left, is much lighter than the other: the colour of honey or translucent amber. The right eye is distinctly brown, and this slight anomaly compounds Kate's confusion as Antonia Offe opens her door to fetch her mail, catching Kate with her hand inside the capacious mail box.

"Oh!" Kate jerks back, as if her hand had been stung by some invisible creature holed up in the depths of the box. "I'm sorry! I ... I was just leaving you a note."

"A note?" The woman stands appraising Kate with her mismatched eyes. She tightens her black cardigan over her breasts. "And here I thought you were stealing my mail," she says, with just a hint of amusement.

"What? No!" Kate blinks, conscious of heat rising at the back of her neck. She opens her mouth to say something, then reaches out and plucks the note she has just dropped in the mailbox. What a stupid, stupid impulse, she scolds herself, clearing her nose. She hands over the note, waiting.

Antonia Offe is just about old enough to be her mother, yet it isn't easy to think of her as elderly. She is tall and sinewy in the yellow silk robe she wears under her black cardigan. She is well tanned. The facial skin is deeply carved by time, but the eyes glow with some sharp, inner defiance. She is somewhere in her late sixties but has none of the timidity, the hints of melancholy and doubt that cling to aging women like whiffs of stale perfume. She stands in front of the open door, reading the note. It is barely four lines long.

"I see," she says at length, making a small, noncommittal sound. She surveys Kate from top to bottom, taking in her long, ochre raincoat, her camera, her stylish Italian rain boots. This, Kate thinks, is one of those women whom nothing ever escapes. "So, when exactly was all this ... when were you last here?" Antonia Offe asks.

"Oh, a long time ago. More than twenty-five years," Kate says, sounding flaky to her own ears. She hesitates for a moment, then opens her bag and fumbles for her international press card, displaying her photograph. At least the woman will know she is who she says she is.

Antonia Offe glances at the photo. Then she raises her eyes, a slight frown settling over her features.

"A journalist! Your note says you're a photographer. You're not here to interview me, are you? Without an appointment?"

"Interview you?" Kate flips the name over in her muddled brain. She has no idea who the woman is. "No, not at all," she says. She begins to explain but just then, a black cat appears at the top of the carpeted stairs. It lets out a meow and, abruptly, Kate's nervous little laugh becomes a tiny hiccup of heightened distress. The cat is an ordinary cat with a bushy tail and slanted green eyes but, years ago, Kate had a cat like that; her first cat, Pablo, who disappeared the week she lost Guillaume Beauregard.

"I had a cat once. Black, just like this," she says.

"Did you?"

"Yes. It's a long ... a very sad story." Kate averts her gaze. "It still hurts to talk about it."

"I'm sorry." Saying this, Antonia Offe lets out the gentlest of sighs. A tree might sigh like that, stirred by an ocean breeze. All at once, tears start pressing behind Kate's eyes; unrehearsed words come tumbling out of her mouth.

"You probably think I'm a little cracked," she hears herself say, fighting her swelling anguish. "And, well, maybe I am but ... I just can't wrap my mind around it, you know? The fact that it's been over a quarter of a century! And it's changed so much! I mean ... everything. I thought it might help to ... oh, I don't know what I thought—" She trails off, raising a hand to cover her stinging eyes.

Antonia Offe hesitates, clutching the top of her open cardigan.

"Well, you're in luck," she finally says. "I'd planned to go out but I'm waiting for an important telephone call." She checks her watch, then steps aside with a broad, inviting gesture. She almost smiles. Her cat jumps sideways, getting out of the way. "Would you like to come in? You may as well. It's as good a time as any."

"Oh, thank you," Kate says. "Thank you so much!"

"Just take off your boots, will you?"

"Yes. Yes, of course."

III

The smells, the sounds, they're wrong! All wrong, Kate says to herself, surveying Antonia's foyer. There is the scent of fading roses, the ticking of a grandfather clock; the clamouring past colliding with the adamant present. Light-headed, Kate peels off her raincoat, doing her best to answer Antonia Offe's questions. Yes, she was brought up in Montreal but lives in Edmonton now. Why Edmonton?

Because her husband was offered a position at the University of Alberta. He's a cardiac surgeon. She is a staff photographer at the *Edmonton Journal*, but was just a student when she lived in Montreal.

"Where does one study photography here?" Antonia asks.

"Actually, I was doing English and Music, at McGill." Kate speaks as neutrally as she can, grappling for composure. "I was very young. I didn't know what I wanted to do with my life."

At this, Antonia smiles kindly, casually instructs Kate to make herself at home, and leaves her to go upstairs, her silk kimono swishing around her calves.

Kate has yet to see the upstairs bedrooms, but the last two words, tossed ever so lightly, fall like stones into the puddle of her rising confusion. At home! Has anyone, anywhere, ever thrown a more challenging directive her way? There are quantum physicists who have tried to advance the theory of backward-flowing time, but others have been quick to dismiss it. Kate knows in her marrow: it must be dismissed!

She circles the living room, stopping at the window to gaze down at the leafy street. She rests there, inwardly shaken, because the bay window, the view of the street, are the only things that appear unchanged. It is garbage pickup day and the waste bins, the plastic bags dumped on the wet sidewalk, look the same as ever. A squirrel has been tearing its way into a lumpy green bag and now scurries up a tree. The trees are the same trees: maple mostly and one mountain ash, its orange berries stirred by the flapping wind. The houses across the street are the same houses; they haven't been converted into chic condos.

Kate's skin is starting to prickle, the way, she imagines, a burglar's flesh must feel while stealthily exploring some absent stranger's private space. No doubt about it: there is a certain thrill in it, but also an underlying tension. There is the temptation to give up the search, to abandon all hope of finding any valuables and look for the nearest exit.

The room Kate explores—a room that used to have one wall panelled in brown cork, another lined with perpetually cluttered bookshelves—looks larger than she remembers. Through a tearful blur, she takes in its polished hardwood floors and refurbished fireplace; its pale decor, all ivory and beige, its occasional splash of colour.

An exquisite Kashmiri silk rug decorates a wall once hung with posters of Don Quixote and Che Guevara; a large combine painting with sculptured, grotesque faces replaces a print of Picasso's *Guernica*. Oh yes, it's all quite beautiful, but all the same, fingers of nausea keep tugging at Kate's throat.

She is aware by now that Antonia Offe is an actress. In the foyer, there are dozens of photos showing her on several Canadian stages. Kate is grateful for Antonia's casual kindness, but she detests the showroom feel of this vast room: its pale, touch-me-not elegance, its impeccable order. Not only that: the kitchen she remembers—a narrow, bright room with a high ceiling and hanging herb bouquets—that kitchen has disappeared! Its window is still here: a large window with a cushioned seat where, once upon a time, she would lounge with a book, waiting for the kettle to whistle, the pasta pot to boil, watching the rain come sizzling down, the snow settle on downtown roofs and treetops. This south-facing window is now part of the expanded living room, a vast room with a formal dining area facing a newly-created galley kitchen.

Ever since she stepped into Antonia Offe's home, Kate has been trying to make sense of the structural changes that have transformed several small apartments into two spacious condos. She has figured out that the wall which had once separated Guillaume's bachelor apartment and the one next door—this old wall has been knocked down, leaving Antonia with an office and terrace on the first floor, as well as two bedrooms on the upper one, accessible through a new, spiral staircase. In the old days, an aspiring playwright and his girlfriend lived on the top floor; a woman with an invalid father in the adjacent apartment facing the alley; a singer named Pauline Julien down on the street level.

But, as she herself has said, more than a quarter of a century ago!

She stands breathing shallowly, a woman with a husband and two grown children, feeling as confused, as bereft, as a dispossessed orphan.

A few minutes go by. Kate sits on one of the window cushions, listening to the thrumming rain, jolted out of her reverie by Antonia's approaching footsteps. She comes up to Kate, perfumed and coiffed and dressed: a narrow black skirt, a long turquoise cardigan, a paisley scarf, and an eye-popping collection of jangling bracelets; more silver and turquoise bracelets than Kate can count at a glance.

"So, have you had a good look?" she asks. Her eyes are both tea-coloured now, Kate observes with interest; she must wear tinted contact lenses in public. Antonia doesn't yet know what happened to Guillaume Beauregard, but it suddenly comes to Kate that, sooner or later, she is bound to ask.

"You have a beautiful home," she says.

"Thank you! Now, how about some tea? There's nothing like a cup of tea on a fall day, is there?" she says, pausing to open a window. The radiators have come on full blast, humming under the window seat. "Earl Grey okay with you? A New York friend brought me some heavenly Lord Bergamot."

"Earl Grey will be great, thank you." Kate smiles. She follows Antonia towards the kitchen, pausing before a large photograph of an egg: a pure, white egg set against a pale sandy background. It is the only thing she likes in the entire place; this exquisite image of fertile, unexplored possibilities. She likes the photograph despite the fact that, on this very spot, a painting used to hang all those years ago. A gouache painting she hugely admired, done by Michel Beauregard, Guillaume's younger brother.

"Can I do anything?" she asks.

"Oh, no. Thank you. You're in luck though. I happen to have some divine French wafers!" Antonia says, smiling in Kate's direction. She bustles about, reaching into a cupboard for tea, the stainless-steel fridge for milk. She is a tall woman with a brisk, memorable presence. Every one of her movements seems easy and graceful, yet at the same time somehow … choreographed. Well, she is after all an actress, Kate reminds herself.

They sit facing each other on the matching ivory sofas, the tea tray set between them on the coffee table. Kate feels intensely self-conscious under Antonia's penetrating gaze. The way she sits there, calmly sipping her tea, makes

Kate feel she is not in control here. But then, she hasn't really been in control since she left Megan's apartment, has she? To think that she actually got up the nerve to intrude on a stranger!

When she says something to this effect, however, Antonia waves Kate's scruples away.

"Oh, please," she says with a little theatrical frown. She remembers at least two occasions when she herself came close to ringing a stranger's doorbell. "I just didn't have your resourcefulness!"

"Resourcefulness? More like chutzpah," Kate murmurs.

Antonia laughs. She has a surprisingly youthful voice for a woman her age. Sooner or later, everyone longs to revisit some place they had once lived in, she says. "I mean, is there anything more seductive than our own past?"

"Oh, maybe not," Kate says.

As she sits there, cradling her tea, Guillaume's face starts to float up from the back of her brain. The image is accompanied by an odd, fluttering sensation in her chest, as if in the presence of some as-yet-undefined danger. She watches Antonia's crayoned lips stretch to form a question but just then—an unexpected reprieve!—the phone starts to ring somewhere in the back. Antonia rises from the sofa and crosses the room in her stockinged feet. She will take the call in her office, she says.

Yes, a reprieve. Antonia must be intrigued by the private drama that has brought a nostalgia-smitten stranger to her own front door. Kate doesn't know how she knows this, but the intuition makes her fidget against the pretty silk cushions. She wants to go. She doesn't want to go. She is like Otto, who keeps slinking into the living room, pausing to sniff delicately around the wafer box, then disappearing, for no apparent reason. Right now, he is back again, purring audibly as he sidles up to Kate, rubbing against her nylon-clad legs.

She is a woman with a weak resolve, that's what she is. Kate sighs. When she was nine or ten, she secretly sheltered a stray kitten she'd found in a back alley, knowing her father would force her to give it up. Something of the sort is what she feels right now, waiting for Antonia to return.

She has swooped up Otto into her arms and sits stroking between his eyes, acutely aware of the scent of drenched earth and dying leaves; of wood smoke and denuded trees. Call it nostalgia, call it a mid-life crisis, but she has reached a time in her life when the past suddenly looms at her back, refusing to be ignored. She's about to turn fifty, but old age is still as unfathomable as the afterlife. Kate remembers the year her mother turned fifty; recalls her father making inane jokes about the Big Five-O. She did not, of course, expect to be spared; she did think it would take much, much longer to get there. Years ago she read somewhere that, once upon a time, only witches were thought to live past the age of fifty. Any woman blessed with longevity was believed to be possessed by diabolical powers.

Times have changed, of course; old women are no longer burnt at the stake. But how mind-boggling to think that, all at once, her future has so little future in it. And how inconceivable that Guillaume, too, would be middle-aged by now, no doubt married, probably a father. Kate has no idea whether he still lives in Montreal, but recalls that he was about a year older than she. To think that, if alive, her Guillaume would now be half a century old!

All this is still going through Kate's head when Antonia's grandfather clock chimes the half hour. The sound startles Otto, who wriggles out of her arms and bolts out of the room, as if chased by invisible spirits. Kate's husband collects old clocks and antique watches. In his own way, he too is obsessed with time. What they seem to have in common is an unvoiced dread not so much of mortality as of the taunting passage of time.

Kate glances at her watch, reminded that her daughter will soon be coming home from her afternoon class, that she herself has yet to shop for groceries, that her son has promised to call from Vancouver. Otto is meowing for his dinner, casting reproachful glances in her direction. Kate can hear Antonia murmur in her office but cannot tell whether the conversation is approaching its end. She is sorely tempted to run off, but is too well brought up to leave without a word of thanks.

A few minutes go by. The grandfather clock keeps ticking. Otto goes on meowing, sounding dispirited. At last, Antonia appears, looking preoccupied.

"I'm sorry," she says, "I couldn't—"

"It's okay, no problem," Kate says, trying for a smile. "But I'm afraid I must leave now. My daughter will be coming home soon. I still have to shop for food."

Although this is true, Kate's mind leaps to primitive Africans' fear of losing their soul on being photographed. How frustrating she used to find it in the early days, travelling on assignment, thwarted by irrational dread.

She is being just as irrational. Kate knows it even as

she stands wriggling into her raincoat, exchanging polite goodbyes. Antonia plucks a business card out of a pretty Venetian bowl, inviting Kate to come back another day for a proper visit. Kate says she may take her up on it, but, as she turns to go, her eyes flick back to the spot where Guillaume used to sit and practise his cello. She remembers him rehearsing a Haydn cello concerto, the last composition she ever heard him play. She recalls his telling her how Haydn's head had been axed off the moment he gave up the ghost, with scientists clamouring to examine the renowned composer's brain. Would one of them succeed in pinpointing the cerebral secret of musical genius?

Kate recalls teasing Guillaume on hearing all this, saying something about the mysteries of his own eccentric brain. She no longer remembers exactly what she said but, as she hastens down Antonia's staircase, can vividly see Guillaume laughing at her little joke. He had the sort of laugh that often made strangers smile at him in passing; that made Kate think that whatever she'd said must have been singularly delightful.

The concerto is still playing in her head as she steps outdoors, greeted by a gust of autumnal air. She closes Antonia's door and inhales deeply, seized by an overwhelming need to photograph the crisp leaves being swept down from the top of a tree. The tree is a glorious Canadian maple; it is rustling in the late-afternoon breeze, next to a ripped garbage bag with a red handle-tie. But what Kate longs to capture is the soundless flutter of a dying leaf, whirling down towards the sidewalk.

Unremarked. Unlamented. Forever red and gold.

TWO

A PHOTOGRAPHER IS a compulsive robber who cares far less about his or her subject than about the occasional chance to trap time. All photographs, Kate believes, are ultimately about this one secret obsession.

"Time is a thief that cannot be caught," was how her late mother used to put it.

A platitude, of course. Nothing breeds platitudes more predictably than knowledge of your own mortality. And nothing brings this awareness home more brutally than the sudden realization that the role reversal you experienced with your mother may, before you know it, replay itself between you and your own adult children. You spend years caring for them, fretting over them, then arrive one day to discover that your young, self-absorbed, daughter is suddenly old enough, alert enough, to worry about your welfare. And that you are now under some sort of obligation to explain yourself.

"Where have you been, Mom?" Megan stands on the threshold to her new apartment, peering into Kate's face with faintly accusatory eyes. Almost at once though, her eyebrows slide towards each other, forming a frown. "Have you been crying, Mom?"

"Crying?" This is one of those moments between mother and daughter when truth must be cast aside like some frayed old garment. The subterfuge is fortunately facilitated by the need to bend down in order to unzip rainboots.

"Your eyes are all red." Megan is beginning to sound bewildered, her toes curling and uncurling on the new hallway carpet. The smell of soaked sneakers and damp umbrella vies with the lingering odour of freshly painted walls.

"Oh. It's been so windy all day ... I guess I got some dust in my eyes."

Kate impresses herself with her own nonchalant tone, the consciously distracted air with which she picks up the plastic shopping bag from the entrance floor. Having left Antonia too late to prepare a proper dinner, she has picked up a roast chicken on her way home. It is windy again. Something metallic can be heard rattling in the alley below.

Megan follows Kate to the kitchen and helps unload the chicken and potato salad. She takes out a bag of blood oranges and cactus pears, both of which she discovered only since their arrival in Montreal. There is also a container of fancy Italian ice cream, Kate's peace offering for her late arrival. Megan adores ice cream, but she's not easily distracted.

"Did you go to the museum?"

"No. I went for a long walk instead. I felt like taking pictures."

Although a camera can easily account for a prolonged outing, it cannot begin to compete with a daughter's intuition. Once she gets going, Megan can be like a dog with a juicy bone. She won't let go, though for several years her mother could have dyed her hair purple and Megan wouldn't have noticed. Kate is impressed by the recent change in her daughter. Being alone with Megan in Montreal has brought them unexpectedly closer.

"Where did you go?" Megan asks now, starting to wash lettuce leaves under running water. The kitchen is so small that they are working side by side under the stark neon lights. Outside, there is the whisper of falling rain, a steady urban rumble.

"Well," Kate says, "I walked and walked along Sherbrooke and ended up in Westmount, on Wood Avenue." Wood Avenue, where she grew up, is within plausible walking distance. "I suddenly felt like going back." Kate pauses, as if musing on her own statement. "I don't know why, fall always puts me in this strangely nostalgic mood." Nothing like a grain of truth to make a lie sound more plausible.

"Oh," Megan says. She is a lovely girl, with russet hair and soft skin as luminous as a seashell. Her wide-set eyes are grey, a little lighter than Kate's. The way they look at her just now prompts Kate to go ahead and flesh out her fib.

"I sat down in the park for a while, thinking about my childhood. What is it about fall? Does it ever do that to you?"

"I guess." Megan shrugs. She has never liked to discuss feelings, but has a rare gift for detecting whiffs of subterfuge. Kate can see her trying to work it out: her mother must have shed a few sentimental tears, sitting there in the Wood Avenue park, across from her childhood home. Nothing to worry about.

Megan reaches for the salad dryer. She offers a passing

comment about the potential usefulness of a mobile phone on days like this. She has already seen one or two students using theirs on campus. "Isn't fall gorgeous here, though?" she says then, finally ready to change the subject. "I love it here! I'm so glad I decided to come to McGill."

The reference here is to her original ambivalence about leaving home to go to university. Unlike Sean, Megan has always been a rather clingy child, reluctant to leave one stage and move on to the next. It's a family joke that she didn't even want to leave the womb; her birth had to be induced two weeks past Kate's due date. And then Megan refused to be weaned until she was two years old. Two years and three whole months! Brad thinks Kate should have put her foot down; he also thinks they should have insisted on sending Megan to summer camp, as they had with her brother.

He is no doubt right. The truth is Kate could never bear to hear her children cry. And her daughter cried quite a lot in her infancy. The grown-up Megan remains something of an enigma to Kate; an exceptionally bright and capable girl thwarted by an insecure child's soul. If there was one thing she and Brad agreed on, it was that Megan had to go away to university. Resisting at first, she then surprised them by choosing Montreal, the most distant option of all. The city offered a first-rate medical school; also, some romantic associations kindled by a childhood trip to Montreal, stoked by an adored high-school French teacher.

Now, as they sit eating their roast chicken dinner, Megan goes over some of her new courses. She rolls her eyes as she speaks of her physics professor's barely intelligible speech, the psychology prof's risqué analogies, the length of the Can Lit term papers she will have to write. Far better organized than her brother, Megan had obtained the reading list for the English course long before leaving Edmonton. She started reading in mid-summer, pouncing on an old cardboard box belonging to her mother. The box was crammed with miscellaneous items going back to Kate's own undergraduate days: yellowing paperbacks and fading term papers; a shrivelled red rose Kate had intended to discard; a fat, lined notebook in which, all those years ago, she tried to keep a journal, including her earliest efforts at writing poetry. Because of the upheaval preceding Kate's marriage, her mother, Fiona, had packed all her possessions, keeping school-related material together in the hope that Kate might decide to resume her studies some day.

The box got shipped back to Montreal together with Megan's personal items, but it was only yesterday that Guillaume's farewell letter turned up, along with the two Youth Orchestra photographs. The letter—five onionskins closely written in English—had been sent in early December, 1970, addressed to the Abbitsons' residence. Kate had forgotten all about the photographs, but the letter she had once searched and searched for. To this day, she doesn't know how it ended up among the yellowing pages of Margaret Laurence's *A Jest of God*. And to think that her daughter would be the one to find it after all this time, sitting cross-legged on her living room floor, burrowing through bags and boxes.

Despite her extensive reading list, Megan's Can Lit course seems to be a definite favourite so far. She has no regrets about having chosen McGill. The city is far more interesting and vibrant than Edmonton, she says across the dining table. She can't understand how her parents ever decided to leave Montreal.

The question makes Kate pause over her dish of coleslaw. She reminds her daughter that Brad did his residency out west.

"Yes, but you could have come back when he finished?"

They could have. They even considered it, along with Vancouver, where Brad has an older brother. There were pros and cons to every option, but Brad finally decided that Vancouver's rainy weather and Québec's political climate made Edmonton a more sensible choice. By the time Kate's husband was done with his residency, the Parti Québécois had won the provincial election; a referendum on future independence was in the offing.

"Well," says Megan, "they're still talking independence!"

"So they are." Kate sighs. "Now they're just talking though." In the late sixties, the radical Front de Libération du Québec was bombing mail boxes and blowing up armouries. "The year before we got married, people were being kidnapped and murdered right here in Montreal. Anglophones were fleeing the province in droves. It didn't seem like a good place to raise a family."

That's the truth, Kate reminds herself, eyes resting on the chicken bones scattered on her plate. The truth, but not the whole truth.

"Oh well." Megan gets up to clear the table so she can do her homework. She has never been very interested in politics, least of all those of Québec, a province which she believes expects too much from the rest of Canada. Not that this view is all that unusual. Québec nationalists demand their own country but they also want the security of an economic union with the rest of Canada. Canadian passport, Canadian currency.

"Québec's like a woman who wants a divorce but still expects her husband to support her," is how Kate's husband puts it.

So, no, Megan's view is not without merit; it is only her tendency to parrot Brad that sometimes grates on Kate. She supposes that Megan finds some security in her father's judiciously expressed views, his stable temperament. When they asked her why she wanted to be a doctor, Megan hesitated, but finally admitted that, for some reason, she liked to feel needed. What her daughter has always needed, Kate suspects, is a path that, though possibly narrow, is both tested and true. Megan is no risk-taker.

Kate pushes her chair back and starts stacking the dinner plates.

"I'm going to have a nice long bath," she says.

II

On the wall facing Megan's bathroom door, a full-length, slightly spotted mirror hangs, probably left behind by some previous tenant. It is this long, white-framed mirror that gives Kate back her own reflection as she goes about peeling off her skirt, tights, striped pullover; appraising herself with the detachment of a curious, mildly sympathetic stranger.

There was a time when she thought black underwear

alluring, but tonight, her fine lacy bra seems to mock the middle-aged breasts it so bravely supports. True: men still seem to find her attractive, but for how long now? Will the time ever come when she too will find herself shopping for the huge cotton pants and hideous bras her mother wore in her final years? And how strange to be able to think with equanimity of death, but not of the aesthetic indignities of old age.

Although she is old enough to be aware of the grip that time can have over a sentimental mind, the Selkirk Avenue visit has left Kate trapped in the murky tunnel connecting past and present. Nearly three decades after losing Guillaume, she is still moved—astonished to be moved—by the most trivial recollections: Guillaume's child-like fascination with insects, his clumsiness with chopsticks in Chinese restaurants; the way he occasionally stammered while speaking English. Thanks to childhood playmates, Guillaume's English was virtually fluent, but his tongue seemed too turgid to distinguish between *tree* and *three*, *true* and *through*.

He did not much like the English language; or, for that matter, most anglophones, who seemed to him staid, pragmatic, unimaginative; "though good at dreaming up ways to make pots of money." When Kate objected to this ludicrous stereotype, Guillaume conceded that Canada had its share of impoverished anglophones. Of course it did. All the same, he seemed reluctant to let go of his private prejudices.

He was given to poking fun at the rich, but just as often at his immediate family, his own lofty ambitions, even his own anatomy. He was tall and as solid as a tree, but his six-toed feet were a source of secret embarrassment, as Kate discovered during a long weekend spent with her parents at their summer cottage. She herself thought he was perfect, all the more so for having been brought up without her advantages; for having chosen to study music, rather than law or physics or finance. Her own brother was a professional violinist, but Paul did not possess Guillaume's child-like capacity for illuminating the ordinary.

Submerged in the hot bath, Kate wishes that her brother and sister-in-law were not away on vacation this month. She longs to speak to Dianne, who is a psychotherapist and who, Kate has always felt, understands her far better than any of her Edmonton friends. Dianne is the only one familiar with the grim details of Kate's breakdown, back in 1970, though she never got to read the letter that had led to it. Kate is still wondering what she should do with Guillaume's letter when Megan's voice comes through the closed bathroom door.

"Mom, do you mind if I come in to take out my lenses?"

"Sure. I was coming out anyway."

Kate smiles as her daughter enters, but there is no mistaking the dismay flickering across Megan's face. It's a mystery to Kate why, having been raised by a mother who never made bones about nudity, Megan remains as prudishly self-conscious as an adolescent. She tries to feign nonchalance, but steadfastly avoids looking at her mother as Kate fumbles into a bathrobe and reaches for a hairbrush. When Megan looks up from her contact lens case, she cannot help but see their two heads reflected in the mirror: Kate's dark one with its two wings of silver, and her own, splendidly russet, cameo. Kate stares for a moment, half-trying to work out how a buck-toothed, bespectacled

adolescent came to be transformed into this exquisite creature with her sparkling eyes and opulent flesh.

"I feel so ancient, looking at you," she hears herself say.

"Oh, you're not ancient ... you're not even old!" How
quick she is to offer comfort, her tender-hearted daughter.
"I was just looking at some of the pictures I've brought with
me. You've hardly changed at all, Mom. Honestly!" Megan
spins away from the pedestal sink, offering the warmest
of hugs.

"You're so sweet," Kate says. She kisses her daughter's
shining head, stabbed by a question she has been kicking
aside for weeks. How will she live without her children?
Sean on the West Coast, Megan in Montreal. It is only
September, but already she finds herself contemplating
Christmas.

"How would you like to visit Québec City before I go
back?" she impulsively asks her daughter. In just over two
weeks, Kate's brother is scheduled to perform in the historic provincial capital, playing with the McGill Chamber
Orchestra. Megan jumps on the invitation.

"This reminds me, Mom ... do you think you could try
to get me some resin and new strings at that music store
you mentioned the other day. If it's still there ... if you happen to be in the area?" she adds, reluctant to push her luck.

"Okay. Can it wait for a day or two?"

"I guess."

The requested strings are for Megan's violin, which
she has been playing since the age of four. Kate herself used
to play the flute, but Megan chose the violin after seeing
her uncle perform in Edmonton. For a time, after she'd
given up an early ballet fantasy, she considered becoming

a professional violinist. She even joined a youth orchestra, but by senior high, she was clearly leaning towards Medicine. What finally clinched it was something she read about Anton Chekhov, a doctor as well as a writer.

"Chekhov used to say that medicine was his lawful wife, literature his mistress," Kate remembers Megan gushing over Easter dinner. "Whenever one let him down, the other was always there, offering consolation. Isn't that cool?" She laughed delightedly, eating with abstracted relish, while Brad and Kate exchanged smiles across the festive table: their brilliant daughter, who had skipped a grade soon after starting school, and was now quoting Chekhov!

"So, that's what I think I should do," Megan was going on. "If he could do both, why can't I, right?"

Kate's daughter is as focused and ambitious as her brother is laid back and dreamy. An aspiring writer, Sean has what is often described as an artistic temperament, though even gifted artists must learn to hustle, as one of Kate's old friends pointed out years ago, speaking of her own husband.

The thought makes Kate pause with a sigh: her memory is not what it used to be. She has just remembered that she'd meant to call her old friend, Eva Walny. She has not seen Eva in years, but still recalls a way she had of rolling her eyes, speaking of her poet husband with the faintly exasperated air of a mother discussing a rambunctious child.

Kate has only two friends left in Montreal. The other day, she had lunch with her oldest friend: Isabelle Deslauriers, whom she met at Montreal's Youth Orchestra and who now works as a senior editor at a French publishing house. Isabelle remains a cherished friend, even if the two of them don't always see eye to eye in political matters.

In the past few months, Kate has found herself questioning the many pointless connections people feel compelled to maintain through life, with both friends and family members. Her relationship with her own sister is a perfect example; Eva Walny, with whom she hitchhiked across Europe, is yet another. After all these years, Kate is vaguely reluctant to see her old friend, but she knows that Eva is bound to find out that she has been in town. Whatever her feelings, Kate has no wish to hurt Eva, who, after all, is as blameless as a daisy. And, well, it has been nearly a decade.

THREE

∞

I

THE EARLY-AUTUMN sun is golden on St. Denis Street, with its fanciful gables and wrought-iron balconies trailing ivy and spider ferns, petunias and morning glories. It is a street that makes Americans and out-of-province Canadians feel they are in Paris, even if the spoken French doesn't sound anything like their high-school teacher's speech back home.

The day Kate and Eva meet for lunch at the Bistro Trois Canards is as balmy as a mid-summer day and, waiting at an outdoor table, Kate enjoys a few minutes of leisurely people-watching. The passers-by are mostly francophones out for lunch, or just a pleasant midday stroll in the warm sunshine. They seem, in comparison with native Edmon-toners, remarkably animated. Their gestures are less constrained than those of people out west; their laughter more exuberant. Some two and a half decades after moving west, Kate can't help but agree with the fervent claims of Québec nationalists: they *are* a distinct society, though she would personally hate to see the province separate from the rest of Canada.

But this is not a day for political reflections. It is a day that feels like an unexpected gift at this time of year. The smell of mushroom soup is wafting out to the terrace, and a whiff of something else: perhaps *Cassoulet*? On her right, a middle-aged man with a round, epicene face lights up at the sight of a waiter delivering his dessert. He tucks into it with the relish of a man long deprived of the pleasure of sweets, reminding Kate of an all-but-forgotten story Guillaume told her years ago, over their first shared breakfast.

One winter evening, long before he joined the Youth Orchestra, the teen-age Guillaume had gone with some Hungarian pals to a European café called Pam Pam, where everyone ordered a big slice of Black Forest torte. It was the café's most popular cake, but Guillaume barely had enough pocket money for a beverage. He kept sipping his coffee, claiming not to have much of a sweet tooth, when in fact he had always been passionate about desserts. He sat feigning indifference, watching the others devour their treat: the moist chocolate cake, the whipped cream, the glistening red cherries.

The feeling of exclusion had clearly gnawed at him but, sharing the story with Kate, Guillaume only laughed, mocking his own childish greed. When Kate reached out in a gesture of mute sympathy, he quickly recoiled, as if to repudiate the image of a drooling east-end adolescent with only a few coins in his tattered pocket.

When Eva finally appears, she looks as breathless as she often is in Kate's recollection. She is dressed in a cool summer outfit: a long, vertically striped skirt and a white, short-sleeved top with navy blue buttons matching the colour of her linen skirt. Kate has, of course, brought her camera. Seeing Eva approach, she leaps up from her chair and starts snapping her friend as she wends her way towards

their table. *Click. Click. Click*. She has captured Eva's laughing eyes, her dimples, her hand raised in that small exaggerated gesture that says: "Oh, don't *ask* what I had to do
to get here!"

"Kate!"

"Eva!"

They kiss each other in the French manner, a peck on
the right cheek, a peck on the left. "Oh, Kate, it's so good
to see you!" Eva cries, with her usual cheerful aplomb.

"You look wonderful!" Kate says. Eva has put on some
weight over the years; she looks *zaftig* but still impressively
radiant.

"Isn't it a glorious day?" she gushes. "Late September!
Can you believe it?"

She pulls out a chair and sits down, beaming at Kate.
They have been faithfully exchanging Christmas cards,
along with invitations to come visit. Eva has never been
to Edmonton; it is, after all, some twenty-three hundred
miles away. The last time Kate was in Montreal she saw
Eva only once. They had come, she and Brad, to sell her
elderly mother's home and move her out west. They had
young Megan with them and a busy month ahead.

The waiter arrives on the terrace, dressed in a black
vest, a *papillon* at his throat. He takes a pencil from behind
his ear. *"Mesdames?"*

Eva looks up with a dimpled smile. She orders a *Vichys-
soise* and a Caesar salad; Kate, always ravenous, asks for a
salad and the *cervelles au beurre noire*, which she first tasted in
Paris. Also — why not? — a slice of chocolate cake. Neither
of them likes to drink at lunchtime.

"But still a chocaholic, I see." Eva looks up with fond

eyes, but all the same manages to make Kate feel a little self-indulgent. She has to remind herself that, so far, she has no particular reason to diet.

As they sit waiting for their lunch to arrive, Eva talks, rather breezily, about her family, and then about a recent promotion that has made her Head of the Ville Marie social services. Her two daughters have recently graduated and, incredibly, both are engaged to two cousins they met on a student exchange in Krakow. Eva is thrilled by the prospect of having two Polish sons-in-law. She is equally proud of Emilio, her Italian husband, who has not only won a recent literary prize for his poetry but is now serving as a consultant for a Canadian documentary about Tuscany.

"Now tell me about yourself," Eva says. "Tell me about your children."

And so Kate does. Stirring her lettuce salad, she speaks of Megan's move to Montreal and Sean's literary ambitions; her daughter's scholastic awards, her son's determination to make a name for himself as a writer. Sean spent several years working for a Vancouver advertising agency but is now with Via Rail's Customer Relations. He claims not to want any job sapping his mental or creative energies. She misses him, Kate says wistfully, all the way out in Vancouver. Her daughter, too, will from now on be home only on school holidays. She seems to have grown up from one month to the next, Kate tells Eva with a helpless shrug. "I don't really understand it but, all at once, she seems to be acting more like a sister than a teen-age daughter."

"But that's nice! Do you have any pictures?"

"Oh … oh yes!" Kate unsnaps her bag, plucking out her wallet with its two glossy pictures: Megan's grad photo and a snapshot of Sean on a boat in the Queen Charlotte Islands. The waiter is back at their table, bearing salads and a fresh bread basket.

"It's going to be hard, getting used to an empty nest," Kate says, letting go of the two photos.

"Tell me about it."

Eva is clearly distracted. Watching her study the two photographs, Kate recalls a long-ago afternoon in Greece when Eva, lazing on a sandy beach, asked to see a photo of Guillaume. Kate did not have one on her. Hoping to put the past behind her, she had left everything connected with Guillaume back in her parents' basement. Now, unexpectedly, she is in possession of an old snapshot but is not at all sure she wants to share it with Eva. She wants to; she doesn't want to. Why shouldn't she, anyway? She did not hesitate to show it to Isabelle Deslauriers.

Kate opens her agenda.

"There's something else I'd like to show you," she says.

II

The photograph was taken at Montreal's Beaver Lake, where, all those years ago, a small group from the Youth Orchestra had gone for a picnic after an early-summer rehearsal.

There were seven of them — a mixed bunch of gifted young anglophones and francophones — lounging around a large wicker basket, rollicking on the sun-dappled grass. Their two communities may have still lived as two solitudes in those days but music, they felt, transcended any differences, any social tensions. Having received a camera for Christmas, Kate had jumped up to capture her six jolly friends sharing sandwiches and beer. Her shutter clicked just as a pale-haired oboeist named Véronique Anfousse was shrieking over a wasp creeping up her arm. The young man seated next to her was her older brother, Marc, with whom she shared a St. Lawrence loft. Both were, at the time, passionate Québec nationalists, though, in later years, Véronique would astonish everyone, becoming a Member of Parliament for the ruling Liberals. Marc had his arm around Kate's friend, Isabelle, who resembled Twiggy; they were both looking over their shoulders, where Guillaume had grabbed someone's violin, playing it theatrically in what might have been a parody of *Fiddler on the Roof.*

"Do you remember Guillaume? Guillaume Beauregard?" Kate asks Eva, her voice light and neutral. She has slipped the Beaver Lake photo out of her agenda, but holds onto it, waiting for an answer.

"Do I remember the cellist you mooned over all across Europe? Of course, I remember! Why?"

"That's him." Kate slides the snapshot across the table. "The one with the violin."

The photo is not large, but large enough to leave no doubt about Guillaume's striking good looks. To think that, after all these years, she can still recall the texture of his sun-bleached hair, visualise every crease around his laughing eyes.

"He had the most extraordinary eyes," Kate says as Eva continues to study the black-and-white photograph. "The colour of olives — green olives, you know?"

They had been deep-set and black-rimmed, with dark

lashes as long as a girl's. In repose, his features wore a re-
mote, fiercely determined expression; the look of a sea
captain focused on unknown horizons.

"Well." Eva hands back the snapshot. "He's certainly
good looking. But then so is Brad," she adds and resumes
eating. "You've always had an eye for beauty, haven't you?
I suppose that's why you became a photographer."

"Oh, photography has very little to do with beauty,"
Kate says, as evenly as she can. It's more to do with a longing for permanence, she adds to herself. It is on the tip of
her tongue to say that she cares less about beauty per se
than Eva does about aristocratic lineage. It is, she has always suspected, what had drawn her friend to Emilio
Sforza. Eva's taciturn husband is not physically prepossess-
ing, but he is said to be related to the renowned Montefelt-
ros of Urbino.

"Does Brad still have all that gorgeous hair?" Eva asks,
reaching into the bread basket.

Brad's hair, in his youth, had been an impressive mop
of brownish-red hair, the colour of a chestnut mare. It is
not quite as thick now, or as lustrous. "But yes," Kate tells
her friend. "He's still got most of it. It's starting to go grey
at the temples though."

"Ah, well, *c'est la vie!*" Eva says. She picks up a knife
and goes about buttering a crisp slice of French country
bread. "A good thing Megan's got her father's hair, eh?"
The statement is accompanied by a warm smile, a surrepti-
tious glance at Kate's thin, chin-length hair—never her best
feature.

"Yes, lucky Megan." Kate sits squinting into the afternoon sunlight.

"Lucky is right: *his* hair and *your* eyes," Eva says, spearing a black olive. "Sean looks a lot like his father though, doesn't he? Especially around the eyes?"

"Oh, no!" Kate says, much too quickly. "No, he doesn't." Brad has hazel eyes; Sean's are actually chocolate brown. She points all this out to Eva.

"Really? Well, anyway, they look like two peas in a pod to me," Eva insists. "Except for the hair, of course."

This is one of the things that has always vexed Kate: Eva is so sure about everything! You can toss irrefutable facts in her face but, though she may on occasion nod and pretend to yield, she never relinquishes whatever conviction she started out with. Nothing has really changed in Eva's character, Kate says to herself. She recalls something her mother used to say, quoting someone — was it Bertrand Russell? — who had observed that the world was full of people who were much too sure they were right.

And, just like that, for reasons she'd be hard pressed to explain, Kate feels a subversive need to burst the bubble of Eva's confidence.

"Actually, they can't possibly look like two peas in a pod," she says. She speaks musingly, as if still tempted to swallow the revelation she is about to offer. "Brad's not Sean's dad, you see."

"Huh?" Eva looks stung. It is the first time Kate has ever seen her friend with her mouth open; so open that half-chewed greens are visible between her small, child-like teeth. Kate becomes aware of a traffic jam somewhere down the street; of aggressively honking horns. "Brad isn't ...?"

"No."

"Oh!" Eva puts her fork down and raises her hand to

stroke her perspiring forehead. "I don't understand what you're saying," she lets out at length. "Are you telling me you had an affair with someone just before you married Brad?"

"Yes." Kate goes on fiddling with her napkin, conscious of as-yet-undiagnosed feelings. She feels at once annoyed and inexplicably gratified. Is it the satisfaction of unburdening herself, she wonders, or is there something more complicated going on here? "I'm not even sure it qualifies as an affair," she adds as an afterthought.

But Eva does not seem to have absorbed Kate's last statement. Perhaps she just can't believe that anyone would so breezily confess to such questionable conduct. She sits staring at Kate with widened eyes, as blue as fresh periwinkles. "Is this one of your weird little jokes?" she eventually asks. *Weird* was the word Eva used in the old days, whenever Kate's inclinations went against her own notions of normal.

"Oh no," Kate says. "Not at all." She watches one of the diners accidentally drop a spoon, then bend down to retrieve it. She and Eva are a tiny island on a crowded terrace buzzing with conversation.

"But that's impossible!" Eva explodes. "You married Brad right after you got back from Paris and ... and in Europe ... well, good God, you wouldn't even look at anyone! Not even that cute Oxford guy who was after you, remember?" She is staring at Kate, tongue working around her mouth. Then something seems to strike her. "Are you telling me you got involved with someone in France?"

Kate half-smiles but keeps her thoughts to herself.

"Did you?" Eva asks. When Kate still fails to answer, Eva makes an ironic little sound. "You mean to say the moment the chaperone flew home, you actually gave in to some bloody Frenchman in Paris?"

"A Frenchman," Kate says, "but no, not in Paris."

"Where then?" Eva demands, her Julie Andrews cheer vanished. Gone! It is not, Kate's reflects, her own dubious morals that have shaken Eva, so much as being forced to consider the likelihood of countless erroneous assumptions, going back ... well, God only knows how far.

"Are you sure you want to hear the truth?"

"Well, of course I do!" Eva exclaims. People always say that but in Kate's experience it is seldom true. "Where, Kate?"

"On the train to Paris," Kate says and bows her head, staring into her plate. Not that she is ashamed, exactly. On the contrary: Eva's smugness has somehow succeeded in banishing the deep embarrassment she has always felt over this secret chapter in her distant past.

There is a moment's silence. When Kate raises her gaze, it is to see a sceptical, faintly bewildered, look creep into Eva's eyes. And, truth to tell, she too is unnerved by her own, possibly malicious, impulse. Suddenly on the edge of tears, she gives a resigned little shrug.

"I was unlucky," she says with a sigh. "I had a fling with a French soldier and ... well, it was obviously the wrong time of month. I—"

"A soldier," Eva echoes, as if trying to decide whether this additional revelation has just compounded Kate's transgression. She sits rolling a breadcrumb between thumb and finger. She rolls it for what seems like a very long moment. "Well, what happened, was he married or something?"

"I never asked." Kate eats a last forkful of buttery calf

brains, then her eyes veer away. "To be perfectly honest, I don't even know his name. His surname, I mean."

At this, Eva leans back in her chair, speechless at last. She looks defeated and, despite herself, Kate is swept up by a wave of guilt.

"I guess I've never understood you," Eva says, with one of her deepest sighs.

Kate remains silent. She looks back at Eva and recognizes the contours of some long-buried resentment. "Wasn't it you who kept saying *carpe diem* to me every other day?"

"You make it sound like it was my fault," Eva says, motioning to the waiter. She looks sulky now; unnerved, Kate thinks, by the suspicion that she might have indeed had something to do with this sudden lapse into promiscuity.

Kate does not reply. She sits casting about the terrace with restless eyes, thinking: What now? Where do we go from here?

The silence lasts and lasts. They wait for dessert and coffee, avoiding each other's gaze.

"So Sean isn't Brad's son at all," Eva says at length, speaking more or less to herself. She raises her round blue eyes and stares at Kate for a long moment. "Does Brad know?"

"Yes. But Sean doesn't. We never talk about it."

Eva sits shaking her head. "I *don't* understand you," she reiterates.

"That's okay. You don't absolutely have to, you know." Kate offers this lightly as she eats her cake. After a while, she pushes the plate aside, saying the cake is a little too rich, even for her. "The coffee is excellent, though, isn't it?"

But Eva just sits there, staring into the distance. Kate

wonders whether they'll ever see each other again. She also wonders whether they would have remained friends all these years if she had told Eva the truth at the outset. She asks herself why, given their obvious differences, they kept up their long-distance friendship after she moved out west. Is there any value in a friendship that cannot absorb an occasional blast of truth?

Eventually, the bill arrives, and Kate moves to snatch it. A brief struggle ensues, which Eva lets her win, since they both know she can better afford it.

"Thank you," Eva says, patting down her hair with a plump little hand. For the second time, she sighs, then rises from the table, smoothing her skirt down over her hips. "Back to the prose of life, as they say in Polish." She smiles bravely.

That gets Kate's attention. The statement is one she has heard Eva make in the past. It is the Polish equivalent of "Back to the salt mines!" Just now, though, it comes to Kate that, for once, Eva has said something rather interesting; that she has touched on what Kate herself recognizes as a life-long dilemma: her own reluctance to surrender to the prose of life.

"It's okay, Eva," she says, contrite. "I was just going through a difficult phase, you know? Please forget what I said, will you? I'm sorry I upset you."

Saying this, Kate squeezes Eva's shoulder, then takes her arm, strolling away from the Trois Canards. This is the kind of gesture that a long friendship demands every now and then. Friendship and perhaps marriage, too?

Oh, marriage for sure, Kate says to herself. Marriage, alas, demands much, much more.

IV

Among the photos Megan has arranged on her dresser is the first colour snapshot of Brad and Kate, taken shortly before they left Montreal for western Canada. Until Megan decided to display it in her own apartment, Kate had not looked at the photograph for at least two decades. What intrigues her now is its subtle evocation of her own inner upheaval. Brad, captured on her right, wears a look that can best be described as sober and dignified: the auburn head is held high, the mouth set in a pale, resolute line. Kate's expression is just a little tentative, a little distracted; the look of a dog alerted by a distant whistle. Is she perhaps listening for her baby's cry? The photograph was taken in late 1972, so Sean had already been born. She would have been tired, of course, but no, it's not fatigue, exactly. There's something about the eyes.

Kate's eyes in this early Kodak photo seem tranquil enough, yet there is something about them that puzzles her; something brilliantly evident, yet painfully opaque. Where is the pain, she feels compelled to ask: the dilated pupils, the exceptionally dark grey of the iris—where? And why are there always women like Eva who seem to breeze through life, looking as buoyant as girls in shampoo commercials, floating through green meadows, picking wild flowers?

The question, which Kate has asked herself on other occasions, elicits an unconscious sigh. Eva Walny had entered her life unexpectedly, back in the summer of 1971. By then, the affair with Guillaume was over and Kate had become something of a recluse. She was still living in her

parents' basement but spent day after day sleeping or reading trashy novels, or trying to create poetry out of private
anguish. She still felt like a fire victim whose skin had
been peeled off in its entirety; who must somehow learn to
live with all her raw nerves exposed. Solitude was teaching Kate both stoicism and humility but did not promote
progress in the outside world. Although she had started a
qualifying year towards graduate school, she dropped out
by Christmas and, to her parents' chagrin, was neither working nor pursuing any sort of career. She could not have
explained it to her family, but all her energy, after she'd lost
Guillaume, seemed to be taken up by the daily effort of
acquiring a new skin. When she stopped playing her beloved flute, her stalwart mother sat down and wept.

"But why?" she implored, wringing her hands as if Jean
Pierre Rampal had just announced he would never give
another public concert. "Why give it up after all these years?"

Fiona Abbitson was a dedicated choral director and an
ardent guardian of her children's musical gifts. Kate could
do nothing to comfort her mother. She had no answer to
give, though she obscurely felt that, if the cello had been
crafted to express human yearning, the flute must have
been invented to convey the rhythms of eternal hope.

She had no hope left and, by spring, her father decided
enough was enough. She had, the year before, talked about
going to Europe with Guillaume, so it was decided to send
her on an extended trip, accompanied by her mother, like
some forlorn Henry James heroine.

And then Kate met Eva. Eva Walny and Dr. Bradley
Thuringer.

She was introduced to both on the same occasion: her

brother's wedding in North Hatley. Eva was Dianne's room-mate; Brad her second cousin. He and Dianne had grown up in the same Lennoxville neighbourhood but had lived in Montreal for the past few years. Had the groom not been her brother, nothing could have persuaded Kate to put on her finery and attend the Eastern Townships wedding.

Brad took an instant interest in her, undeterred by her blatant indifference, her barely civil responses to his over-tures. Much later, he was to say that her churlishness had both amused and intrigued him. Possibly, he was unaccus-tomed to indifference. As for Kate, there seemed to be some perverse satisfaction in giving the cold shoulder to this young, up-and-coming physician: so attractive and confident, so persistently interested.

He began to call and, after a while, Kate agreed to go on a movie date, if only to escape her father's baleful looks. Brad was a man after her father's heart. When he heard that she was leaving for Europe, Brad asked Kate to marry him. She told him she would let him know when she re-turned, though to this day she cannot explain her own motives. Was she too selfish to give up an attentive young man who, if nothing else, provided occasional diversion? Or could there have been something a little sadistic in keeping Brad Thuringer on her leash? There are people who refuse to take No for an answer. Their arrogance, or just lack of pride, is so maddening it makes otherwise de-cent people want to punish them.

Kate ended up going to Europe with Eva instead of her mother but, wherever they went, her single consistent pleasure came from photography. Eva often annoyed her, all the more for failing to do anything truly blameworthy.

Unlike Kate, she slept like the proverbial log, waking up every morning with the eagerness of a child leaping out of bed on Christmas morning. She showered quickly, ate an enormous breakfast, then proceeded to drag Kate to churches, museums, historic monuments. Everywhere they went, Eva would stop to chat with waiters, policemen, shopkeepers, backpackers. Outgoing by nature, she must have found Kate's reserve occasionally trying. Had she not been a trained social worker, endowed with an almost-missionary zeal, she might have decided to hightail it early on. Instead, she set out to make Kate look at life through her own sunny window.

One day, sitting at a sidewalk cafe in Urbino, they fell to chatting with two young Englishmen from Oxford. The two were graduate students visiting a former Italian classmate. They wasted no time inviting Kate and Eva to a party at an old palazzo belonging to their friend's parents. Eva pounced on the invitation, but Kate declined to go.

"But why not?" Eva demanded when they were alone.

"I don't know. I just don't feel like going."

"But why? Didn't you like those two guys? What was wrong with them?"

"Nothing. Nothing was wrong with them. I just feel like being alone, reading for a change."

"Reading!" Eva's eyes made an appeal to heaven. "But you can read when you get back home!" She let out a sigh, looking as chagrined as Kate's mother had the day Kate decided to renounce the flute. "You know what your problem is? You've become too attached to your own pain, if you ask me," she pronounced.

"Eva, please. I –"

"No, listen to me. Listen."

And so Kate did, though there was nothing new in what her friend had to say. Eva, in fact, was all too given to platitudes. They weren't going to be young and carefree forever; Kate wasn't, as Eva understood it, likely to see her Québecois lover again. What was the point of wasting her time brooding about something that could never be? "Who knows when you'll be in Europe again?"

What eventually swayed Kate was the scorn she sensed lurking in the shadows of Eva's solicitude. What was needed, Eva concluded the evening of the party, was sheer will power. The thing to do was to make up one's mind to move forward, and then ... just do it!

And, well, wasn't this the truth? Like the man Kate was destined to marry, Eva was a brisk, determined sort of person who, when she felt herself to be in the right, simply refused to budge.

Kate ended up going to the party, where she flumped into a huge velour arm-chair and nursed one Campari after another, while Eva circulated in the large, smoky drawing room. Before long, Kate observed her flirting under the glittering chandelier with a local poet; an impoverished aristocrat whom she seemed to find irresistible. Kate took a photograph of the two of them, then got up to go to the bathroom. When she came back, her camera was gone, never to be recovered. All Kate had were several rolls of film waiting to be developed. There would be no more photos after Urbino. Not until the following Christmas, when Kate's parents took pity on her, buying a new, superior, Canon for her holiday gift.

FOUR

∞

I

A̲ᴌᴛʜᴏᴜɢʜ ꜱʜᴇ ᴡᴀꜱ not unaware of the emotional web underlying her need to provoke Eva, several hours go by before Kate acknowledges that the last straw was her friend's statement about the love of beauty.

That, and Eva's ongoing failure to understand anything about photography. Somehow, her friend has always managed to convey the idea that Kate was a rather frivolous sort of person; unlike her, a woman devoted to serious social work, to charitable activities. Saying Kate had an eye for beauty might, coming from someone else, have been meant as a compliment. With Eva, the subtext seemed to be: "You've always been a little shallow, Kate, haven't you?"

The truth is Eva has never shown much regard for Kate's achievements. Anyone, after all, could get hold of a camera and snap what's in front of them. If Kate has chosen photography as her profession, Eva seems to believe it is only because she is too dreamy, too self-indulgent, to have taken up a more rigorous profession. She is, of course, aware that not all photographers manage to make a living taking pictures, but seems to attribute Kate's professional success to sheer luck. After all, she herself was there when Kate snapped the photo that launched her career. If she'd had a camera on her, surely she could have photographed those picturesque gypsies every bit as well?

And who knows, maybe she could have; if only she'd stopped gabbing long enough to take in what really mattered. A colleague of Kate's once said that a photography course should be a requirement in all high schools because it would teach students to see the world rather than just look at it. Had Eva ever taken such a course, she might have been trained to see not just Europe's monuments and breathtaking scenery but the distilled truth that goes beyond mere technical skill; certainly well beyond what is generally meant by the word "beauty."

When Eva and Emilio became engaged, Kate had the gypsy photograph blown up, and gave it to Eva as a souvenir of their shared travels. This was before she won the National Geographic Traveler Prize, so Eva did not bother to have it framed, though her walls were hung with examples of the purest kitsch. By the time Eva got married, Emilio had begun to exert his own aesthetic influence, and Kate had won the prestigious prize. Only then did Eva have the gypsy photograph framed. She hung it in the guest room, and promptly ushered Kate to see it, beaming with affection and good will.

"To think I was there when you took it," she said.

Yes, she had been there, but when the gypsies turned up, all Eva Walny seemed to care about was having one of the women in the caravan tell her fortune. Wasn't that what you did with gypsies?

Eva knew about gypsies from her Polish parents, but Kate's photograph was taken in northern Spain, not far from the town of San Sebastian. They had been hitchhiking that day; had found themselves dropped off at a cross-roads during siesta time, resigned to spending half the afternoon in the shade of a wild mulberry tree, waiting for the traffic to resume.

No one seemed to be going anywhere in the blinding heat, so they sat on the roadside to eat bread and cheese and dry salami, then jumped up to pick mulberries off the low, fruit-laden branches. There was a yellow field across the asphalt road; a long stretch of cultivated land, with sunflowers yearning towards the sun.

There was something unexpectedly blissful about being there, in the middle of nowhere, surrounded by delirious bees, trilling birds, shrilling cicadas. Not a cloud in the sky. The wild berries were huge and red, sweeter than any berries Kate had ever eaten. The juice trickled through their fingers, running down their chins, their perspiring necks. Eva stood under the mulberry tree, laughing, shoving fistfuls of berries into her reddened mouth. They surprised themselves with the shared hope that no car would pick them up for a good while yet. Eva would not stop eating or laughing. She looked so splendidly greedy, so consumed by appetite, that Kate, who had quit eating, took out her camera to capture her friend in all her sensual, purple-stained, glory.

And that was when the gypsies appeared in the distance. They were coming down the road in a caravan, their dust-covered wagons creaking, their horses' hooves hitting the asphalt in what seemed like slow motion. The heat by then was so intense the sun no longer seemed like a beneficent force.

As the caravan approached the crossroads, a man leapt

out of the wagon, holding on to the reins. Kate had her hands on the camera, her gaze meeting the man's febrile eyes. *"Hola!"*

In the darkness of the wagon sat a shadowy woman rocking a naked infant. Her husband wore faded blue jeans and an undershirt exposing his arms and shoulders. Kate was mesmerised by his burnished muscles, the gleaming white teeth in his nutmeg-hued face.

The woman twisted around and passed the infant to someone in the back of the wagon. She jumped off then and crossed the road towards them.

"Hablan espagnol?"

"Si," Eva answered, and the gypsy beamed, shooing off a fat bumblebee.

She was a young woman in a flowered skirt and creased purple blouse, a long braid running down her back. Did they want to have their palms read? she asked, speaking Spanish.

Kate was afraid of her, of what she might tell them, but Eva was visibly excited. She sat down on a flat rock and held out her small hand like a trusting child, waving Kate away with her other hand; Kate and her intrusive camera.

There were children clamouring to get off the wagon, but the father motioned them to stay put. He said something to one of the boys and the child arched back and reached for a flute. Kate knew that gypsies were said to be gifted musicians, but was unprepared to find herself breathless with admiration. She had not played her own flute for months and would never do so again after hearing the gypsy: a barefoot man in a sweat-soaked undershirt, standing next to his wagon, with the yellow sunflowers at his back, in the heat and dust, playing his gypsy music with his eyes shut tight, oblivious to the giggling children, the clicking camera.

Kate snapped him over and over; snapped his children with their shaven heads, his wife with her raw fingers clutching Eva's suntanned wrist. The air was hazy with pollen. The bees went on humming.

Back in Montreal, Kate would find herself from time to time thinking about the gypsies: their sudden appearance on that deserted road, their noisy departure. She had given them most of the *pesetas* she had, then stood on the roadside, shielding her eyes, watching the caravan move on, the wheels rolling on the dusty road, the children waving from the back of the wagon.

"Adios! Adios!"

When one of her photographs eventually won the National Geographic prize, the jury spoke of the marvellous juxtaposition of shape and colour, the dark poetry of the nomadic life.

"We can't hear the flutist," they wrote in their commentary, "but we know what's in his heart as he stands there playing. We feel the romance, as well as the heat and dust, the need to feed all those hungry children."

II

Oh, the countless times she read the American judges' comments! What sublime comfort she found in the knowledge that so much could be conveyed, with such exquisite accuracy, without her having to utter, or write, a single sentence. Kate had always been rather good with words but in the previous year, the year that had so irrevocably changed her life, she had become acutely aware of their limitations.

She was, by the time she won the prize, a married woman nursing her first child. When she told her husband that she'd decided to become a professional photographer, Brad did everything in his power to encourage her. He thought photography was something she could easily pursue while raising their son, born seven months after their simple Montreal wedding. Eva might have her doubts, but what Kate told her over lunch was the absolute truth: Brad knows that Sean is not his natural child.

Oh, the past, the ever-lurking past!

She had been staying with her mother's Parisian friends when she discovered that she was pregnant. For two or three days, she thought of Guillaume. She thought of the gypsies. She considered an abortion but, somewhat to her own surprise, found herself rejecting this obvious solution. A few days went by, then she sat down to place a long-distance call.

A slow, mysterious calmness came over Kate as she spoke to Brad, telling him she would be back home by the end of the week. She did not yet know the expression "back to the prose of life," but this in essence was what she felt when she spoke to Brad. The pregnancy had—overnight, it seemed—thrown the comforting cloak of fate over her turbulent self, her on-going search for life's poetry. She was not exactly lying when she said she was looking forward to seeing Brad again. If she had not by then given up on words, if she had been sure that there was such a thing as "soul," she would have said that one had died and another was about to be born.

You had to grow up sooner or later, a stern voice kept pointing out in her ear.

And so it was Brad who stood waiting for Kate at the airport, his russet hair blazing amid the huddling crowd. He looked, when he caught her eye, at once hopeful and triumphant, waving his long arm above the shoulders of waiting friends and lovers.

Brad Thuringer was over six feet tall and had the broad frame of a hockey-player, the clear eyes of a curious child mesmerised by some trapped, unfamiliar creature. The Abbitsons, and perhaps Dianne, must have persuaded him that Kate had been going through a difficult phase but was bound to come around, given time and patience. Who, after all, could fail to love a man like Dr. Brad Thuringer?

But that weekend—the weekend she returned from Europe—Kate's parents were attending an American school reunion, so it was Brad who drove Kate back into town; carried her off like a testament to his own tenacity, his unflagging optimism. He had, he was to tell her much later, always hoped she would be his wife; ever since the two of them met at Paul and Dianne's wedding.

Oh, she *tried* to tell him the truth almost immediately. The very next day, after a night spent with Brad in her parents' basement, she said she had something important to tell him.

"Really? Can't it wait?" Brad asked, yawning by the window. He was standing on his toes, stretching in the pale light of a late-fall morning. He looked uncharacteristically indolent at that moment; laid-back to the point of smugness. Kate took a decisive step towards him.

"No, it's important," she said. "I—"

He would not let her finish. He reached out and put a finger over her lips, and gave her a deeply earnest look. He must have assumed she wanted to tell him about Guillaume. Brad knew about Guillaume, of course, but no more than he wished to know, and certainly not from Kate.

"Whatever it is, I don't want to hear it right now. All I want—"

"But Brad!" Kate protested, "I think—"

He stopped her again. All he wanted to know, he said, was whether she would marry him—whenever she felt ready. He gazed at her with a sort of tender reproach. He drew her to him and kissed her.

"Oh!" Kate was jetlagged and tired. She looked Brad straight in the eye. "Is that really all you care about?"

Her smile was a little ironic, but Brad did not seem to notice. He smiled right back, complacent in the way of men who have triumphed over a reluctant woman. "Right now, yes, that is all I care about."

Of course, the key words were "right now." The key issue, for Brad Thuringer, was the challenge of making Kate Abbitson fall in love with him. He had no illusions about her feelings when he asked her to marry him. What he had was supreme confidence in his own ability, given time, to bring her around.

Ironically, what fuelled Brad's fierce masculine optimism was Kate's own ability—unfeminine, she secretly believed at the time—to enjoy sex as distinct from love. Not that she hadn't experienced the glory of having both, but Brad was after all unacquainted with the details of her turbulent past, the secrets of her wayward body.

III

Her body began to change. She thought again of getting an abortion and, once more, banished the thought. She had no moral qualms about doing away with a pregnancy, but not this particular foetus; not one nourished by her own blood. She had always been squeamish. The one time she'd had a blood test she had fainted at the hospital's test centre. Whatever happened, there would be no abortion.

As the days passed, Brad grew more and more buoyant, more overtly pleased with himself. Kate was beginning to doubt both her integrity and her courage. Now and then, she found herself toying with the idea of leaving Brad; writing him a note, then taking the train to Boston, to stay with her mother's sister.

Day after day went by; one week, and then another. Kate looked at Brad's love-lit face and could not bring herself to speak her mind. They saw each other three evenings a week, but every morning she woke up, convulsed with nausea and self-loathing. The trees on their street had shed most of their leaves by then; the air carried whiffs of approaching winter. And still she remained silent.

It was late November before she finally spoke up, tasting shame and panic. Brad stood facing her in fraught silence, a vein pulsing above his left eyebrow. It was as close as Kate would ever come to seeing Brad Thuringer look helpless; stupefied, she would think later, like an obedient child who somehow lost his way when home had already been sighted. In her own home, the surrounding walls seemed to shift and sigh. She waited, barely breathing, thinking wildly that she fully deserved to be slapped. But when Brad raised his hand, it was only to touch her cheek, and brush a strand of hair away from her face.

"Thank you for telling me," he said.

He was, Kate would discover, a man who took exceptional pride in his own virtue. Solemnly gazing into her eyes, he reiterated what he'd said on her first morning back. The past was over and done with; the future, their shared future, was what he hoped she would focus on from then on. He loved her, he said, taking her trembling hands in his own; he certainly wasn't going to abandon her. Now that she needed him.

Kate knew Brad well enough to be sure he would keep his promise. If she still felt an occasional spasm of anxiety, it was only at the thought of her unborn baby; the child of a stranger even she knew nothing about. Something told her, though, that Brad was the sort of man who, aware of his own conflicted feelings, would try all the harder to behave in an exemplary manner. She did not yet know the price of his fierce high-mindedness.

It took several years for Brad's attitude to show signs of strain. For hadn't she proven to be aloof and unyielding? Hadn't she, despite all his efforts to win her over, failed to offer him the hidden blossom of her passionate heart? He never once reproached her; never made a single reference to her pre-marital past. In her dialogues with her own conscience, Kate has often reminded herself of this fact, though she sensed that, in his private moments, Brad must have occasionally brooded on her messy past; not so much her thwarted love for Guillaume, but the havoc she wreaked in the months leading up to their wedding.

But does she regret having married Brad? Does she?

Ah, this is a difficult question to answer, Kate says to

herself; an impossible question, when you stop to think about it. Answering it in the affirmative would, after all, be tantamount to wishing her own daughter's annihilation.

And then there is her son, who believes Brad to be his natural father but whose very existence is a perpetual reminder of her own fecklessness. The past might eventually be redeemed but can never be forgotten. And yet, Kate loves her son as much as any woman has ever loved her child. How could she possibly want to undo the past?

This is the sort of question that eventually led Kate to turn her back on words and philosophical musings; that made her embrace the more forgiving truth of photography.

IV

Most of Kate's family photographs are in Kodacolor, but in her professional work, she has long preferred to use black and white. When Sean was three years old, she had a late-term miscarriage, believed to have been caused by a neural-tube defect. This would have been Brad's first child; would, the doctors patiently tried to explain, have been born with Spina Bifida. It was what Brad, too, tried to impress on Kate, his eyes willing her to understand that she should be grateful; that it would not be reasonable to mourn the loss of such a tragically compromised life.

Five years would pass before Kate was able to conceive again but, during those years, she began to reject what she was starting to think of as the aggressiveness, the perniciousness, of colour. When Brad bought a 35" Sony TV at Christmas, she found herself mentally stripping scenes of their colour. As if life were actually black and white; as if her mission in life were to uncover the authentic nature of everything around her.

"But you haven't captured the authentic me," Brad argued when she showed him a black-and-white photo she'd taken of him; when she tried to explain what must have seemed like a rather eccentric preference. "No human being is black and white, are they?" Brad smiled tightly. "Not even me, you know."

It was an intriguing comment; one that made it clear Brad had come to intuit something about Kate's unvoiced perception of him.

But that, it seemed, only strengthened his resolve to win her over. His work as a cardiologist must have, after some years, begun to present few new challenges. He was at the top of his game by his late thirties, but the mysteries of his own wife's heart continued to elude him. They made bitter lines run along his tightening lips. They made the invisible vein in his temple throb with increasing frequency. Brad was not emotionally obtuse. At some point he must have realized: His wife's tattered hopes had left her with all her senses intact, but with a softly murmuring heart no cardiologist could ever hope to cure.

This is the secret grief behind Brad Thuringer's tightening lips. It explains everything, except perhaps why, after some twenty-six years of marriage, the unrest in Kate's chest has become a steady ache, an occasional plea that cannot be ignored.

But a plea for what?

This is what Kate is still trying to figure out. It is one reason why she is not yet ready to go back to Edmonton.

FIVE

I

A WEEK GOES by before Kate sees Antonia Offe again. She suspects that Antonia must be a little bored, maybe even lonely, what with her only daughter living in the UK, married to a Brit. Why else would an aging actress invite an impulsive stranger to come back for another visit?

Kate had meant to send a thank-you note to Antonia, but forgot all about it after coming down with a stomach flu. She often gets sick when she is under stress, especially while travelling. But today, at last, she is on the mend; she's feeling so much better that Megan did not hesitate to re-mind her about the promise to buy resin and strings for her violin.

And so here she is, back on Mackay Street for the first time in nearly thirty years. Incredibly, Ludvig's music store is still here, unchanged, but just now is closed for a funeral. It is going to be closed until four o'clock, so Kate goes in search of a quick lunch before running a few errands.

But then, heading west on St. Catherine Street, she comes upon a lavish flower stall and impulsively decides to call Antonia, who lives barely ten minutes away. If she drops off a nice bouquet, she won't have to bother with writing and mailing a belated note. There must be a public phone booth at Le Faubourg. She can grab a muffin or bagel to tide her over.

Antonia answers on the fifth ring, a little breathless, but sounding rather pleased to hear Kate's voice. When Kate says that she is phoning from Le Faubourg, Antonia cuts her short, telling her to come right over and have a cup of tea. She has a rehearsal this afternoon but doesn't have to leave for a couple of hours yet.

"Oh!" Kate says. "I wasn't ... I was just going to drop something off."

"How intriguing!" Antonia exclaims.

Kate goes back to the flower stall and buys a bouquet of exquisite yellow roses. She will have a quick cup of tea with Antonia, then shop for some groceries and head back to Ludvig's. She has bought a protein bar and a banana in lieu of lunch and eats them on the run as she heads up St. Matthew Street. It is mid-afternoon; another grey, windy day, with showers in the forecast.

"How sweet of you to think of me!" Antonia says, flinging the front door open. She exclaims in delight on being handed the rose bouquet. Yellow turns out to be Antonia's favourite colour. She brings the fragrant cone to her nostrils, leads the way upstairs, then goes to the kitchen and fills a beautiful blue vase with water.

"Shall we have some more of that heavenly tea?" she asks.

"Well ... if you're sure it's not too much trouble. I was actually on my way to buy violin strings for my daughter but the shop is closed for a funeral. They'll re-open at four o'clock."

"Perfect! We'll have a nice cup of tea, then I'll walk

down with you. My car's in the garage this week." She puts the kettle on, then excuses herself to go to the powder room.

Kate waits, dawdling in front of the combine painting, scrutinizing its spiteful, grotesque faces, its grasping, aggressive arms. She reminds herself that it is possible to like people whose tastes one does not share; she has no explanation for last week's unease; or, for that matter, her eager acceptance of today's impromptu invitation. She knows she is not always as rational and consistent as she'd like to be. Certainly not as rational as her husband.

II

"Did you know that Pauline Julien used to live downstairs?"

Kate voices this question as soon as she and Antonia sit down with their tea, having made up her mind to steer the conversation away from personal matters. Pauline Julien was a celebrated *chanteuse* in the turbulent 70s, as famous for her fervent nationalism as she was for her singing.

"Oh, I know Pauline quite well," Antonia says.

She is sitting across from Kate on one of the ivory sofas, looking a little tired but warmly engaged in the conversation. She claims to be acquainted not only with Pauline Julien but also with Yves Letourneau, the playwright, who used to live upstairs and who was the one to mention the new condos weeks before their restoration was complete.

Like Pauline Julien, Yves had become a nationalist when the small tremors of Québecois rage began to be felt across the country. Kate's Westmount upbringing may have been typically privileged, but it was unusual in at least one respect: her mother was not Canadian. She was an American from Massachusetts who had settled in Montreal after her marriage. Radcliffe-educated, she could never understand why anglophones like her husband seemed incapable of rallying any sympathy for Québecers, a beleaguered minority desperate to preserve its cultural identity on a vast American continent; to gain its fair share of economic power.

It was French Canadians' political aspirations that gradually made Yves Letourneau a household name in Québec. Antonia, it turns out, has acted in two of Yves' early stage plays. She seems only too happy to fetch her portfolio, going on to show Kate several photos of herself with the acclaimed playwright. Today, Yves Letourneau would be in his early fifties, but the man Kate remembers—a young man whose girlfriend she was once friendly with—seemed on his way to becoming an alcoholic, ranting into the small hours because no one would produce his plays.

"Ah, yes. It's not enough to have talent. You have to have talent for having talent," Antonia says, flipping through her album. Yves had made a lot of enemies when he was young, Antonia states, but who can blame him? She, too, has had more than her share of professional battles, though she shouldn't complain; she really has been surprisingly lucky.

Antonia says all this and smiles, hastening to knock on wood. Right now, she is in an interesting production at the Centaur Theatre, a new play dealing with immigrant life and complicated mother-daughter relationships.

"It's probably my most challenging role so far," she says, putting her teacup down on its pretty saucer. "I play a Greek grandmother, an old woman in the throes of dementia."

"A grandmother?" Despite Antonia's age, it is not easy to imagine her playing an immigrant granny, let alone a demented one. "I wish I could see you perform!"

When Megan was very young, she longed to be a ballerina, an ambition Kate did her best to quell early on. It is, she has always thought, one of life's cruellest professions; she is so glad her daughter is talking about becoming a neurologist instead. Acting must be a better career choice than dancing but, listening to Antonia describe her new role, Kate finds herself wondering about the life of an aging stage actress; one who must have spent years rehearsing for applause, only to find herself waiting for the phone to ring. How many roles can there be for a woman in her late sixties? And yet, Antonia does seem to be quite successful; Kate is disappointed that *The Crabapple Season* will open only after her departure.

"My mother died of Alzheimer's," she hears herself tell Antonia.

"I'm so sorry. Terrible disease. Tragic."

"It's what made my daughter decide to become a neurologist," Kate says. "That's why she is at McGill. She's only seventeen, though. Just starting out."

"Ah, my dear, seventeen!" This is all Antonia says, but something about her tone tells Kate that her hunch was right: Her new friend must be lonely, even if she isn't the sort of woman one would be quick to feel sorry for. Not with that mobile face of hers, those narrow, unflinching eyes. The eyes seem exceptionally avid, but Antonia has a way of crinkling them with a sort of tender amusement, an expression that reminds Kate of her late mother.

Which is how Antonia ends up catching her off-guard,

asking about Guillaume when Kate's mind still hovers around the memory of her beloved mother.

"So, you haven't told me about this boyfriend of yours," Antonia says, ever so lightly. "Was he a student, too?"

"Guillaume? Oh! Yes. Yes, he was working towards his Master's in Music," Kate says, her eyes returning to the spot where Guillaume used to sit and practise.

His cello was a fine, hand-made instrument, purchased by his parents at great personal sacrifice. They'd given it to him for his twenty-first birthday and Guillaume worshipped it, sitting for hours with the fat, gleaming instrument between his legs, the bow hypnotically sliding back and forth. Day in and day out. One evening, soon after they met, Guillaume pointed out to Kate the little cylinder between the sounding board and the back of the cello; a small dowel common to all string instruments, known in English as the "sound post" and in French as the "soul."

"And that," he said, speaking in a faux-didactic tone, "that is where the soul of the most soulful of all instruments rests. Right there." He reached out and carefully placed his hand under the treble end of the bridge.

Kate answers Antonia's questions, but rather reluctantly. A part of her would like nothing better than to sit reminiscing about Guillaume, yet her on-going flirtation with the past fills her with both guilt and shame. When Antonia asks about her husband, therefore, Kate is relieved to change the subject. Soon, she finds herself speaking of Sean's literary ambitions; the unresolved conflict between him and his father. Brad has made his views clear: It's high time Sean started acting responsibly, thinking about the future instead of wasting his best years on dead-end jobs and self-indulgent pursuits.

Kate shares all this with Antonia, then stops with a small, nervous laugh.

"I don't know why I'm telling you all this," she says.

But, of course, she does! It is easy to be so open precisely because Antonia is still a relative stranger; one she may never see again, if she chooses not to. Also, though her heart remains in revolt against Antonia's sterile surroundings, there is, now that she has overcome her initial discomfort, something liberating about speaking openly to someone whose judgement is untainted by any knowledge of a decidedly messy past. Someone, in fact, who seems totally non-judgemental.

Kate is still musing on all this when they finish their tea and Antonia goes upstairs to get ready. Kate sits fondling the remarkably docile Otto: rubbing his inner ear between her fingers, his shiny, luxurious fur. The cat has settled himself against the cushion of her abdomen and lies there, purring with wanton abandon, while she mulls things over.

He is still purring when Antonia returns, her face powdered, her eyes carefully made up. She stands for a moment, smiling indulgently at the cozy scene. It is almost time to go, but maybe Kate's daughter would like to have a newborn kitten? she asks. There is an eccentric old woman living alone just down the street. Well, not quite alone: she must have a dozen cats of all stripes and sizes. Last week, the old woman went around knocking on doors, asking whether anyone they knew might like to have a newborn kitten.

"She's got a litter of exceptionally cute ones, I'm told," Antonia adds. She is standing in front of the hallway mirror, arranging her scarf, adjusting her purple beret.

"Is this Elizabeth Berg by any chance?" Kate asks, staring at Antonia's reflection. "Elizabeth's still around? I can't believe it! She must be ... what? A hundred by now?"

"Well, not quite." Antonia chuckles. She pulls a few silver curls out of the beret, her head tilted sideways. "Only eighty-nine ... rather eccentric but surprisingly sharp. Did you know she's lived on the street since World War II?"

"Yes ... I think I remember her telling me. Good old Elizabeth." Kate sighs, shaking her head on a wave of nostalgia. Miss Elizabeth!

The German immigrant must have been only about sixty when Guillaume lived here, but she seemed ancient to the two of them.

Soon, Kate finds herself telling Antonia how she had met Elizabeth all those years ago. She says nothing about the life-altering day on which she lost her beloved Pablo. Losing her cat may have been the least of her problems that weekend, but she will never forget her anguish on realizing that Pablo had slipped out through an open window.

It was Guillaume who had left the window open but, caught up in the web of momentous events, Kate didn't notice either the window or Pablo's absence. Oh, of course, she went looking for him once she realized. She checked with every neighbour on the street, called the SPCA, the adjacent Catholic seminary. Her cat was gone! She supposed he must have got trapped in the heavy Côte-des-Neiges traffic; had most likely been hit by a speeding car.

The following day, she ran into Elizabeth after she'd gone looking for Pablo for the second time. It was dusk and there was Elizabeth in her apron, stepping out to give a short, musical whistle, peering down the street.

Instantly, half a dozen cats appeared out of nowhere, circling around Elizabeth's swollen ankles, their tails in the air. But no, she had not seen a black cat in recent days. Had Kate thought to ask at the seminary? If the priests didn't have Pablo, she'd be happy to give Kate one of her own kittens.

Elizabeth insisted on showing her the new litter, and Kate was too distraught that day to resist. She ended up having coffee with Elizabeth, listening politely to the story of her life. It was not at all a boring life, but Kate still remembers her own suppressed impatience as she sat there in the dark parlour. That's what Elizabeth called it, a parlour, and surely no girl in her early twenties would have willingly spent time in one, listening to a German eccentric.

When Elizabeth heard that Kate was a student, she pressed her to take a jar of her own home-made jam. Kate didn't have the heart to tell her that she lived with her parents, in Westmount, where she was exceptionally well fed. As things turned out, she never saw Elizabeth again; never even got to taste the home-made plum jam.

III

It is going on four o'clock when Kate and Antonia make their way down towards de Maisonneuve Boulevard. They stroll to the corner but say goodbye at the Metro entrance. Antonia is on her way to the Centaur; Kate still has her errands. A soft drizzle falls as she leaves her new friend and crosses towards Le Faubourg's indoor market. She has only a few items to buy, but by the time she is done, the drizzle has turned into a steady downpour, with thunder rumbling in the grey distance.

Kate knows by now that her new designer raincoat is not as impermeable as she had been led to believe. She decides to take a cab. Standing on the blustery corner, she tries to hail one, then gives up and crosses the street, resigned to taking the Metro. It is only two stops, then something like a ten-minute walk up to Megan's street in the McGill Ghetto.

Head lowered against the slanting rain, she starts to trudge to the Guy Metro station when someone considerably odder than Elizabeth Berg happens to turn the corner. Just a downtown bag lady, but one who, at that distracted moment, on that rain-veiled September evening, looms before Kate like some familiar phantom in an ever-recurring nightmare.

The Guy Metro has always had vagrants lounging by its escalators, but the elderly bag lady is out in the rain, shuffling back and forth, hunched over a chaotically packed shopping cart. Despite the evening chill, the homeless stranger is sporting black summer sandals and a thick turban as green as a grasshopper. Staring straight ahead, she wears the expression of someone on a private mission: a heavy, tight-lipped stranger who appears to have heard a call inaudible to anyone else.

The facial expression sends Kate's thoughts towards her recently deceased mother, though Fiona Abbitson was fortunate enough to be spared a bag lady's fate. There were no bag ladies at the Glenview Manor; only fading spectres in various stages of dementia, babbling to themselves, pacing aimlessly, shouting obscenities. Those who, like Kate's mother, were no longer ambulatory, lay in bed day after day, or lolled in recliners, blankly staring at the flickering TV screen.

Kate's mother had broken her hip and spent much of her time strapped to a vinyl recliner in the patients' lounge. She never stopped protesting, wailing, threatening. She no longer knew where she was, who she was. The last time Kate had come for a visit, her mother mistook her for a man.

"Sir! Sir!" Kate had stepped off the main elevator, to find her mother yelling in her direction. "Can I speak to you for a moment, Sir?"

Kate hurried up to her mother. She leaned over and kissed the pale forehead, the soft, parchment-like cheek.

"It's me, Mother dear. Kate." The sagging flesh was giving off an odd, acrid smell.

"I had a daughter named Kate." Her mother's cloudy eyes blinked, peering without recognition. "I had two twin daughters but—"

"I am one of them, Mom. I'm Kate," she repeated. Sometimes this worked and her mother's face would freeze for a moment, then dissolve into a look of chaotic bliss. But not that day. That afternoon, Kate's mother kept calling her *Sir*; kept appealing to her to contact her children, her husband, the family lawyer. She was in one of her fiercely paranoid moods. Everyone was in cahoots here, she informed Kate; everyone, even the staff doctors.

"I won't stop shouting until they let me contact my lawyer! Or the police!" she went on, her eyes as grey as storm clouds. One of the nurses had tried to choke her to death; an orderly had stolen her personal possessions. She lifted her chin, gesturing towards the nursing station. "I want to file a report: right now, right away!"

The paranoia was new but the pride was not: Kate's

mother's ancestors had arrived in the New World onboard the Mayflower. She had met her husband at Harvard, married him before the year was out, and went on to spend the rest of her life in Montreal. She had always been an iron-willed woman, but her husband's death turned her into a hermit, and then, gradually, into a true eccentric. She began to sport ancient, moth-eaten hats she'd found in old steamer chests; to stash cash and jewellery in her frayed undergarments.

Brad and Kate had brought Fiona Abbitson to Edmonton, to live with them, until she began to defecate in the bathtub, and one terrible night, came very close to burning down their home. They decided to place her at the Glenview Manor. It was there, the day she called her *Sir*, that Kate's mother had a massive heart attack and died in her daughter's presence, a puddle of urine forming below her seat.

There was a time when Kate believed that she could never lose anyone if she photographed them often enough, attentively enough. It has taken her a long time to discover that family photos only become reminders of just how much one has lost.

Back in Edmonton, there is a black-and-white photograph of her mother as a little girl, sitting on the grass by a picturesque Massachusetts pond. She is wearing a polka-dotted halter and has a white ribbon in her hair. She seems oblivious to the photographer's presence, wholly absorbed in talking to her doll. She is four years old, but Kate can never look at this fading photograph without finding herself engulfed by a wave of preposterous dread. The poor child. She is going to get sick and die, she finds herself thinking. A terrible catastrophe awaits this beribboned little girl and she has no inkling of it!

The sense of impotence Kate feels at such moments goes on bruising her heart. Her mother is gone, but a photograph is immutable, an eternal testament to both our innocence and our shared doom. Time has taken the edge off Kate's sense of loss, only to saddle her with a new worry: Is she destined to end up like her poor, deranged mother, strapped to a vinyl lounge chair, urine dripping from a soggy diaper onto a clean institutional floor?

This is not a fear Kate has shared with anyone; not even her husband. What she can't work out is her private conviction that Brad is all that stands between her and eventual dementia. A truly perplexing notion, given that, with her children gone, she can hardly bear the thought of the two of them alone, drifting through all those empty rooms like ghosts in search of a past they had once inhabited and cannot quite believe has vanished.

Kate has stashed away the picture of her mother sitting in her dripping lounge chair. It is the last photograph anyone will ever have of Fiona Abbitson. This, Kate wishes she had said to Eva, is what photography is really about. It's about our deepest joys and sorrows and unvoiced fears; the inescapable awareness that a photograph, any photograph, will outlast both subject and photographer. A photograph does not discriminate between the living and the dead.

Photography is about defeating time, Eva.

IV

A woman may stop talking to her friends, but she can never stop talking to her mother, not even long after she has been buried. Yet nothing a woman says, nothing anyone says, can ever quite dissolve the bitter kernel of guilt lodged in a daughter's gut; the occasional ambush of the purest, blackest sorrow. This might well be the greatest challenge life throws our way, Kate says to herself; the insistence that we raise one reluctant foot, and bring it down, and then raise the second, letting the sheer effort of locomotion distract us from devouring sorrow.

So this is what she finds herself doing on this bleak Friday afternoon. She ends up turning her back on the pitiful bag lady. She takes a resolute step forward. And then another, and yet another.

At that moment, she spots an approaching cab.

"Taxi! *Taxi!*"

The cab screeches to a halt and Kate splashes her way towards it, settling in with a conscious effort to channel her thoughts in a positive direction. This is something her sister-in-law trained her to do many years ago, but today it turns out to be all but impossible. The images of her dying mother cling to Kate's brain cells like cobwebs. She is still fighting tears when she suddenly realizes that, what with the rain and all, she has forgotten to go back to Ludvig's for the violin strings. She will now have to make a special trip on another day.

The rain goes on falling, hurtling across the windshield. The taxi is inching along in the heavy rush-hour traffic, heading east on St. Catherine Street. The street has hardly changed since Kate's last Montreal visit. Its gaudy neon lights flash as aggressively as ever; they dance in the gutter, the oil-slicked rain puddles. Friday is one of two evenings when the downtown clothing and shoe stores remain open until nine o'clock. Dozens of shoppers caught in the rain are now huddling under canvas awnings, waiting out the storm; others scurry down the flooded pavements, sidestepping each other's wobbly umbrellas.

The wind has been steadily rising since Kate said goodbye to Antonia. Now and then, her taxi hits a puddle, and the water comes splashing up against the cab windows with a great muddy *whoosh*. Kate shifts her weight in the back seat, while the cab continues eastward towards McGill University, slowing down at a red STOP sign. Well, an ARRÊT sign, to be exact. The provincial switch to the French version is relatively recent; Kate still recalls her husband shaking his head in disbelief on first learning of Québec's new language laws.

"It's the only place in the world where drivers will now need a dictionary as well as a road map," he said, his mouth quirked over the weekend paper.

But of course there is more to it than traffic signs, Kate says to herself, clearing her stuffed nostrils. She has just gotten over her stomach flu, but now seems to be coming down with a cold. Letting herself get caught in the rain was a bad idea. If only Megan would deign to carry her own umbrella!

Kate reaches into her handbag, rummaging for a tissue. As she does so, her fingers brush against the envelope containing Guillaume's letter. Because of its gouging power, Kate has resolved never to read the letter again. What to do with it is another question. Somehow, she can't bring herself to chuck it out with the daily trash: the brittle egg shells, the cabbage leaves, the fish heads with their dull, accusatory eyes. One day, back in Edmonton, she had photographed a plate of fried mullet heads before offering them to the cat. And then she took a picture of the cat pouncing on the leftovers. She does not like any sort of waste. She dislikes it almost as much as she does missed opportunities.

Kate slides the square blue envelope into her agenda. She has no idea why her mind keeps tossing up such trivial memories. But one thing is clear to her: she has been as confused, as high-strung, as a teenager in the throes of hormonal chaos. She has to remind herself that, whatever the mirror says, she is almost fifty years old. Is it possible that all this internal tumult is due to nothing more worrisome than a normal, perhaps even inevitable, physiological battle; one whose rumblings may not be all that different from those heard decades ago, during adolescence?

The latter thought, for some reason, offers a modicum of comfort. It is as though she still had her mother standing over her, gently murmuring: "This too shall pass, my darling. This too shall pass."

SIX

I

IT IS NOT easy to make friends in middle age. It is even more difficult in a town where you have few social connections. Kate is glad to have met Antonia Offe, but she still can't make up her mind how she feels about her. One way or another, she always ends up doing, ends up saying, more than she had intended. She is about to see Antonia for the third time, but this will be the first meeting the two of them have actually planned ahead.

They have agreed to meet in Old Montreal, where the Centaur Theatre is situated, and where Antonia is still rehearsing *The Crabapple Season*. The play is set in a Montreal suburb and revolves around the Greek-born grandmother played by Antonia, her divorced Canadian daughter, and a love-struck adolescent granddaughter called Rikki. The plot deals with mother-daughter relationships, as Antonia told Kate earlier, but also with the three women's respective search for love. When she learnt that Kate would be returning to Edmonton before the play opens next month, Antonia invited her to come down and at least see a stage rehearsal. It was an invitation Kate was happy to accept, despite the dismal weather. Megan has piles of homework to do. Kate's brother and sister-in-law are still in Sicily.

After the rehearsal, the first stage rehearsal Kate has ever attended, Antonia suggests dinner in nearby Chinatown. Although the rain has all but stopped, the cobble-stoned streets, which throughout summer are thronged with revellers, are now dark and hushed, dimly lit by ancient street lamps. As a young woman, Kate enjoyed coming here on sultry nights, but this evening the wet streets are as deserted and desolate as a rain-washed *quartier* in some French wartime film. As she and Antonia head south, a gust of wind blows up from the river, laced with the scent of rain and fallen leaves, the droppings of *calêche* horses. Janis Joplin's voice is wafting out of a brightly-lit bar, singing *Boots*. The song makes Kate and Antonia laugh in unison: weren't they just talking about the courage it still takes to live without a man?

Antonia has been twice married and twice divorced. She believes that marriage, like acting, requires special talent; one which she, alas, does not seem to possess. It took the better part of her life, she tells Kate, but she finally learnt to centre her life around the theatre and her friends. She has many good friends, all over the world.

"I hope you'll be one of them," she says, taking Kate's arm as they turn a corner. She also hopes Kate can come to her birthday party next weekend. Her sixty-ninth, she adds, widening her eyes theatrically. "I'm thinking of inviting my ex, my second one—he's a wonderful raconteur —though my horoscope warns of potential complications later this month, so maybe I'd better not, eh?"

They laugh, then go back to discussing *The Crabapple Season*. In the play, the Greek grandmother, known throughout as *Yaya*, is left alone one evening and invites a friend, an old Italian immigrant with whom she used to work, to come for a visit. The two elderly women sit drinking plum brandy, catching up on each other's news. Eventually, they move on to the granddaughter's room, where *Yaya* insists on showing her friend a birthday gift she has bought for Rikki. Giddy with drink, they end up trying on the teenager's clothes and accessories. They turn on her music. They clown around in an outlandish, poignant parody of flirtatious youth.

"That's a wonderful, a truly heartbreaking scene, when Rikki's mother comes home and finds her own mother and the guest dancing drunkenly," Kate observes at length.

"It's a lovely scene. When I first read the script, I thought: This is as good a role as I'm likely to get these days."

The statement is accompanied by a slow, resigned breath. They walk on in silence, their rhyming steps echoing in the night. After a while, Kate asks how Antonia had come to be an actress; when did she decide on an acting career?

"Oh, I don't think I ever really decided, you know. I think I was born an actress ... if that doesn't sound too pretentious." Antonia is one of those people who place a tiny emphasis on every key word: I don't think I ever *decided,* I think I was *born.* She is altogether a rather emphatic sort of person.

"But how did you know that? When did you first know?" Kate is curious about this because it never occurred to her, when she was young, that she might some day be a photographer. People have often told her she was born with a photographer's eye, but what if she had never entered the gypsy photograph in the American competition? What if she hadn't taken any pictures when she was in Europe? She gazes up at the yellow moon, floating in and out of the storm clouds. What would she be doing with her life without photography?

Antonia doesn't have the answer to Kate's question. All she can say is that she'd always, as far back as she can remember, longed to know what it would be like to inhabit other people's skin.

"Any time I met someone who stood out in some way —an amputee or a blind child, or just a silly, flirtatious woman, I would end up compulsively imitating them."

Antonia's laugh tinkles with reminiscent delight. Once, when she was about six and her mother was teaching at Miss Edgar and Miss Cramp's, her parents invited the headmistress for Sunday tea. Antonia could not take her eyes off the prim lady: her long gloves, her small purple hat.

"Like all spinsters of her time, she had a ramrod-straight posture, but also an odd way of turning her head sideways when spoken to ... like someone coming out of a deep trance, you know?"

Antonia pauses, glancing at a young couple strolling up the street, their arms wrapped around each other. The sidewalks in this part of town are narrow and the lovers end up stepping down onto the road. As they reach the corner, the girl bursts out laughing, and Kate finds herself listening intently. There is something arresting about this youthful laughter. It rings down the mist-shrouded street with such aplomb, such exquisite clarity, it's impossible not to visualize the lips giving shape to such carefree laughter. The shape of the lips, the curve of the neck, the head thrown back with the sort of abandon only the young seem to possess. Antonia, too, is listening.

"Well? What did you do to the poor woman?" Kate asks, breaking the long silence.

"What? Oh!" Antonia chuckles, then goes on to share her childish fascination with the aging headmistress: her somnolent air, her deep, masculine voice. She turns towards Kate, raises her chin, and mimics her mother's guest. "My dear child, how you've grown since I last saw you!"

The theatrical voice makes Kate laugh as she buttons her collar. She takes her gloves out of her pockets and pulls them on, trying to imagine her grey-haired companion as a small child. It is a mental challenge that just about fails. It demands an imaginative feat that must efface over sixty years!

"Anyway," Antonia continues, "the day the schoolmistress came to visit, my mother asked me to run to the kitchen and bring some packet she had prepared for Miss Perkins. That was her name: Miss Annabelle Perkins." She reaches into her pocket for a handkerchief.

The wind from the St. Lawrence River is blowing in their faces, making Antonia's eyes and nose run. Sniffling, she tells Kate how, when her mother made the request in front of Miss Perkins, she — six-year-old Antonia — stopped and glanced at her mother, and slowly, very slowly, turned her head sideways with that *de haut en bas* look the schoolmistress habitually wore.

"Oh certainly!" she said in the deepest voice a child could muster. "Certainly, Mama!" And then she ran off towards the kitchen, giggling into her hand.

"You didn't! Did you really do that?" Kate says, sounding incredulous. She remembers herself as a shy child, slavishly respectful towards adults. She often met her parents' friends and professional acquaintances, but the most she would have done in Antonia's place would have been to stare at the snooty guest.

"You're much bolder than I ever was," she says.

They laugh again, startling a bundled vagrant asleep on a closed boutique's steps. The dishevelled old man opens his eyes, squints at them for a moment, then re-settles himself and goes back to sleep. Beside him, rainwater drips from an ancient eave.

"That was the first but certainly not the last time I got into trouble with my childish pranks," Antonia says, sounding rather pleased with herself. "I've got my come-uppance though," she hastens to add. "My daughter is the world's worst prankster. Worse than I ever was." Antonia laughs some more, her eyes sweeping the looming edifice on her left: its bulging-eyed gargoyles, its softly glowing windows. As they move on, huddling closer against the wind, a beam of light catches a small creature scurrying towards a manhole.

"Look!" Kate cries. "Is that a rat over there?"

"Looks like it, doesn't it?" They slow down, staring straight ahead. "It's a big one, though." Antonia shudders.

Incredibly, Kate has never seen a live rat before; at least not that she can recall. But as she squints at the quickly vanishing creature, she remembers the day Guillaume discovered that rats, or perhaps squirrels, had gnawed right through his pantry wall. He had been hearing them race through the rafters for weeks. One day, he found a bag of egg noodles ripped open on the bottom shelf, half its contents gone. The hole in the wall was too large to have been made by mice, the old janitor told Guillaume. He offered to sprinkle poison in the pantry, which Guillaume briefly considered but rejected on learning that the pink, harmless-looking pellets caused the animals' stomachs to rupture. He examined the janitor's traps, designed to decapitate the rats, but rejected those as well, opting, as so often, for his own, eccentric, solution.

Every night, before he went to sleep, Guillaume would leave a sandwich bag with leftovers by the hole in the cupboard. Every morning, the sandwich bag and its contents would be gone, with no trace left behind. The nocturnal visitors seemed to respect the silent deal offered by Guillaume. They never went beyond the hole in the wall; never touched anything else in the pantry.

Guillaume called this arrangement "peaceful coexistence." Canadian politicians just lacked imagination, he said to Kate, laughing.

The memory makes Kate smile to herself. She doesn't share the story with Antonia, who, she thinks, would be too fastidious to appreciate Guillaume's compromise. For that matter, she doesn't suppose Guillaume's wife would approve either. Not that Kate knows anything about her, of course, but she can't think of any woman who would approve. And yet, her younger self had been charmed by what seemed like an inspired idea; charmed and deeply touched. Guillaume always seemed to be ahead of her and everyone else, finding paths to peaks of transcendent insight, and islands of humble compassion.

II

The weather remains capricious. As they approach Chinatown, the evening air is suddenly thick with whiffs of roasting duck and Oriental spice, the sweetish odour of discarded fruit rotting in wooden crates. Just before they turn the corner, a few drops of rain start falling out of the bloated sky. A shopkeeper goes about picking up boxes full of fresh produce, lugging them indoors before the storm breaks out. Antonia walks with her head craning right and left, scrutinizing the shops, the signs.

"Somewhere around here, there's a new restaurant I've been wanting to try," she says. "It serves both Cantonese and Szechuan food. Is that okay with you?"

"Absolutely!" Kate enjoys Cantonese cuisine because of the extensive vegetable menu, but she also adores bold and spicy flavours. Now and then, she accompanies journalists on travel assignments to exotic places. One of the pleasures of these assignments, she tells Antonia, is getting to taste things like grape-weed with fermented coconut in Fiji, or fish bladder soup in Penang.

"Fish bladder soup!" Antonia exclaims. "Yuck!"

"Oh, no, *au contraire!* It's a great delicacy in Malaysia, usually reserved for weddings."

"Well, another good reason never to get married," Antonia tosses out, peering into every shop she passes. "How does your husband feel about all the travelling you do?" she asks after a moment. She has stepped aside to let a butcher's delivery man pass, a small carcass hauled over his shoulder. Kate is about to answer when Antonia stops, exclaiming: "There! I think that's it ... yes. Yes, it is!"

It is a simple eatery, decorated with red lanterns, crowded with Chinese diners.

"That's always a good sign," Antonia declares over her shoulder. She pauses at the entrance, then leads briskly towards the back, where she has spied the only available table. They have arrived just in time. The rain is suddenly gaining momentum, pelting the dark windows. There is the clatter of a wheelbarrow going by, the rattle of shutters being drawn next door.

"Oh, I'm positively famished!" Antonia says, speaking in Miss Perkins' deep-throated voice.

Kate laughs, hanging up her damp raincoat. Antonia makes her laugh more often than anyone else she knows. They settle across from each other, hands fluttering over damp hair, eyes scanning the trilingual menu. Antonia pours the tea, then compulsively smoothes down the transparent plastic covering the table.

"Where were we?" she says. "Ah yes, I was asking how your husband felt about your travel but—"

"Right," Kate says. "He ... well, I don't travel all that much, you know, and never for very long. Anyway, the children are grown now. He doesn't mind anymore."

"But he used to?"

"Well, of course he minded," Kate says. "To be fair, though, he never really complained. We've had a house-keeper for years now, so—"

"Aren't you a lucky woman!" Antonia smiles at Kate, fiddling with one of her earrings. It is not really an un-pleasant smile, but there is something ... a little compli-cated about it.

"Yes, I suppose I am."

A waiter materializes, jotting down their order, but Kate still feels obscurely guilty, as she often does with women who have had to juggle career, housework, chil-dren. Sarah, Antonia's only daughter, lives in London now, with her husband and two children. When Antonia was young and still married, they lived in Toronto with her mother-in-law, a German woman from what used to be

Danzig, but is now the Polish city of Gdansk. It was mostly she who had taken care of little Sarah.

"I think I understand *Yaya* much better because of my
own experience," Antonia muses sadly. "I'm afraid I wasn't
as understanding then as I might have been."

Kate's own mother-in-law was dead by the time she
married Brad, but the mention of Poland has conjured the
long lunch she recently had with Eva, reminding Kate that
she, too, did not behave particularly well. For the first time,
she finds herself wishing that Guillaume's letter and old
photographs had never turned up when they did. Would she
be feeling more self-possessed right now if they hadn't?

A moment passes. All at once, Kate looks up from her
steaming cup. "Would you like to see a photo of
Guillaume?" she hears herself ask.

"Guillaume? Your Québecois beau?"

"Yes. My daughter found it among my old school stuff."
Kate has opened her handbag and is rummaging for her
agenda, in which she keeps Guillaume's farewell letter,
along with his photograph.

"Which one is he?" Antonia has put on her reading
glasses and is peering at the photograph in her hands.

"The one with the violin."

"I thought you said he was a cellist."

"He was. He was just clowning around for the photographer."

"You?" Antonia says. She looks up over her tiny, red-
framed spectacles.

"Yes. My American aunt had given me a camera for
my twenty-first birthday. That's how it all started."

"Well," Antonia says after prolonged scrutiny. "He
looks dishy all right."

The word makes Kate smile a little. She has, since her lunch with Eva, conceded that her old friend had not been entirely wrong: She probably is more susceptible to good looks than the average person. Does that make her a shallower woman than her friend Eva?

Kate casts the thought aside, focusing on her steaming corn-and-crabmeat soup. Every now and then a zigzag of lightning rips through the street's darkness, followed by distant thunder.

"So, are you going to tell me what happened?" Antonia asks over the rim of her soup bowl. She had asked the same question soon after they met, but Kate managed to avoid answering. It was a long story, she said that time.

Now, as she slips her agenda back into her bag, Kate's hand makes a small, helpless gesture, as if to say she can't make up her mind, or doesn't quite know where to start. Antonia continues eating, but pauses long enough to give Kate one of her probing looks.

"Did another woman come between you?"

The question makes Kate smile from a deep well of suppressed bitterness. "No, not a woman," she says, with a sigh.

"A *man*?" Antonia says.

Kate stares into her own soup bowl. "Not a man either," she answers. She might have found it easier to get on with her life had there been another woman, or even a man; had she thought that Guillaume had simply stopped loving her.

"What then? Don't tell me his mother didn't approve of you!"

Kate laughs. "She probably wouldn't have, come to think of it. I never got to meet her."

"What was it then?"

"You're not going to believe me."

"Why not?"

"It was politics." Kate achieves a smile, fidgeting with her rings.

"Politics!" Antonia echoes. There is an ironic twinkle in her avid eyes. "What? He wanted you to vote for the Separatists?"

"Not exactly," Kate replies.

As she speaks, an old mental door flies abruptly open. On the threshold stands Guillaume Beauregard as she last saw him, wearing eyeglasses because he had lost one of his contact lenses, pausing to fling back the striped wool scarf she'd knitted for him, then leaning in to bestow a hasty goodbye kiss. Of course, neither of them could have known that it would turn out to be goodbye. Damp-haired, still wearing her white bathrobe, Kate stood and watched Guillaume turn towards the shabby staircase, a spring in his gait, ready to face the world.

"Oh, never mind all that," she says now, with abrupt resolve. "It all happened … it seems to have happened in another life." She draws a deep breath, determined to slam the door on the still-vivid recollection. But then, although she is a woman approaching fifty, and although all this happened over a quarter of a century ago, Kate picks up the white paper napkin beside her plate, fiddles with it for one chaotic moment, then raises her hands and weeps into them, thinking: Let them stare if they want to. Let them! What the hell do I care!

To Antonia she says: "Please forgive me. I don't know what's happening to me. I don't seem to be able to stop crying these days."

PART II

The instinctive need to be the member
of a closely knit group fighting for common
ideals may grow so strong that it becomes
irrelevant what these ideals are.

—KONRAD LORENZ

ONE

I

I<small>N RECENT YEARS</small> Kate's attitude towards astrology has become as capricious as her belief in God. She thinks astrology is childish nonsense. Most of the time she does. But every now and then, thumbing through some women's magazine at the hairdresser's or the dentist's, she comes across a horoscope which seems to have been written with just her in mind. A tantalizing message from a seemingly omniscient power to a professed sceptic.

Her husband likes to tease her. He looks at her with his bright, knowing eyes whenever she insists that she doesn't believe in astrology.

"Sure," he says, "who does? Astrology is a secret religion with few believers but millions of followers."

That's what Brad likes to say, but Brad is in Edmonton right now, 2300 miles away. Kate is on a south-bound Metro train, where someone has left behind a section of the *Montreal Gazette*, sliding the folded pages between the wall and Kate's window seat. There are still several stops before she must transfer, so she sits back, idly leafing through the abandoned paper. A hefty passenger scrambles onto the train just as the Laurier doors are closing, lets out a noisy sigh of relief, then lowers his bulk into the aisle seat. Kate shifts her weight and crosses her legs, but goes on reading the daily horoscope:

> *Accent on creativity, change, challenge, and a powerful emotional involvement.*
> *Scenario also features children, variety of experiences. Aries figures prominently.*

She has just spent several hours with Megan on St. Hubert Street, picking fabric for curtains, shopping for throw cushions and picture frames and an old rolltop desk Megan begged Kate to buy, though they will have to pay for re-finishing and delivery. So, okay, a fairly creative scenario involving at least one of her children.

As for challenge, there was the minor goal of finding everything in the few hours Megan had at her disposal before her mid-afternoon Physics class.

Variety of experiences? Well, the day is only half over, Kate says to herself with an inner chuckle. But a powerful emotional involvement, an Aries in the picture!

It is this last astrological detail that has caught Kate's attention. The only Aries she knows, or at least knows to be an Aries, happens to be Guillaume. Despite her pro-fessed scepticism, she finds herself ever so slightly stirred by the allure of the words *emotional involvement*, especially as they appear in conjunction with the Aries sign. And, well, who wouldn't be intrigued?

For here it is, an ordinary September afternoon and she is once more on her way to Ludvig's while a sly voice in the back of her head cannily points out that *if* she were in fact meant to run into Guillaume, *if* he were still living in Montreal, the old music store would be the most likely venue for such an encounter. All string instruments must have their strings replaced every now and then; all require resin for bow lubrication. This, of course, is why she herself has come down again: to buy resin and new G and E strings for Megan's violin.

This time, she finds Ludvig's open.

After all these years, there is still a tiny thrill on entering this downtown shop, with its glossy instruments, its heady scent of wood and glue and varnish. Kate recalls stopping here with Guillaume one snowy afternoon, to buy sheet music for one of his courses. The violin-maker was at the time a robust Austrian in his early 40s. Now, he is an old man with white hair and a prune-like face. Kate is tempted to ask him whether Guillaume Beauregard is still a customer. She opens her mouth to do so, but then thinks better of it.

Ever since they landed in Montreal, she has resisted the temptation to look up Guillaume Beauregard in the telephone directory. Oh, she can't deny being curious, but she absolutely does not wish to see him; she's decided she doesn't even want to know whether he still lives here. All the same, turning to leave the store, she pauses at the entrance to scan the old bulletin board, with its pinned notices of concerts, instruments for sale, private music lessons. It's unlikely that Guillaume would still be giving private cello lessons, but what *is* he doing these days?

Out on the street, Kate raises her eyes to the sky. It is another overcast afternoon; a little damp, occasionally gusty, the sun's feeble light beaming now and then through the mass of clouds. The kind of day that makes you crave a good cup of coffee. On her way to Ludvig's, Kate passed a new coffee shop called Java U, just around the corner from the Guy Metro station. She will stop there before heading home; buy a magazine at Multimags; have a cup of good cappuccino.

Turning up her collar, she hurries towards the traffic island dividing de Maisonneuve Boulevard. The cars whiz by, honking horns, spewing out noxious fumes. Next to Norman Bethune's statue, a hunch-backed pensioner stands feeding pigeons out of a brown paper bag. As Kate goes by, another gust of wind carries off the old man's beret and he promptly takes chase, cutting through the flock of pigeons like Moses in biblical depictions of the Red Sea crossing.

Kate crosses the street, breathing in the heady aroma of freshly brewed coffee. In the old days, there used to be a chocolate store on this busy corner. When she was a child, her mother would stop here on their way back from a flute lesson and buy Kate a small bag of chocolate-and-pecan turtles: a weekly reward for her daily practice. Some of Guillaume's pupils would eventually require more serious bribes: LP records or tickets to hockey games.

A sigh escapes Kate's throat. For here she is, sitting down with a cup of coffee and an issue of *TIME*, wondering not only what happened to Guillaume but also to his three siblings: his radical brother Michel, and the other one, the wild-eyed junkie whose name eludes her just now but who got caught shoplifting at Eaton's a few days before Christmas. There was also a pretty sister, Chantal, who was in her early twenties when Kate met her, but already the mother of two young children, having been rushed to the altar with her high-school sweetheart, both of them barely seventeen.

Kate may not believe in the stars, but she often reflects on the vagaries of fate. Guillaume's musical talent would have gone wholly unsuspected had it not been for a lucky Irish Sweepstakes ticket purchased by his father. The father was a house painter and the lottery win was not substantial enough for a major change in lifestyle, but it did enable the family to leave their rented east-end apartment and buy a modest home in the Plateau Mont-Royal.

The Plateau was, in those days, a working class district, but the Beauregards' neighbours happened to be Hungarian refugees with three children, one of them Guillaume's age. Mr. Lehotay had been a cellist in Budapest and, observing Guillaume's musical interest, sat down one day to give him a rudimentary cello lesson. Guillaume was reportedly enthralled; so keen he kept nagging his parents to let him have regular lessons.

It was finally agreed that the Beauregards would babysit the Lehotays' children twice a week in exchange for private sessions. That was how the son of an east-end house painter and a part-time Woolworth's clerk began to play the cello at the age of nine. Kate has seen photographs of Guillaume at that age: a thin, pale-faced child with exceptionally long limbs and an unflinching gaze.

By the time he met Kate at the Youth Orchestra, Guillaume did not resemble his shy childhood self so much as a vigorous young Viking, out to conquer the world. The only battle he seemed to be waging in those days was against his own noisy, musically indifferent family. Gifted and industrious, he began to dream of some day playing for the Montreal Symphony Orchestra.

Kate joined Mr. Lehotay in offering encouragement, though she sometimes felt that she, too, was a fluke in

Guillaume's life; like the Irish Sweepstakes win, the Hungarian neighbours. Guillaume loved her. She had no doubt about that. But a part of him, she knew, was not quite at ease with his own attachment to an anglophone, especially one raised in Westmount. She suspected that Michel, Guillaume's radical brother, must have tried to talk him out of his relationship, but Guillaume was a singularly stubborn man. The more one tried to sway him, the more obstinate he became. His sister would eventually try to warn Kate about her brother's famous mulishness, but Kate would only laugh, saying she already knew all she needed to know.

II

And, truth to tell, she had a stubborn streak of her own. What she lacked was Guillaume's remarkable will power. Just how exceptional his will power was became apparent to Kate on the first morning she woke up in his studio bed. The first blizzard of the season had raged all afternoon and evening, providing her with a perfect excuse for spending Saturday night away from home. She had yet to tell her parents about Guillaume, but was planning to do so that week, after returning home.

All Saturday night the snow went on gusting, blanketing the cowering city. By dawn, St. Matthew looked like a pristine ski hill; everything was at a standstill and would remain so for hours, awaiting municipal snow ploughs.

Waking up on that wintry Sunday morning, Kate found Guillaume propped up against the back of the hide-a-bed, reading Franz Fanon's *The Wretched of the Earth*.

When he became aware that she was awake, Guillaume put his book down and twisted around to plant a kiss on her drowsy eyes.

"Bonjour, chérie!"

Kate squinted towards the window, speaking through a yawn.

"What time is it?"

It was ten o'clock. Outside, the silvery sun was bouncing off rooftops and snow-blanketed trees. Church bells were ringing somewhere in the distance. When was the last time she had slept this well? Kate leaned in and put her lips to Guillaume's neck, snuggling against the length of his warm body. How she loved the hollows above his collarbone, the smell and texture of his breathing skin! The room was poorly insulated, but she nonetheless felt like a woman who had, through divine caprice, found something she didn't even know she'd needed.

She sat dreamily fidgeting with her hair, suddenly voracious. She did not as a rule have much of an appetite in the morning but now, inexplicably, found herself craving a substantial breakfast.

"Do you have any mozzarella or cheddar?" she asked, turning towards Guillaume. She was thinking of cooking a cheese omelette when her eyes landed on his bare feet, poking out of the pile of blankets. Guillaume's size thirteen feet, with their twelve sun-tanned toes. She paused for a moment, stole a sideways glance at his face, then playfully lunged forward, tickling his soles. And then she stopped and turned, staring back at him with dilated eyes.

"What, aren't you ticklish?"

"Not at all," Guillaume answered. There was a slight

twitch of eyebrow as he met Kate's gaze, but that was all. Not even a smile.

She tried again, tickling soles and toes.

"How can you not be ticklish?" she squealed. "Everybody's feet are ticklish!"

"Nope, not mine!" Guillaume's eyes rested on her, green and complacent.

"You're one incredible guy, you know that?" She laughed, placing her mouth on his. Outside the bay window, a slab of snow came sliding off the roof, crashing on the sidewalk. The church bells went on ringing.

As it turned out, Guillaume had good reason to act complacent. Weeks later, he would confess that he was every bit as ticklish as the next guy. The secret lay in his exceptional will power.

"Mind over matter," he said to Kate, smiling, speaking in his low, melodious voice. "Mind over matter, *chérie!*"

III

Summer was drawing to a close when Kate was invited to Chantal's birthday party. Guillaume's brother, Michel, had come from Québec City and was sleeping on an air mattress, on Guillaume's hardwood floor. The Selkirk apartment was a bed-sitter, so there was no question of Kate's spending the night with Guillaume that weekend. She drove a battered VW she had inherited from an Ottawa cousin, so the plan was to pick up Guillaume and head to the east end together. Michel had borrowed Guillaume's bike and would be joining them later.

All this took place during a late-August heat wave. Chantal and her children had spent the day at La Ronde with her parents, whom Kate had yet to meet; Guillaume, Michel, and Kate were invited to come in the evening, when Chantal's husband, Claude, would be there to cook a birthday roast.

Chantal was twenty-two, a year younger than Guillaume, but the resemblance between brother and sister was remarkable: the same sage-green eyes, the small bump in the nose, the mane of unruly blond hair. Chantal's voice was not as melodious as her brother's but she made a show of speaking to Kate in English, doing her best to convey good will.

Kate liked Chantal but was nonetheless feeling ill at ease. Her French might be better than Chantal's English, but watching a woman her own age change diapers and wipe snotty noses filled her with rippling pity. The cooking smells wafting out of the kitchen were tantalizing, but the small living room was so hot her cotton dress clung to her damp skin like gauze. Michel had another engagement in the late afternoon and kept everyone waiting. Chantal kept glancing at her watch. She was worried about the roast, but also about her brother, who had to cycle through heavy downtown traffic to get to the east end.

"What if something happened to him?" she said, draining her wineglass. "He should have been here by now. It's my birthday after all!"

"Oh, come on, you know how he is." Guillaume leaned over to refill their glasses. "He's always late."

"Artists!" Claude put in, hitching up his jeans. He was a young man with finely-etched features and dark hair combed as neatly as a priest's. He brought out bowls of chips and cashews, then went back to the kitchen to check on the roast. At that moment, the bell downstairs rang.

Kate, who had met Guillaume's younger brother once before, felt a sudden knot of anxiety. Michel made her think of a truculent James Dean. He shook her hand and seemed polite enough, but she still sensed his suppressed disapproval. As soon as dinner was over, he gave Chantal her present, waited for her to open it, then grabbed his leather jacket and took off with some muttered excuse.

No one said anything about this abrupt departure, but Kate was still dwelling on it after she and Guillaume left Chantal and Claude's walkup. It was by then going on midnight, one of those muggy summer evenings when the humidity rises with every passing hour, making the body fleetingly yearn for snow.

"He still doesn't like me," Kate said, sounding childish to her own ears.

Guillaume put his lips to her cheek. "It's not you ... it's nothing personal, trust me."

Kate stopped to adjust the strap on her sandal. "It's not fair," she said.

"No, but give him time, he'll come around." Guillaume had spotted an open *dépanneur* and was steering Kate towards it. "I need cigarettes. Are you tired?"

"Not really. I had too much to drink though," Kate said and sighed. "I'm not sure I should be driving."

"We can walk for a while ... try to find an open café, *d'accord?*"

"*D'accord.*"

They resumed strolling through the sweltering streets,

Guillaume's arm around Kate's shoulder, his mood a little hard to diagnose. There didn't seem to be an open café anywhere; despite the heat, the streets were becoming deserted. Here and there, people could be seen, sitting on roofs, balconies, fire escapes.

This was the neighbourhood where Guillaume had spent the first eight years of his life. It was notable only for its long lines of drying laundry, its pawnshops and barber shops and at least one pool hall. Their aimless stroll took them past a hardware store, a pharmacy, a coin laundromat where Guillaume's mother used to do the family laundry. Kate had never been to this part of town, but it neither interested nor especially bothered her. What troubled her was the ironic tenor of Guillaume's commentary; the close watch he seemed to keep on her reactions, expecting what? Shock, distaste, disdain? Was this supposed to be some kind of cultural Rorschach test?

She was still pondering this question when, walking away from the laundromat, Guillaume shot her a quick sidelong glance. Perhaps next time she could bring her mother; her mother and the family laundry, he said. "She might find it interesting ... maybe even educational, eh?"

The question took Kate by surprise, but she declined to dignify it with a reply. He was being deliberately provocative. Let him be provocative; she would not rise to the bait, she decided. She shifted her bag, a little unsteady in the moonlight, letting her silence reproach him.

And yet, as they approached the parked Beetle, she became aware of a surge of sympathy for what she suddenly realized must be eating Guillaume. Distracted, she stumbled on a stone, righting herself only with Guillaume's support.

She was unhurt, but still feeling a trace of guilt over her own privileged background; above all over what she now perceived as obtuseness on her part, a failure to offer the simple reassurance Guillaume must have been fishing for.

It seemed obvious by the time they arrived at her car. Overcome, Kate stopped with the keys in her hand, and turned to wrap her arms around Guillaume's neck. Several inches shorter, she rose on her toes and kissed him, tasting his doubts no less than his flaring desire.

At last, they drew apart, smiling breathlessly. Guillaume's gaze landed on the shabby *pension* across the street: its cherry-red entrance, its blinking black and white sign: VACANCY. Kate saw a speculative look appear in Guillaume's eyes, the corner of his mouth rising ever so slightly as he turned to face her. How would she feel about spending the night here, he asked with a rakish grin. Yes, right here, at the Bienvenue, he said, pointing across the street. It would not be expensive.

Kate stood searching Guillaume's face. "Are you serious?"

"Well, you're still tipsy," he said, his eyes appraising her. Kate recalled an uncle who had been killed some years back, driving home after a New Year's party. She stole another glance at the blinking sign. Guillaume might be trying to act responsibly, but there was no mistaking the sexual undertone. He might have also been thinking of his brother, Michel, who would be sleeping on the air mattress next to Guillaume. "Well, what do you say?" he asked.

"All right, why not?" Kate tossed her head. "We can pretend we're illicit lovers out on the town!"

The statement made Guillaume chuckle. He had once told her she had the wildest imagination he had ever encountered, especially in an anglophone. He paused, gave her black VW one final glance, then led her purposefully across the street. Afraid she would change her mind; thinking he would call her bluff? If so, he did not know her as well as her family did: her insatiable curiosity, her adventurous streak. To say nothing of her pride and, yes, even her mulishness. They were alike in this, she and Guillaume. In this, as in so much else.

IV

There is, Kate knows, no explaining anything to do with physical desire but, much as she has tried not to dwell on sexual questions over the years, there was no denying one weighty fact: Guillaume was the only man who had seemed capable of meeting her halfway in the realm of the imagination as passionately, as playfully, as he had in the purely physical realm.

They may have both been sexually aroused that night in the east end, but as they walked hand in hand up the winding stairwell, they felt like children playing house, unexpectedly caught up in their own make-believe. By tacit agreement, they avoided looking at each other, as if to do so might break the spell. Soon, they found themselves standing at the deserted reception desk, waiting. Kate asked for a cigarette. Guillaume gave her one, then reached out and hit the brass bell next to the telephone.

The man who emerged from the shadows was no more than thirty but at first glance his missing teeth and unshaven jaw gave him the appearance of a much older man. He took his time lighting a cigarette, assessing the new arrivals. He addressed Guillaume but kept eyeing Kate, as if trying to decide where he might have met her. They were asked to pay in advance; then, clearing his nose, the clerk handed them a numbered key. Guillaume winked at Kate, leading the way upstairs.

"*Ça va?*"

"*Ça va!*"

The stairs were covered with a faded carpet. They creaked under their feet as they climbed to the second floor. Kate glanced down through the banisters and saw the clerk following them with his rheumy eyes. His apparent interest made her feel as if she and Guillaume were characters in a foreign film. What was the matter with her? She thought of her twin sister. Heather, she was sure, would not dream of setting foot in such an establishment.

"*Voilà!*" Guillaume said on spotting their room. It was number 9. They would have to share the bathroom, which Kate paused to inspect, filled with sudden doubt. She could not abide the thought of sharing the bathroom with strangers, but Guillaume seemed unfazed. He was busy inserting the key into the keyhole, turning it back and forth twice before it opened.

It was a stuffy but clean room with a double bed, a night table with a lamp, a faux walnut dresser. The bed was covered with a floral bedspread; the dresser top had a small cigarette burn. Standing next to Guillaume, Kate became aware of his perspiration. How odd that desire could flourish in such drab surroundings, she thought. Through the thin plaster wall, an elderly man could be heard snoring and coughing, muttering in his dreams.

"Wait!" She strolled over to the window and opened the curtains, but even so, the heat continued to oppress her flesh. The moon shone down on the sleeping street; somewhere a dog barked and barked. Kate thought of her parents, getting ready for bed in their air-conditioned bedroom; of her own basement apartment with its ceiling fans and comfortable furnishings. She turned away from the window, watching a trapped fly buzz around the small bedside lamp.

"Would you rather go home?" Guillaume asked, making Kate's eyes flicker. Did he find his own ardour waning in this seedy room? Had he been merely testing her?

"Oh, no." She spoke airily. "We may as well stay … we've paid after all."

She shrugged, her gaze landing on the calendar hanging behind Guillaume's shoulder. It was some sort of promotional calendar and had a picture of a winking blonde, skimpily clad in black lace. It made Kate smile as she crossed the room, heading straight into Guillaume's arms. She was wearing a gauzy summer halter with spaghetti straps, a pair of brown sandals, and white cotton underwear.

Guillaume reached out and switched off the bedside lamp. In the dark, the fly buzzed on for a moment or two, then abruptly stopped.

V

She may be an Edmonton matron about to turn fifty but, sitting with her second cup of coffee at the Java U, Kate can still feel a certain *frisson*, recalling that distant summer night. Is it possible that her *pension* experience had spawned an enduring taste for sexual adventure; perhaps a certain boredom with the predictability of marital sex?

An intriguing question, to which Kate has no answer. But as she finishes her coffee and gets ready to leave, she can't help wondering what a life of conventional domesticity would have been like with Guillaume Beauregard. Years and years of it, in Montreal or some unknown city.

Another question to which she does not have an answer. As she heads towards Megan's apartment, though, a line from Michael Ondaatje's *The English Patient* suddenly echoes in her head: "Words are tricky things ... they are much more tricky than violins."

And, she thinks, far more tricky than photographs, two of which she ends up snapping as she walks east along de Maisonneuve. Because of the glory of autumn in this part of the world, she has bought colour film for a change. A good thing, too, because she soon spots an elderly nun in a black habit rummaging through her handbag right in front of a fancy boutique's vitrine displaying sexy imported lingerie. Pink and red and turquoise.

In the life of most photographers there is at least one moment when they feel that they've been positioned at a particular spot, on a particular day, just when the powers that be are on the lookout for someone with a camera, ready to click the shutter.

This happens to be one such moment, but there is always pleasure in the search itself, in the patient wait for that rare, eloquent image that, once seen, cannot be forgotten. Kate has published a book of her photographs and is now working on a collection of artists' portraits: mimes and concert musicians, poets and dancers and sculptors. It occurs to her that she might include a photo of Antonia Offe; maybe even Yves Letourneau, the Québecois playwright?

She is still musing on the Ondaatje quote about words and violins. Like most people, she often uses words to rationalize her own conduct. Her actions seem, at times, hard to justify, even to herself. Unlike her prudent husband, she seldom stops to weigh an impulse, and certainly doesn't do so on the day she returns with the new strings and resin for her daughter's violin.

This is what she does instead.

She closes the front door, hangs up her fall jacket, goes to Megan's bedroom and, dismissing reason, opens the telephone directory to look up Guillaume Beauregard in the white, residential pages. Not that she has any intention of calling, of course, should she find his name listed.

She does find it and no, she does not call, though she is, for the moment, alone in Megan's apartment. She hastens to the kitchen and goes about preparing dinner for her ever-ravenous daughter. Nothing like the eye-stinging revenge of an old onion, the sensuous ripeness of a fat eggplant, to keep a wayward mind anchored.

And anyway, what would be the point?

TWO

I

THE PHONE IN the Wood Avenue basement was ringing. It was October 16, 1970. The phone shrilled on and on and on, clamouring for attention. Wrenching herself from the clutches of sleep, Kate reached out for the receiver, then slowly levered herself from the pillows. It was going on nine o'clock. The house seemed eerily quiet, though Pablo could be heard upstairs, chasing his toy mouse across the hardwood floor. Having no classes on Friday, Kate had slept in while her parents and siblings all got ready and left for the day. It was not unusual for her to sleep late on Friday mornings, but it was for Guillaume to be phoning so early. Wasn't he supposed to have a class on Friday morning?

"Yes, yes. You haven't heard, have you?"

Guillaume's voice sounded oddly brittle in Kate's ear. He was speaking French; she was speaking English. Two months into their relationship, after hours of debating the issue, they had arrived at a bilingual compromise; a private solution to Québec's interminable language problem. He would speak to Kate in his mother tongue; she would address him in hers. If they had to write to each other, as they did on occasion when Kate was in the country, they would do so in English. Kate lacked confidence in her written

French; Guillaume was doing his Master's at the McGill Conservatory and was happy to improve his English writing skills.

But that morning he was speaking so rapidly that, still groggy with sleep, Kate could not quite follow what he was saying. She had to stop him twice before fully absorbing the news: Pierre Trudeau, Canada's Prime Minister, had just invoked the War Measures Act, a radical manoeuvre prompted by two high-profile FLQ kidnappings. One of the captives was James Cross, a British diplomat stationed in Montreal; the other was Pierrre Laporte, Québec's own Labour and Immigration Minister.

"They came to get Pauline Julien at the crack of dawn," Guillaume was going on. "They—"

"What? Pauline Julien! Whatever for?"

"They're picking up anyone who's ever expressed any nationalistic sympathies." Guillaume spoke in a tone of suppressed outrage. The War Measures Act was giving Canadian authorities the unprecedented power to arrest suspects without so much as a warrant; to search houses and detain occupants for as long as a month, without formal charges. "I won't be surprised if they go after Michel, too."

The last statement hardened Kate's clutch on the black receiver. Michel was a fervent nationalist, but he was just a twenty-year-old fine arts student in Québec City. "How would they even know he exists?" she asked.

"I don't know. Let's hope they don't."

Guillaume sighed and was about to say more, but seemed to think better of it. They would talk when she came over that evening. He would be finished a little later today; around nine fifteen. There was a quarter of an hour he owed one of his private students.

Guillaume was putting himself through university working in construction every summer, and giving private music lessons the rest of the year. He had two lessons on Friday, so Kate's evening routine comprised a family dinner, a leisurely bath, and a change of clothes before heading to Selkirk Avenue for the weekend. Her father had made it clear he did not approve, but his children's morals were his wife's domain and Kate's mother had always prided herself on her progressive views. She could not accept having one of her daughters and a boyfriend sleeping together under her own roof, but the world, as she kept telling her husband, wasn't what it used to be when they were dating. She did not think it her place to meddle in her children's love life.

"I'll see you around nine-thirty then," Kate said to Guillaume on that historic Friday morning. "Do you feel like going out?"

He paused and thought it over. "No. I think I'd rather stay home tonight. *Je t'aime,*" he said, as he always did by way of goodbye.

"I love you, too. Try not to worry."

James Cross, the British Trade Commissioner, had been kidnapped from his Montreal home by four conspirators posing as delivery men; Pierre Laporte had been on his front lawn, playing football with his nephew, when he was abducted at gunpoint. The sweeping arrests were as shocking as the two abductions, but Kate saw little reason for personal concern. She got dressed, had a quick breakfast, then headed for the library, to research a term paper for a Shakespeare course.

She was not keen on the project. She was taking qualifying courses towards a graduate degree in English, but was not at all sure it was what she wanted to do. All those academic papers, the countless scholarly books on arcane subjects, seemed to offer nothing useful or especially interesting. Their main purpose, she was beginning to think, was the advancement of the authors' academic careers. Unlike her brother, she was not gifted enough to contemplate a career in music, but she did enjoy reading. Maybe she could become a book critic or a literary translator?

But that Friday morning, Kate's mind was not on her professional future. Every time she looked up, there would be a helmeted soldier brandishing a rifle, or a police car zooming by, its lights flashing. On street corners and in shops, at the library, Montrealers huddled together, speaking in hushed voices, as if their personal safety were at stake.

The danger was palpable. The FLQ terrorists were threatening to execute the British Trade Commissioner unless their demands were met. A huge ransom had been stipulated. Half a million dollars! And there were two other non-negotiable conditions. The terrorists insisted on a public broadcast of the FLQ manifesto, as well as the liberation of jailed political activists.

All over the country, Canadians were fuming and vilifying, or scurrying around in panic. Unless revoked, the War Measures Act would stay in force for the next six months, and who could tell what still lay in store? Twelve thousand police officers were already deployed across the province. Voices were being heard, calling for the reinstatement of the death penalty.

Kate's parents were opposed to capital punishment but her father, it would turn out, fully supported the Prime Minister's radical action. No, he did not like to see civil liberties compromised; of course, he didn't. The way things had been going, though, Québec seemed to be heading towards anarchy; possibly even bloodshed.

"It's been ten days since they kidnapped James Cross; they've had Laporte for five days. What did you expect him to do?" he demanded. "Nothing?!"

Dwight Abbitson was a large, hulking man, with a florid face and slightly protuberant eyes ever in search of an object worthy of his interest. He could look kindly, even benevolent, but most days found him regarding the world with the shrewd, sceptical gaze of a man well acquainted with human folly. He was a Vice-President at Canada Trust. His argument that evening was aimed at Kate and her brother, Paul, as well as at their left-leaning mother. They were all huddled in the den, in front of the television, but only Heather, Kate's twin sister, seemed to share their father's point of view.

"Of course he had to do something," she echoed at length. "If he'd given in, he would have just been inviting more kidnappings!"

"Maybe," Paul said, looking up from the new tennis shoes he was busy lacing. "But we do live in a democracy, remember? And this isn't wartime, it's—"

Heather would not let her brother finish. "Oh, democracy!" she cried. "Was the FLQ acting democratically when it resorted to violence? We had an election, didn't we? What right did the terrorists have to go against the majority vote?"

"Heather's right," their father put in. "You can't let a minority impose its view through violent means." He spoke emphatically, like a statesman at the centre of some momentous press conference.

"Oh, I don't know," his wife ventured. "I think it's more complicated than that."

The problem, as she saw it, was that repressive measures, even if justified, often ended up just adding oil to the fire. After all, both James Cross and Pierre Laporte were still being held captive. Who could tell what horrors Trudeau's manoeuvre might unleash?

"I'm sure glad I'm not the Prime Minister right now, I'll tell you that!" Saying this, Fiona Abbitson sighed, then turned to face Kate, having become aware of her prolonged silence. "What do you think about all this, dear?"

"I don't know. There's nothing ... absolutely nothing Trudeau could have done that everyone would approve of," Kate said. "He was being blackmailed after all. On the other hand, I do understand—"

"Oh you and your *on the other hands*," Heather interjected. "Why must you always sit on the fence? Can't you for once—"

"Heather!" Their mother broke in with her sternest voice. "Kate was just trying to be objective. I don't think it's something to sneer at, dear, is it?"

"Oh, objective, my foot! She was just being indecisive, as usual." Heather tossed her long honey-coloured hair, then pulled a comical face, as if to make it clear no malice had been intended.

Kate stuck out her tongue, then turned to check the wall clock. "On that friendly note, I think I'll go have a bath. You'll just have to solve the national crisis without me."

The last few words were tossed back with well-practised *sangfroid*. Kate had long since inured herself to her sister's gibes. They were twins, but did not even look like sisters. Fair-haired Heather resembled their father in both looks and temperament. Decisive and single-minded, she had studied Law and would soon be articling with a major Ottawa firm. One of their uncles was a prominent judge in the capital. You had to hand it to Heather: she'd had her professional future all mapped out by the age of fifteen.

Kate went to have her bath, then remembered that Guillaume had promised to go with her to the vet on Saturday morning. Pablo (named after cellist Pablo Casals) was supposed to be spayed but, yes, she had mixed feelings about that as well; had asked Guillaume to accompany her to the animal clinic up on Côte-des-Neiges. She had planned to take her cat to Guillaume's place for the night, but Pablo quite wisely vanished and hid while she was having her bath. It took her half an hour to find him and coax him into the pet basket. Was it possible cats really had psychic powers?

II

She was running late, feeling hot and exasperated because Pablo would not stop meowing in the back of the car. It was going on ten o'clock, but Kate could clearly see the soldiers, standing impassively in front of the neighbourhood park, the Squash and Badminton Club, the Sacred Heart School for Girls.

Pablo was still protesting when she parked her car on Selkirk Avenue and let herself in through Guillaume's front door, as she had been doing every Friday for months. And then she climbed the stairs to the second floor, an overnight bag in one hand, the cat basket in the other. The odour of chicken curry hung over the stairwell, possibly wafting out of Guillaume's own kitchen. Guillaume loved Indian food, the spicier the better. Sometimes, he would cook while waiting for Kate, and she would end up eating all over again.

Guillaume wasn't home. He hadn't called to say that his plans had changed. He hadn't left a note. The apartment was in shambles, as if a crazed burglar had been through the place, frantically ransacking drawers, plucking books off wall shelves, emptying fridge and cupboards. The hide-a-bed had been opened and the mattress stripped; the medicine cabinet in the bathroom stood empty, its contents spilling into the white sink. Guillaume did not have a large wardrobe, but the few clothes he possessed were strewn on the floor — everything but the second-hand suede jacket he wore at this time of year. He must have been wearing it when he left home, but where did he go?

Kate let the meowing Pablo out of his wicker basket. She ran upstairs to Yves Letourneau's apartment, where Suzanne, Yves' girlfriend, informed her that, just before noon, two police squads had arrived to pick up both Yves and Guillaume.

"But why?" Kate wailed. "Guillaume was not involved in politics. I'm sure he wasn't! Was Yves?"

Suzanne shook her head. The police, she said, had arrested hundreds of men and women: prominent writers, actors, physicians. Yves and Guillaume were not the only innocent ones picked up on mere suspicion.

"But don't worry ... I'm sure they'll soon realize they've made a mistake and let them go."

"You think so?" Kate stood hugging herself, panic

clinging to the roof of her mouth. She thought she knew Guillaume well, but a taunting inner voice was beginning to ask whether he might have been secretly involved in the Separatist struggle after all. Could Michel have talked him into contributing to his political cause? Was that perhaps why he stayed with Guillaume when he came to town, rather than with their parents?

But Suzanne was going on, offering reassurance. "*Mon Dieu,* they can't just keep two innocent guys in jail, can they? This isn't Russia, we're not dealing with the KGB here, are we?"

"You're right," Kate said. She pulled out a chair and sat down to have a cup of coffee with Suzanne. "I'm sure you're right."

THREE

∞

I

It is Saturday evening and Kate's daughter is bundled up on the living room sofa, nursing a bad cold. Kate is in the kitchen, waiting for the water to boil, thinking about the telephone conversation she has just had with her son; then, consciously redirecting her thoughts, about shoddy home appliances. The fridge has developed a fitful rattle and will now have to be repaired, or maybe even replaced, just after she'd filled it, top to bottom, with fresh groceries. The management will deal with the problem, but why is it that nothing is made to last anymore?

Kate leaves the kitchen to add dish towels to the compact washer/dryer, repaired just before Megan moved in. One of the things life has taught Kate is to appreciate durability and reliability, even if the latter is not among her personal virtues. She jots down a reminder to call the superintendent, then sets about preparing a hot toddy and cookies for her daughter, who has just woken from a medicated nap. It is a little after nine o'clock.

"It looks like Sean won't be coming for Christmas after all." Kate shares the news with her daughter as neutrally as she can, but the words make Megan sit up against her new decorative cushions.

"Not coming?!" She tugs at the slipping blanket, surrounded by crumpled tissues, breathing through her mouth. Kate has set the steaming toddy on the coffee table but Megan ignores it. "Why?" she asks. Her voice sounds congested, her red-rimmed eyes appraise her mother: her damp hair, her scented, terrycloth-wrapped body. Kate had just come out of the bath when the telephone rang.

"Something to do with his crazy new boss. That's what he says, anyway." Kate pours herself a glass of wine and settles across from her daughter. It is still three hours to bedtime but fatigue is weighing down every bone in her body. "I thought he sounded ... a little evasive."

The last statement hangs in the air while Megan blows on her hot toddy. "You think he's not telling the truth?"

"Who knows?" Kate feels her left eyelid begin to twitch, as it often does in moments of heightened stress. She remains quiet for a while, listening with one ear to the whining wind and, with the other, to the sound of laundry being tossed about in the open utility closet. "I think he doesn't like being with us anymore," she finally says, a catch in her voice.

Megan, who has been wiping her nose, raises her eyes to her mother. "Us or just daddy?"

"I don't know!" Kate says, with a small helpless gesture.

"Have you tried talking to him?"

"Sean?"

"Daddy! I don't think he's, like, even aware of what's going on, you know?"

"What do you think's going on, exactly?"

"Oh, come on, Mom! A blind man could see how he feels about Sean."

Kate stirs in her chair, trying to decide whether she wants to pursue this particular discussion. "What are you saying, sweetheart?"

"What am I saying?! Can't you see how he gets under Sean's skin, nagging him every chance he gets?" Megan pauses, bringing the hot toddy to her lips. It is only the second one she has ever had with alcohol mixed in with the honey and lemon. "I can't say I really blame him, not wanting to come home."

"Oh, you exaggerate, darling." The past is hissing in Kate's ears but she does her best to ignore it. "I think … I think it's just that dad understands you so much better, you know? He doesn't get Sean. They're just too different … they look at life through two completely different windows. That's the long and the short of it."

"Whatever. But *have* you tried talking to dad about it?" Megan insists. "You're so polite with each other! Does he even know how you feel?"

"Yes … no. Oh, I don't know! He's not good at taking even a hint of criticism. You know that."

Megan says nothing. She sits clutching a crumpled tissue, pensively biting into a cookie. "The thing is Sean really likes to provoke him," she says after a while. "You realize that, don't you?"

"Yes. Yes, I do." Kate sighs. "And he seems to know just which buttons to push too, doesn't he?"

"Yup." Megan continues to munch on her oatmeal cookies. She chews, and coughs, and stops to blow her nose at regular intervals. "I think dad's not good for Sean. He's making him more and more insecure. Maybe even jealous," she adds after a moment.

"Of you, you mean?"

"Duh!"

"But Sean loves you so much!" Kate lets out in a despairing tone. "He's always loved you. You must know that? The way he—"

"I know. I know he does." Megan's voice is so congested the *know* comes out sounding like *doe*. "He used to, anyway."

"Used to!" Kate shifts her weight in the high-back armchair they bought at IKEA soon after landing in Montreal. She thinks of the day Megan was born; of Sean's tender solicitude all through her childhood. He was nine years old when she was born, but would rush home after school, and hasten to check on his baby sister, telling her his concocted stories even before she could understand a word. "What do you think has changed?" Kate asks. "When?"

"Oh—" Megan opens her mouth to answer, but lapses into reflective silence. "I'm not sure, Mom," she finally says. Her eyes have landed on one of the table lamps, where a stray moth is vibrating, with a sort of frantic tenacity. Megan stares and stares, as if mesmerised by the moth. When she speaks again, she appears to be thinking out loud. She thinks Sean's problems must have started sometime in high school. "I think he was okay before that, but who knows? Maybe I was just too young to notice?"

"I don't know. I wish I did." Kate's eyelid is still pulsing. "I wish I could remember." She tilts her head back and rests it, closing her eyes. "Adolescence is never a walk in the park, is it?"

"No kidding," Megan says, and Kate almost smiles. Her mind has summoned up the memory of her daughter

coming home from junior high, asking whether it was possible to be both sincere and popular. She seemed to believe
sincerity was her only obstacle to social success, and Kate
wished she could tell her daughter to lighten up a little if
she really cared about popularity. Megan has always been
not only outspoken but too earnest, too single-minded,
for her own good; "relentless" was the word Sean used
one day when nine-year-old Megan would not give up
pestering him for attention while he was trying to write in
his journal.

She is relentless still, trying to understand something
that keeps eluding her. But that's Megan: always trying to
understand something or other.

"Remember the year he failed those two big exams?"
she is saying now, still speaking about her brother. "Chem-
istry and physics, I think it was. I think he was a sophomore,
wasn't he ... when he had that terrible fight with dad. Remember?"

Kate nods sadly, taking a sip of wine. She reflects that
this was the only time Brad had come close to hitting Sean,
but for the life of her can't recall what Sean had said to
provoke him. "Are you saying ... do you think that's when
their problems actually started?"

"I'm not sure ... I think so. They might have had an
occasional tiff before that, I really can't remember. That
day, though ... it, like, stands out in my mind, you know?"

"I see." Kate shifts in her chair, her thoughts idling in
the past. She thinks about her son, who, despite an above-
average IQ, has always refused to pursue anything that did
not fully engage his interest. She thinks about her highly
disciplined husband. She returns to her son, whom Brad

considers lazy, but who works impressively hard on his own stories, writing and re-writing them dozens of times before he sends them out. "It's such a pity. If only he had a little interest in science."

"I don't think you get it, Mom! It wasn't his two F's that made dad lose it. It was the fact that Sean lied about them."

"He did? I don't remember that!"

"Yeah, well, selective memory," Megan says, making Kate bristle. She reminds herself that her daughter is suffering from PMS, and tends to be combative whenever she feels under the weather.

"What do you mean?" Kate says. "Why would—"

"What do I mean, what do I mean! You coddle him, Mom! You're always there, ready to whitewash whatever he does!"

Kate sits staring at her daughter, feeling ambushed. "So that's what you think?" she finally says.

"It's not what I think, it's how it is, Mom!" Megan bites on a cuticle, sounding exasperated. "You should, like, video yourself sometime."

"You think so?" Kate falls silent, contemplating her wine, listening to the wind plough its way over the balcony. When she speaks again, it is more to herself than to Megan. "I don't know ... you may be right," she says in a hollow voice. "I guess I feel I have to protect him ... to compensate somehow, you know?"

"I know, Mom," Megan says, her tone softening. "Sometimes, you over-compensate, though, you know? You seem to care more about protecting him than you do about anything else."

"Megan! That's not fair!" Kate ripples with indignation,

even as another part of her brain goes on brooding on her daughter's statement. Megan may be too outspoken for her own good but, sick or not, she is often right.

Kate retreats into prolonged reflection. "It's so hard, not being able to ... you know, shelter him," she finally says. "He really is ... hypersensitive. And Brad ... he can be so intimidating."

"You should speak to him about it," Megan says. "To dad."

Kate sits wrapped in thought, gently swirling the remaining wine.

"Does he intimidate you?" Megan asks after a while.

"Me? No. But I do feel ... I sometimes feel like I'm letting him down," Kate hears herself confess. To her own daughter!

"But he means so well!" Megan says with sudden intensity, as if it has just occurred to her that her father, too, deserves an advocate. "He tries so hard to do the decent thing. You should talk to him ... I mean seriously. I'm not sure you give him enough credit."

This statement startles Kate more than anything Megan has said so far. "What makes you say that?" she asks after a moment's pause. "I give him lots of credit. He's an exceptional man."

"I know he is, but—" Here Megan wavers, but only for a moment. "Do you love him, Mom?" She gives Kate a long, steady look, then falls to chewing on her lower lip, as if it has just occurred to her that, this time, she may have gone too far.

"Of course I love him!"

"Well, maybe you should show it more," Megan replies

with stunning matter-of-factness, as if offering an opinion on home décor or some new outfit. And then she drinks her toddy and lets her glance stray around the room. She dabs at her dripping nostrils. She toys with the fringes on her wool blanket. Just as it seems as if she has said all she is going to say, she turns back to Kate. "Have you thought of going to Vancouver for Christmas?"

"What, alone?"

"No, of course not. We could all go. Maybe Sean will finally get the message?"

"What, that we all love him?"

"Yeah. That we care enough to make the trip just to be with him during the holidays. Especially dad."

Kate sits wiggling her bare toes, pondering the suggestion. How observant her daughter has become lately; still a little too intense, perhaps, but incredibly astute for someone so young. It's true Brad hates to travel, but could he be talked into flying to the West Coast for a week over the holidays? Would his surgical commitments even allow him to? They would, she supposes, have to stay with his brother's family. Brad likes his brother but his wife, not so much. He would probably prefer to stay at some nearby hotel, but his brother would be offended.

"I'll speak to him," Kate says at length. "He may not be able to do it." She takes her agenda out of her bag and makes a note to raise this with Brad tomorrow. She has become so forgetful lately, so tired by the end of the day, that all she wants to do is have a bath, then crash. Is this the beginning of old age? she wonders. A stopover on the way to a rocking chair by the fire?

II

Having transferred the laundry from washer to dryer, Kate stops in the bathroom to use the toilet and get a jar of vitamin E ointment for Megan's chafed nostrils. She can hear her daughter cough and cough in the living room, but by the time Kate returns, the coughing spell is over and Megan sits with a paperback in her hands, sucking on a lozenge. For a moment or two, she does not speak, watching her mother settle back into the blue armchair.

"You should go home after my birthday," she says then, looking less like a college-age daughter than a stern, solicitous parent. "Dad needs you more than I do at this point, you know."

Megan is to have a roommate in January, but will be alone for the first semester. Kate studies her wine as if it might offer solutions to all her problems. She sits for a moment, scratching between her breasts, still weighing pros and cons. "You may be right."

"I am right." Megan casts her novel aside. She is still intent on her mother's movements, as if trying to diagnose her precise state of mind. Kate's mind seems far away just now, her air abstracted, her smooth-skinned face looking rather drawn. She refills her wineglass and sits back to take a slow, thoughtful sip. Megan reaches for the vitamin ointment. She is smearing it over her red nostrils when, all at once, Kate seems to rouse herself, like a woman who has suddenly reached some vital decision. She puts down her glass, glances at her watch, then sits up and slips her agenda back into her handbag.

"Who was the letter from?" Megan asks.

Kate's eyes flick up from her bag. "Letter?"

"The old letter I found in the Margaret Laurence book. The one in your agenda," Megan adds with the faintest smile.

"Oh. Have you read it?"

"Only a line or two. When I first came across it." Megan shrugs. "It sure sounded intense."

A moment passes. Kate picks up her wineglass.

"He was an old boyfriend. Someone I knew before I met your father."

Megan goes on contemplating her mother, her open book lying face down at her side. "Did you love him a lot?" she asks after a while. Her voice is hoarse, her tone almost reverential.

"Yes. Yes, I did. What makes you ask?"

"Honestly?" Megan meets Kate's eyes. "I thought you looked kind of shaken after you read it, you know? And ... well, you haven't exactly been yourself since then."

"Is that so?"

Megan makes an ambiguous little noise between her teeth. "I heard you crying the other night, Mom." She lets this soak in, tugging and tugging on a stubborn hangnail. "What was his name?"

"Guillaume. Guillaume Beauregard."

"Oh! So he was Québecois?"

"He was," Kate says, briefly diverted by a fluttering sensation in the vicinity of her heart. "The letter went missing long before you were born. I had no idea what happened to it, but—" She breaks off, her hand flying up to her chest. It is not the first time she has had palpitations in recent weeks. "I'm sorry, sweetheart. I'm really bushed to-day. I don't feel like talking about him, okay?"

"Whatever," Megan says. She sets about rearranging the cushions at her back, then drains the last of her toddy. As she does so, her book slides to the floor and she reaches down to retrieve it. When she sits up and turns back to Kate, there is new resolve on her puffy face. "Can I ask you something, Mom? Just one more question, okay?"

"Just one more?" Kate does her best to smile.

"Yeah. All you have to do is say yes or no." She pauses and gives Kate another one of her searching looks. "Was he Sean's real father?"

"Guillaume? No!" Of their own accord, Kate's hands rise to cover her burning cheeks. "What makes you think that?"

"I don't know. Just a feeling. Sean told me once he did not think dad was his real father."

Kate forgets to breathe. The whole room is spinning around her.

"Guillaume is *not* Sean's father," she states emphatically.

Megan scans her face. "Is that the truth?"

"I swear! I swear on my children's heads! On my mother's memory!"

"Okay, I believe you," Megan says, pausing to clear her nostrils. "But ... why are you, like, being so secretive, Mom? I mean, he must have broken your heart, I guess, but it was so long ago! And anyway, it happens to everybody sooner or later, right?"

Kate gathers her hair to the back of her head, and holds it there for a long, pensive moment. *Secretive*. The word glowers at her. She wants to answer her daughter's question. They have been so close lately she finds herself wishing away this entire conversation. She thinks there is no reason in the world why she shouldn't answer Megan. She opens her mouth to do so, but all that comes out is a weary, drawn-out breath. She is not yet ready to discuss Guillaume; not while he continues to cast such a huge shadow over her days.

"I'm sorry, sweetheart. I really don't feel like rehashing the past right now. Maybe some other time, okay?"

Megan shrugs. She picks up her novel and pulls the wool blanket up to her chest. "Okay," she says. "I'm sorry I asked." She leans back and makes a show of starting to read. Kate observes the glitter in her daughter's eyes but can't tell whether it's unshed tears or rising temperature. She goes around to the sofa and places a palm over her daughter's forehead, testing for fever.

Megan raises her eyes. "I love you, Mom," she says. "I'm sorry I made you unhappy."

"Oh, darling!" Kate leans in to hug her daughter. "I love you too, my angel. And, honestly, you have nothing to apologize for, but—" She stops and sits down on the edge of the sofa, stroking Megan's hair.

"But—?"

"Look. I'll tell you all about it some day—when you're not sick and I'm not so tired. I promise, okay?"

"Okay, Mom."

And then they are both silent, each lost in her own musings. Kate becomes aware of her suddenly flaring senses. She registers the honking of impatient drivers on the street below, the tremor across windowpanes, caused by a passing truck. It is almost time for bed, but she feels an obscure need to ask forgiveness. In the hallway, the dryer whirs for another minute or two, then stops. Kate rises and picks up the mug, the plastic snack tray. Megan's face looks flushed. She is blowing her nose again, wheezing a little. Kate thinks she must remember to buy a thermometer first thing tomorrow morning. In the kitchen, the fridge starts with a loud shudder, and then subsides and begins to hum, like a well-fed, complacent beast.

FOUR

I

ALTHOUGH HE HAD not been privy to any abduction plans, Michel Beauregard did play a minor role in the infamous FLQ drama: he had helped reproduce and distribute subversive flyers in both Québec City and Greater Montreal. It was possible that Guillaume had been aware of his brother's FLQ activities but he had never contributed anything beyond an air mattress for Michel to sleep on whenever he was in town.

During the October Crisis, this turned out to be more than enough to warrant detention. Everyone in Michel's address book was arrested as soon as the War Measures Act came into effect. Guillaume was picked up at his Selkirk Avenue apartment six hours after Michel had been detained in Québec City. Kate would learn all this much later, from Chantal Beauregard. Other details were provided by Guillaume himself, sent through Canada Post in two separate letters.

The first one was mailed two days after Guillaume's release from jail. It was written on eight sheets of lined paper and sent in a large manila envelope, like a college student's term paper, or a drafted project proposal.

Kate read Guillaume's missive over and over in the

days that followed; read it so many times that his words came to be permanently etched into her febrile brain. Soon, even her dreams became bloated with Guillaume's rage, her fitful sleep splashed with blaring headlines and grainy black-and-white images of hooded faces, and vast caches of obscure, deadly weapons.

The night she read Guillaume's letter for the first time, Kate leapt, hollering, out of a dream in which fists pounded on neighbours' doors and dishevelled strangers found themselves hauled out of their beds and dragged, shrieking their innocence, to the firing squad. She had, of course, been reading the papers, but the portentous images might have been inspired by long-forgotten films of KGB and Gestapo arrests.

In Québec, too, the police squads conducted most raids shortly before dawn. Yves and Guillaume's arrests, however, took place in mid-morning, just two or three hours after Guillaume had phoned Kate to break the news about the War Measures Act. Yves and Suzanne were still in bed when the police arrived on Selkirk Avenue; Guillaume was taking a shower, unable to come to the door when the pounding started. The janitor had let the squad into the building. By the time Guillaume came out of the shower, two plainclothes detectives and an armed policeman were getting ready to bust the door.

All this was recapped by Guillaume in his first letter, posted in Montreal without a return address:

> ... *They didn't even explain their presence. All they said was that the new 'special law' made explanations unnecessary. Can you believe it? Would you believe it if it happened to you, or your*

family? The armed cop stayed put at the entrance, to make sure I did not take off after the two detectives began to pull out drawers and empty all the cupboards, bookshelves. They inspected the oven, the freezer, even my cello, Katherine—the inside of my cello!

At one point, one of the policemen got his finger accidentally cut in the kitchen and came out swearing, glaring at me and darkly hinting I would pay for his spilled blood. He went on to the bathroom to get a Kleenex, then came out clutching his upright finger in what looked like an obscene gesture. The fucking pig! He looked like one too, with his bloated pink face and little snub nose. His fat fingers made me think of pork sausages, but ... well, maybe I was just hungry.

I hadn't yet had any breakfast, and by noon, as they went on riffling through my things, my stomach was beginning to protest. I asked permission —asked very politely—to go to the kitchen for a bowl of cereal while they finished their search. And do you know what they said to me?

"There's no point, Monsieur: we'll soon have you as one of our honoured guests. We'll serve you eggs with caviar, coffee with whipped cream—the works." And then they laughed at their own moronic wit, the bastards!

When they finished searching every nook and cranny, they told me to put on my jacket—they were ready to take me down for a friendly visit, they said with their fake smiles. One of them ran upstairs, but his colleagues were not yet done with

Yves and Suzanne. Personally, I was more than
willing to go to the police station and let them
question me, let them find out what a stupid
mistake they'd made.

But then they handcuffed me! They took my
two wrists, Katherine, and handcuffed them, then
shoved me into one of their cruisers like any bank
robber or murderer!

Oh, you can't imagine what it's like, chérie.
No one can, who hasn't lived through it. You know
you're innocent—you know it!—yet your helpless
hands, cuffed in front of your grumbling stomach,
make you feel like a criminal on his way to jail!
Instead of outrage at being victimized, you feel this
strange sense of shame, as if you were an
amnesiac, or maybe a sleepwalker, who committed
some unspeakable act you have no memory of.
Why else would they be going after you?

Anyway, they drove me down to Parthenais and
ordered me, along with I don't know how many
others, to strip down so they could search for lice,
for small objects hidden between my buttocks! Oh
God, I won't even try to describe all this. I was
ordered to take a shower, to put on fresh prison garb.
Me, Guillaume Beauregard, a fucking prisoner!

By then, I was beginning to feel like a character
in Kafka. They fingerprinted me but no one would
say what it was all about. In Canada, every man's
innocent until proven guilty. Isn't that the way it's
supposed to be? I felt not only guilty, but already
convicted: without a trial, without any charges.

Oh, and something else, trivial but somehow

humiliating. They had hired barbers to chop off our hair and beards. I am not sure you would even recognize me now! Eventually, they threw me into a cell with a cot, a toilet, a sink. True: It wasn't as bad as the jails I've seen in movies, but I was innocent! I felt like howling. I've never felt so fucking impotent in my whole life, Katherine. Impotent and, I confess, really scared.

At the beginning, you see, I kept thinking they would soon realize it was all a terrible mistake. As soon as they questioned me, I thought, they'd apologize and send me home.

But that's not how it played out. There I was, in a barred, airless room, a spotlight aimed at my eyes, just like some character in a political thriller. I was all alone with a policeman and a crude bully for an interrogator. The bastard quickly made it clear that they had evidence proving Michel's involvement in the FLQ; that they knew he had stayed at my place when he was in town. I told them I knew nothing about my brother's activities, that I'd always kept my own nose out of politics. As far as I knew, Michel had come to Montreal for holidays and anniversaries.

I told them all this, but then something new struck me.

"Have you arrested my parents, too?" I asked the interrogator. I was worried, you know, because of my father's heart. Not that they would give a damn about that. "Have you?" I insisted when they did not answer.

"You're here to answer questions, not ask them!"

the interrogator barked. I asked if I could call my parents, but again, they didn't deign to answer. It terrified me that no one had any way of knowing where I was being held. The guards only sneered when I asked to consult a lawyer, or even write a letter. The second time I was questioned—questioned for three consecutive hours—the interrogator told me I would be executed in three days.

And I believed him, Katherine. I did! Why not? I was living through a Kafkaesque nightmare. Anything was possible: a mock trial, no trial. I felt like a condemned man awaiting his turn on death row. I began to re-examine my life …

I have to stop now, chérie. I do need to get these things off my chest—to tell you what I've been through—but I get so fucking mad, thinking about it all. Right now, I feel like running out, you know, and screaming out my story for the whole world to hear. I know I'm not the only one who feels this way; the newspapers are full of innocent people's protests. I'll finish my own story tomorrow, okay?

Guillaume's grim account continued the next day, as promised, after a short digression about two crazy women living across the landing from where he was staying:

… I was kept at Parthenais for twelve days, but every day was pretty much the same: an eternity of rage, dread, boredom. There was nothing to do but sleep, eat, and think about life and justice. Every night,

the prison guards came and woke me up to search the cell all over again. I have no idea what they thought they'd find, but they stripped the mattress every single night; inspected my body over and over and over. Oh, I forgot to tell you: The first time I ate prison food, I threw up. I accused my jailer of trying to poison me, but the sadist only laughed.

"That would be much too easy!" he said.

The prisoner in the next cell heard the guard's answer. He began to shout and rattle the iron bars. He was ordered to stop but wouldn't. He shouted louder, cursing these men, who were treating their own people like rabid animals. That's what he kept saying, and he was right! When he wouldn't shut up, they opened his cell, stripped him naked, and threw him into solitary confinement. I learnt this much later, when we were both waiting to be released. At the time, I thought they were taking the poor bastard to be tortured, or even executed!

Are you wondering if they ever tortured me? They did not, but they were very—very sadistically—rough with me, and, well, soon I began to find myself tortured in my dreams. I suspected they would use torture only as a last resort, but I was sure they would resort to it sooner or later, when all their threats failed to get them a signed confession.

Of course, I knew this was what they were after, but I could neither give it to them, nor say anything to defend myself. Since they had not laid any formal charges, I couldn't even offer an alibi. After they told me I'd be executed, I wondered if

*they would at least let me see a priest. Maybe if I
told them I was a believer? The strange thing was,
I couldn't bring myself to lie about my religious
beliefs. Ridiculous, eh? Maybe I'm not a true
atheist after all, just another confused agnostic.*

*I went to sleep without eating that night,
thinking I might try a hunger strike. But then they
took me for another, more friendly, interrogation. I
kept thinking they would release me, but all they
were doing was trying out a new strategy.*

*Katherine, Katherine! You can't imagine what
it was like, to be locked up in that prison cell!
Every day, men came and went. Some came back,
some didn't. Later, I would find out that most of
them had been released very quickly. It was
Michel's politics that apparently made me such a
strong suspect. I kept worrying about my father. I
wondered if they'd also arrested poor Jacques,
maybe Chantal as well.*

*After I got out, I learnt that they had in fact
arrested my sister, forcing her to leave her small
children behind, can you imagine? They ransacked
her place too, then told her to call her mother and
tell her to hurry over. Mother dropped everything
and took a taxi down, but the bastards didn't even
bother waiting until she arrived. They took
Chantal downstairs and left a policeman to watch
over an infant and a terrified three-year-old child.
In Canada! They kept Chantal with them in the
cruiser until they saw my mother's taxi pull up.
My sister pleaded with them to let her speak to*

her mother for a minute, just to give childcare instructions, but the bastards took off at once. They didn't even bother to answer.

Fortunately, they did not keep Chantal very long. She was released after one interrogation. I have no idea why. Some say it's because she's a woman, but I doubt it. There were women they kept just as long as they did me and Yves. Don't ask me to explain. Maybe they thought no one as young and sexy as Chantal could possibly be involved in subversive activities?

Anyway, I'm out now, Katherine, but I wish I could honestly say that I feel—what's the English word? Unscathed, I think—right? Truth to tell, I don't feel at all like the man I was when I was last with you. It's strange, you know: for twelve days I had nothing to do but think, and now that I'm out, I don't seem to be able to stop thinking. I feel profoundly changed, though I can't exactly say how, and certainly not if the change will turn out to be permanent. I am staying with Marc and Véronique Anfousse. They, too, were arrested, then released at the same time as me for lack of evidence. Sometime, chérie, I hope to be able to explain more coherently everything I feel, but for now, I hope you'll simply forgive me; I hope you will understand that I just can't see you or my family right now. I can't even play the cello!

Je t'embrasse,
Guillaume

II

Idle and impotent in their prison cells, Guillaume and his co-detainees would have had no way of knowing the details of the political drama unfolding beyond the Parthenais jail walls. James Cross remained an FLQ captive but, one day after the War Measures Act was declared, Pierre Laporte's strangled corpse was discovered in a South Shore parking lot, stuffed into the trunk of an abandoned car.

The news shook the nation, but the Montreal tragedy quickly turned into black comedy. The provincial authorities had succeeded in apprehending the three murderers, but were soon forced to make a public announcement, admitting that the captives escaped after their guards had left them to have dinner out.

"Don't they deliver pizza in Québec?" an incredulous caller-in demanded on national radio.

"Does their union forbid them to eat in their captives' presence?" a street interviewee wondered.

Having succeeded in getting the FLQ manifesto broadcast, Cross's kidnappers hastened to dissociate themselves from the underground cell responsible for Laporte's murder. Robert Bourassa, Québec's Premier, had no choice but to offer safe conduct to Cuba in exchange for the immediate release of the British diplomat. Day in and day out, frenzied negotiations took place, while innocent detainees waited to be freed, and combat troops stood at the ready all over the jittery city.

October came to an end. November passed. The negotiations went on and on.

They continued until the third of December, 1970.

Kate had a morning class that day, but came home at lunch, hoping Guillaume might suddenly turn up. She was just in time for the coverage of what the media had dubbed "the final chapter."

After fifty-nine days in captivity, James Cross was about to be released on St. Helen's Island, where, only three years earlier, EXPO '67 had attracted thousands of international visitors. The historic event was about to be broadcast live on national television. The terrorists were said to possess arms and dynamite. What if something went wrong at the last moment?

Alone with her mother in the family den, Kate burst into tears in front of the television. Her mother glanced up, reached for a box of tissues, then put her arms around Kate in mute sympathy. Kate cried on her mother's shoulder, but at length rallied herself and stepped out onto the balcony for a quick cigarette. Then she went back to watching the live newscast.

The CBC cameras were beginning to roll. They tailed the zooming FLQ Chrysler through the ramshackle streets of Montreal's waterfront, accompanied by police motorcycles and cruisers, their lights flashing, their sirens shrilling. The winter sun bounced off squalid tenements and skeletal trees shuddering in the wind. Here and there, children stopped to watch the cacophonous motorcade streak by. A scrawny dog gave chase, then came to an abrupt halt, barking dispiritedly.

On the man-made St. Helen's Island, the former Canadian pavilion had been designated as a temporary Cuban consulate. A British representative was waiting for the three abductors to deliver their English captive. With the promise of Cuban passports, the kidnappers were ready to relinquish their weapons and hand James Cross over before being allowed to depart. On the sidelines, a helicopter stood ready to transport the three young men to the airport. The signed agreement stipulated a direct flight to Havana, where Fidel Castro had promised official asylum.

"The final chapter," the broadcasters kept repeating.

The plan was executed without a hitch. Pierre Laporte's killers had yet to be ferreted out and brought to justice, but the night on which James Cross was finally handed over to Canadian authorities, the entire nation heaved a collective sigh of relief. Interviewed on television, Prime Minister Trudeau confirmed the British diplomat's successful release.

"The rest is now, I think, a nightmare which has passed into history," he told his fellow Canadians. He seemed to be looking straight at Kate as he spoke, but for her personally, the nightmare was far from over.

By the time the Prime Minister's speech was aired, over a month had passed since Guillaume's release from the Parthenais jail, but Kate had yet to lay eyes on the man she loved. She knew Véronique and her brother Marc, but didn't know where they lived. She thought of trying to get their address from their cousin, who was a clarinettist at the Youth Orchestra, but Kate's mother urged her to respect Guillaume's stated wishes. She thought "the poor boy" was traumatized and needed to be alone for a while; to think things through.

Kate kept reminding herself that it was not her that Guillaume was rejecting. She told herself they needed to be together now, he and his jailed buddies, licking each other's wounds. Didn't he say as much in his letter? No one who hadn't been there could possibly understand what they had all gone through.

Kate read Guillaume's long letter again and again. She would be understanding then; as patient and understanding as anyone could be in the circumstances.

I can't even play the cello!

FIVE

I

It is early Sunday morning and the downtown church bells are chiming as Kate heads west, towards Selkirk Avenue. She has left Megan to sleep in and is on her way to an early breakfast-cum-photo-shoot with her new friend, Antonia. Stepping over a leaf-clogged manhole cover, she trudges uphill, doing her best not to think of Brad, who sounded aloof when they talked last night, disappointed to hear of her intention to prolong her Montreal stay.

She had planned to return to Edmonton after Megan's birthday, but is reluctant to leave without seeing her brother and sister-in-law. They had planned to fly home early next week, but some professional issue has unexpectedly come up, forcing them to stop over in London. They won't be back now before early October, Kate informed Brad; she will be home soon after, in time for her own birthday and, of course, Thanksgiving. She has given her word.

Kate is approaching the corner of Selkirk and Côte-des-Neiges, still thinking of her husband, when she spots a familiar figure: an old woman crossing the busy street, an unwrapped carton of milk clutched against her bosom.

Elizabeth Berg! A much older Elizabeth, dressed in an engine-red windbreaker and white woollen hat with pompoms. She seems to be coming from the *dépanneur*, is perhaps rushing home to feed her cats, but, impulsively, Kate calls out to her.

"Miss Elizabeth!"

The old woman slows down on the curb. She stops and turns, squinting quizzically, while Kate crosses the street towards her. Elizabeth stands waiting, her face like a crumpled envelope, her faded eyes blinking in confusion. As Kate comes closer, the frown on the familiar face dissolves and a smile as tentative as a child's on the first day of school takes over her sagging features.

"Oh, I remember you!" she says, wagging a gnarled finger. She speaks with a faintly Germanic accent. "I don't know your name but—"

"Kate. Kate Abbitson, that was my name when—"

"Sure, I remember you." She laughs now, exposing several missing teeth. "You ... you used to live up there, right?" Elizabeth twists around as she says this, raising her arm to point towards the second-floor bay window. "Where the actress lives."

"Yes, sort of." Kate smiles into the watery brown eyes, delighted to have run into the old woman. "It was actually my boyfriend's place. Guillaume Beauregard?"

"So, I remember him, too! A handsome French-Canadian musician, right?" Elizabeth cackles. "Sure, I remember him. I'm not very good with names or dates, but I *never* forget a face!" She stands studying Kate's features. "You haven't changed much," she says after a prolonged scrutiny. "You had longer hair in those days, though, didn't you?"

"Yes." Kate jams her hands into her jacket pockets. "Yes, I did."

"Sure. You used to wear this ... this red thing without sleeves. What do you call them ...?"

"A poncho?"

"That's it. I always thought you looked like Audrey Hepburn in *Funny Girl* ... at the beginning, you know? Before they make her into a high-fashion model. How come you never came back for your cat?" she asks in a wheezing voice.

"My cat?" Kate stares for a long, muddled moment. "My cat disappeared. I did come back ... I guess you don't remember. I couldn't find him anywhere. I even—"

"Of course I remember! You came in and had coffee at my place. I gave you some plum jam just before you left, remember?"

"Yes, but I thought—"

"You thought he was hit by a car. I remember your telling me, but ... well, he obviously wasn't, was he?"

"He wasn't?" Kate stands motionless on the leaf-strewn pavement, listening to her own heartbeat.

"Certainly not! He showed up on my porch one evening and, well, I couldn't turn him away, could I? He was quite a mess, believe me. His ear was all chewed up and—"

"Pablo showed up at your place?" Kate stares and stares at Elizabeth, her stomach in utter revolt. "He was alive?"

"Sure he was alive! I left a note in your mailbox, but you never came back. I never saw you again, you or your beau. What happened to the two of you anyway?"

"Oh, Miss Elizabeth!" Kate opens her mouth to explain, then gives up and lets out a long sighing breath. "It's a long story," she says at length, fidgeting with her camera strap. "I'm sorry you got stuck with my cat."

"Ach, don't be silly," Elizabeth croaks. "He was a lovely cat ... lots of personality, you know?"

"Yes. Yes, he was." In the back of Kate's head, an un-expected vision is rising: Pablo meowing on Elizabeth's porch, Pablo purring in front of her fireplace. Suddenly, an inarticulate exclamation leaps out of her mouth.

"The cat you gave Antonia Offe," she says breathlessly. "The actress. Is her cat by any chance one ... one of Pablo's offspring?"

"Sure," Elizabeth says with palpable satisfaction. "Isn't he something?" She gives another one of her raspy cackles. "So you know the actress, do you? She a friend of yours?"

"No ... yes, a new friend, I guess. I've actually held her cat in my arms, but I had no idea ... I thought he looked just like Pablo but ... oh my God, I just can't believe it!" Kate says, nervously pushing her hair away from her fore-head. "When did Pablo die?" she asks after a while.

"Oh, he lived to a ripe old age: nineteen or so," Eliza-beth says. "I can't believe it's almost a decade already." She sighs, clearing her nostrils once more. And then, all at once, she seems to recall the purpose of her visit to the *dépanneur.* "I must be going. My pussy cats will be wanting their milk. Come have coffee with me one of these days, will you?" She turns to go, then stops and gives Kate a long, earnest look. "I would have phoned you, you know, but I didn't remember your name ... I'm sorry."

"Oh ... please!" Overcome by impulse, Kate reaches out and kisses the old woman's withered cheek. "Thank you for taking such good care of Pablo. Really." She places her right hand over her heart. "I can't tell you how much this means to me."

"Ach, don't mention it. I've got to run now. Drop in any time and we'll have us a nice little chat, okay?"

"Okay," Kate says; then, once more: "Thank you!" She lingers for a moment, watching Elizabeth waddle down the street; then she runs up Antonia's steps, as light-footed as if she were still the girl in the red poncho, with all her life before her.

II

"I can't tell you how happy it makes me to know that Otto is related to Pablo!" Kate says this to Antonia as they stand clearing the breakfast dishes, watching Otto emerge, stretching, from under the dining table. Antonia says something about life being full of surprises, but Kate wants to say that's not the point; not entirely. She wants to say that Elizabeth's disclosure has made her feel somehow redeemed, or has redeemed the past. No, not redeemed exactly, but validated it. As if, until she ran into Elizabeth, a part of her had secretly suspected that her own romantic past might be a figment of her imagination.

But what a ridiculous thought!

She has never doubted her own memories; never stopped to question a single one of them. And yet, she feels as if Elizabeth has unexpectedly provided a secret bridge, connecting her past and her present; that their chance encounter has brought the past out of its thickening mists and sharpened its fading contours.

"That was a lovely breakfast, thank you," she says.

Antonia starts stacking the dishwasher while Kate

stands wiping the granite counter. As she does so, she has a mental vision of herself wiping the Arborite counter in Guillaume's kitchen, stopping every now and then to look through the window at the street below. Antonia's galley kitchen has no windows. One could spend an entire year here and never be aware of the changing weather.

Kate doesn't share these thoughts with Antonia. She is inwardly flipping through seasonal images from her private past: Guillaume in his winter sheepskin throwing snowballs at her outside the Catholic seminary wall; Guillaume in his light suede jacket stopping one early spring day to buy her a bunch of daffodils at the Atwater Market; Guillaume, sunburnt from his construction job, wading into Lake Massawippi, where her parents had a summer cottage, splashing water like a playful, overgrown school boy.

"What's the matter?" Antonia says, putting a dishtowel away. "You look kind of weepy. What are you thinking of?"

"Oh, I was just remembering something about Guillaume," Kate says with a sigh. "He couldn't swim, you know. I was so surprised to find out he couldn't! I'd never met anyone who couldn't swim, have you?"

"Well, yes, now and then." Antonia leads the way back to the living room, bearing a coffee tray. Settling into one of the plump sofas, she tells Kate how, though she had been taught to swim as a child, she once came close to drowning in Tunisia, caught in a whirlpool with an Austrian boyfriend. Otto is named after this former lover.

Kate listens to the meandering story, paying less attention to its details than to Antonia's mobile features. She is trying to decide how best to pose the actress in this vast, elegant room. She has brought her camera, but Antonia herself obliged her by picking up the rest of the equipment yesterday, on her way home from a McGill play. It is all waiting now, propped up next to the bay window, though Antonia claims that she doesn't much like being photographed. She seems, in fact, happy to sit and chat, as if she has quite forgotten the purpose of this carefully planned visit. All the same, as she concludes the story of her near-drowning in Tunisia, Antonia becomes aware of Kate's abstracted air.

"You still think of him quite a lot, don't you?" she says.

"Guillaume? Oh ... yes." Kate can feel herself flushing. "He is ... he seems to be everywhere I go these days. He still lives here, you know, in Nôtre-Dame-de-Grace."

"Oh? How do you know this?"

Kate drops her eyes. "I looked him up the other day. Unless there is another Guillaume Beauregard, of course."

"I see."

Nôtre-Dame-de-Grace has traditionally been an anglophone enclave, though in recent years, a growing number of professional francophones have moved into this leafy part of town bordering Westmount. Antonia says she has a godson living there; a McGill philosophy professor.

"Would you like to see him?" she asks. There is a tender, amused gleam in her prolonged gaze. "I mean Guillaume, of course, not my godson." She laughs.

"Would I like to see Guillaume again?" Kate echoes, feeling adrift, foolish. "No. No, I don't think so," she adds after a moment's reflection. "In fact, I'm sure I wouldn't."

"Why not?" Antonia's left arm rests across the colourful cushions, her mouth stretched in a sphinx-like smile. This, Kate decides, is one expression she must strive to capture in her final photograph; this complicated smile with its old woman's wisdom and girlish flirtatiousness, and something else; some enigmatic quality she can't quite put her finger on.

Why not? Kate shifts her weight on the sofa, turning the question over.

"Well, to be perfectly honest, I think I'd be a little afraid."

"Oh? Afraid of what?"

Kate hesitates, eyes hazy with thought. "I'm afraid that if I met him tomorrow ... if he were to ask me to go with him someplace like Timbuktu, I might be tempted to follow." Kate laughs, making clear this was meant as a joke. To herself she adds: Well, who knows? I might.

After a while she says: "I couldn't do this to Brad after all these years. I couldn't leave him. Not for another man."

"I see." Antonia studies Kate, toying with her antique jade pendant. "From what you've told me, though, you might actually be doing him a favour. Have you ever thought of that?"

Kate sits very still for a moment. "Yes. I have." She shifts her gaze, breaking away from the look in Antonia's eyes. A moment or two go by. "It's impossible to predict how anyone will react," she says. "Brad might feel relieved, as you say, but then again, who knows, he might be devastated. I couldn't do that to him. I feel ... well, I do feel indebted to him, you know. Obviously I do." She pauses and heaves a sigh. "Oh, let's not talk about Brad. Let's take some pictures, okay?"

III

As Kate goes about setting up the tripod and floodlights, Antonia shifts her weight on the sofa, her hand flying up to pat down her unruly curls. Outside, just below the bay window, a man whistles, then calls out to his dog. There is a short, playful bark, a man's throaty laughter. The dog barks and barks; a child bursts into prolonged giggles. Kate stands studying her subject, frowning a little.

A great photograph, as Ansel Adams famously said, is one that fully expresses what one feels about what is being photographed. And that, it seems, is where Kate's problem lies at the moment. She is not sure how she feels about Antonia; is not sure she quite understands her. A painter's job may be to construct, but a photographer's is to reveal. When she decides to do a serious portrait, what Kate aspires to is access to the subject's innermost being. Right now, she does not feel she is anywhere near having such access to her subject.

Antonia says: "If you're thinking of shooting me in profile, please make sure you take this side, okay?" She angles her head sharply towards the window, theatrically raising her chin. "Isn't it strange, how different two sides of the same face can look? Anyway, I have a mole on this side," she adds, raising a hand to cover her cheek with her long, bony hand. "It keeps growing, too."

"Never mind the mole." Kate smiles, promising to let Antonia see a contact sheet; let her veto any photos she doesn't like. She is nothing if not accustomed to her subjects' vanity, though perhaps the vanity is meant to conceal a deeper vulnerability. Every picture, after all, is not just the photographer's interpretation but a judgement. Years ago, on a Calcutta street, even an Indian beggar sat up straight on spotting her camera, and adjusted his rags, looking severe and proud in a photo he would never see.

"You look wonderful anyway," Kate assures Antonia.

Still smiling her small professional smile, she moves to adjust the reflector, while Antonia lets out a little chortling sound. She then makes an extraordinary statement. She hadn't, she says, realized she was an old woman; not until the day her mole began to grow, sprouting a grey hair.

"I think I was in denial until then, you know?"

Kate sighs, at a loss for words. She is thinking of a picture-book illustration that had, on a couple of occasions, crept into young Megan's dreams; a colourful depiction of a witch with a large mole on her chin, sprouting dark bristles.

The thought leaves her feeling a little guilty. She sits down next to Antonia, hoping to help her subject relax. "I know what you mean," she says with a chuckle. "I'm almost fifty and ... well, I still don't think of myself as a middle-aged woman."

Just before they left Edmonton, Megan had her last dental appointment. Kate accompanied her and, later that night, dreamt that she was being fitted for dentures.

"Dentures!" she says to Antonia.

Antonia stretches her lips to expose strong, if slightly yellowing, teeth. "I still have my own, touch wood," she states, patting the coffee table.

Kate laughs. Waving it all away, she levers herself from the plump sofa and goes about snapping Antonia: on the sofa, the window seat, next to the combine painting, in front of the spiral staircase. When Otto reappears, Antonia bends over to pick him up from the floor. Kate captures her swooping up the bushy-tailed cat, muttering in his ear, her eyes narrowed, her lips slightly parted. The expression, in a different context, might easily be associated with sexual ecstasy.

Kate snaps Antonia and her cat over and over. She has her now, she is sure of it, but doesn't stop until she hears the camera click, the film starting to rewind.

"That was great!" she says. "I think you'll like them."

"Oh, I'd *love* a nice one of me and Otto!"

"Your wish is my command, *Madame!*"

"*Merci. Merci Beaucoup!*"

Antonia lets go of Otto, then stands running her hands down to smooth her narrow wool skirt. The skirt is charcoal grey with thin white stripes; she wears it with a crisp white shirt and a long black cardigan. The film in the camera is black and white, Antonia's hair is a shiny, silver halo. Perfect. The outfit Antonia has chosen to wear will make for exquisite contrasts. And yet, it is often said that art is not in the subject but in the eye of the beholder. Sometimes, Kate doesn't quite know what she beheld until she has had a chance to study the contact sheet.

"I can't wait to see these!" she tells Antonia.

"Just make sure you show me what you've got. I don't want anyone to see it before I do, okay?"

Kate smiles a little. "Of course not. I promise."

IV

Just before heading home, while Antonia feeds her cat, Kate returns to the egg photograph, her thoughts straying back to the gouache painting that used to hang on this wall all those years ago; Guillaume's brother's exquisite painting of a woman in a long white dress and a straw hat, facing the entrance to a small rustic dwelling.

Kate can't remember the title of Michel's painting, but she has often thought that the work may have inspired her own lasting interest in photographing doorways. She has a series of them from around the world: Cycladic portals, wrought-iron Roman gates, and cave-like entrances on the edge of the Sahara. She is fascinated by thresholds; by the subtle pressure they exert on her dormant imagination. When she photographs any kind of entrance, it is always with the hope of compelling viewers to imagine what lies beyond.

Nothing she has ever done, however, has come close to the power of Guillaume's brother's painting; the image of a woman standing on the threshold to a small rural home, her back to the viewer, her slender arms hanging down simply, gracefully, naturally. Following Antonia downstairs, Kate still can't tell what it was about this faceless woman's shoulders and the back of her neck—above all, her youthful arms in their long white sleeves—that so eloquently conveyed her private turmoil: her pride and her dread, her heroic resignation. The first time Kate saw the painting, she found herself thinking of young women coerced into marriage; of impoverished single mothers forced to sell their bodies in order to feed their children. The woman in the painting was ageless, her circumstances obscure. Only her inner chaos seemed beyond dispute; that and the shady interior she stood facing with such heartbreaking female stoicism.

Guillaume's younger brother did not like to discuss his paintings; at least not with her. Kate has no idea what he had in mind, or what has happened to that early painting. She supposes that Guillaume must still be in possession of it, but if she chanced to stumble upon it at an art gallery or

an auction, she would snap it up without hesitation. Whatever the asking price.

She makes a mental note to check whether Michel
Beauregard's name is known at the Sherbrooke Street gal-
leries. Meanwhile, Antonia helps her carry the photo
equipment down to the parked car. She has a lunch date in
the Plateau and will be dropping Kate off on her way east.
The entire day has been planned by Antonia, who seems
like a born organizer, an impressively competent woman.

"When will the photos be ready?" she asks. "Do you
think you could bring the contact sheet to the party next
Sunday?" She opens the trunk to her car. The Volvo has
finally been fixed and is parked directly across from Elizabeth's house.

"Your birthday party? I doubt it." Across the street, on
Elizabeth Berg's porch, two cats are curled against each
other, the sleepy green slits of their eyes lost within a mass
of streaked caramel fur. The only person Kate trusts with
her film, she explains to Antonia, is a Dutch photographer
friend back in Edmonton. "I'll send you the contact sheet as
soon as it's ready," she promises, sliding into the passenger
seat.

The white Volvo has a soft grey interior smelling of
leather and pipe tobacco. *Pipe tobacco?* As her new friend is
a non-smoker, Kate wonders whether, despite her disclaim-
er, Antonia might have a man in her life.

But why should she doubt Antonia? She has no answer
to her own question; she just does. Then she remembers
her mother again: the occasional meanness of her old age,
the growing suspiciousness. She turns and rolls down her
window.

"What a beautiful day it's turned out to be!" she exclaims, resolutely upbeat.

"It's perfect!"

While the two of them were busy having breakfast and taking photographs, the sun gradually emerged through its thick veil of morning mist. It is now drying rain puddles, sifting through rustling treetops: orange and red, green and yellow, the splash of brilliant colour outlined against the postcard-blue sky. Kate lets out a sigh, reminded that, very soon, she must leave all this and head back to Edmonton.

"Maybe I can talk my daughter into going for a walk on the mountain," she says. Montreal's Mount Royal is more hill than mountain, but has a vast, wooded park with picnic tables and bicycle paths winding around a small, picturesque lake. It was on the grass surrounding Beaver Lake that the old Youth Orchestra snapshot was taken, all those years ago. It occurs to Kate that Megan might have too much homework after last week's bout with the flu. She may have to take her daughter's bike and go for a ride on her own.

"Would you like me to help you up?" Antonia asks, parked in front of Megan's apartment building. "As far as the elevator?"

"No, I'm fine, thank you. I'll just buzz Megan and ask her to come down." Kate dashes off, then comes back to the car and leans into Antonia's window.

"We're going to Québec City next weekend," she says, "but I'll be back on Sunday, in time for your party. What time?"

"Oh, any time between seven and eight? We always have cocktails and then a buffet dinner."

"Great! I'm looking forward to it."

And she really is. Despite what she has just told Antonia, Kate hopes to have a portrait ready before the party. If she sends the film to Edmonton by express mail tomorrow morning, she just might be able to get it developed in time. Yes, she will call Edmonton tonight and ask Pieter to do her a favour and rush it through. A perfect birthday gift!

Kate loves giving presents; she always looks forward to seeing her friends' faces when they are at the peak of delight, often taken by surprise. She is still looking for the right gift for Megan's birthday later this month. There was a time when she knew exactly what to get her children for their birthdays, but not anymore; not unless she asks, and she would much rather not ask. With a little luck, she'll find something in Montreal, or maybe Québec City. She hopes to get something original for Megan's new apartment.

SIX

I

THE PHOTOGRAPHS KATE likes best are ones that offer a hint of some complex story. Unlike many of her colleagues, she is not interested in photographing buildings, bridges, streets, except perhaps in a city like Venice or St. Petersburg. In Montreal, the street she finds most intriguing cannot lay claim to architectural distinction, but it is nonetheless a vibrant, historic street that has loomed large in her personal history.

Although her childhood was mostly spent in tony Westmount, once she enrolled at McGill University, Kate's life quickly began to expand eastward, towards St. Lawrence Boulevard, a far-reaching street that has historically separated the francophones in the east from the anglophones in the west. In recent years, the seedy commercial street has undergone extensive gentrification, but in Kate's memory it is still the Main, a long stretch of cut-rate clothing stores and ethnic groceries, peeling warehouses and steaming hot dog joints. The block just below St. Catherine was where Guillaume's friends, Marc and Véronique Anfousse, were living when the War Measures Act was passed. At the time, it was mostly known for its go-go clubs and pool halls and scantily-dressed streetwalkers. Occasionally, students or struggling artists might rent a shabby loft on the street, transforming industrial space with posters, batik bedspreads, Chinese parasols.

Marc and Véronique's father was a music critic at *La Presse*, which probably explained their being able to afford an exceptionally attractive loft with exposed brick walls and cathedral windows. Véronique was a sociology student, Marc an aspiring songwriter who had recently begun to set Émile Nelligan's poems to music. The building in which they were renting a third-floor loft had once been an underwear factory. Marc and Véronique shared the top landing with a Christian mission run by two ex-prostitutes. The recent converts had painted a bold cautionary sign on the street door: THE WAGES OF SIN IS DEATH. Had Guillaume been with her, Kate would have laughed herself silly on reading the bilingual sign. LE SALAIRE DU PECHE Ç'EST LA MORT.

But Guillaume wasn't at the loft when she went looking for him a month after his release from Parthenais jail. He had, Véronique Anfousse was still trying to persuade Kate, stayed with them for just a few days before moving on.

"I give you my word of honour," she was saying. "He hasn't been here for over three weeks." The statement was made in English, but the key word came out sounding more like *honneur*. Véronique sat cradling her Red Zinger tea, pale and inscrutable.

"But where would he go? He hasn't been in his own apartment ... I've checked," Kate said, fiddling with her silver rings. And it was true. The Selkirk apartment was being sublet until January. Kate leaned towards Véronique, her whole body a plea for cooperation. "Why won't you tell me where he is?"

"Because I don't know!" Véronique stared at Kate for a long moment, tight-lipped. "I wish you'd believe me."

She was a slight girl with a high forehead and pale hair as fine as a child's. The hair flowed loose to her bony shoulders. She had a stiff way of holding herself, as if to make her tiny breasts appear more prominent. The thought stole into Kate's mind that, after their joint ordeal, Guillaume had become sexually involved with Véronique. She had a rather square jaw but striking blue eyes, the gaze of an aloof adolescent, determined to keep a prying parent out of some private domain.

"He didn't tell us where he was going, Kate. Maybe —" Whatever Véronique had set out to say was abruptly swallowed. "Don't worry about him," she said instead. "I'm sure he's all right."

But these words only brought Kate's head jerking up.

"How can you be so sure he's all right if you don't know where he is?"

Oh, she thought she had her there! But no: Véronique only sighed with an air of exaggerated patience. She scratched one of her knees.

"I know he is with friends. This is what he told us ... but that's all he said. I'm sure he's all right."

"All right!" Kate sighed, shaking her head. She rubbed her eyes, thinking: I shouldn't have let my mother talk me into staying away when I got the letter. I should have set out the day it arrived and maybe he'd still be here. We could have sat down and talked about whatever was going on in his head. Everything would be fine if only I'd come in time!

A few minutes passed. Kate sipped her tea, but the anger she felt at the missed opportunity soon had her rummaging through her bag, blindly searching for a pack of cigarettes.

"Are you involved with Guillaume?" she heard herself blurt, instantly regretting her own words: As if Véronique would tell her! She closed her eyes for one frenzied moment, damming her tears. "Are you?"

"Me?" Véronique's eyes were wide, the irises rimmed in black. If she was lying, she was a gifted actress. "Don't be ridiculous. He's not even my type," she stated, meeting Kate's eyes. Perhaps sensing her doubts, she quickly added: "I've never been attracted to blond guys myself. Never."

"Really?" Kate did not believe that any woman could be impervious to Guillaume Beauregard's charms. She contemplated Véronique through a cloud of smoke but the oboeist only stared her down, unflappable in her tight blue jeans, her bulky red sweater.

"Really." Véronique all but smiled. She handed Kate an ashtray, her gaze straying towards the rustic, potbellied stove, which she'd lit before offering tea. Kate had accepted the invitation, thinking Véronique was going to be warmly sympathetic. Instead, she had turned out to be polite but intractable. And yet, she did not seem especially eager to be rid of Kate. Reserved and silent, she got up to refill the teapot. Kate did not budge. She sat smoking by the blazing stove, feverishly weighing the situation.

The loft had beautiful high windows, and that afternoon bright sunlight streamed through the glass, dancing on the colourful posters, the faded velour sofas. The furniture looked much like Guillaume's, no doubt purchased at the Salvation Army. Here, too, there were sagging bookshelves and amateurish sculptures, and tropical plants flourishing to spectacular heights. Kate thought of the Benjamina which Guillaume had been ready to throw out in the summer, but which she had impulsively rescued and gradually nursed back to health. She remembered it with a breath of resignation: Whatever the subject, her thoughts seemed to willy-nilly find their way back to Guillaume. The previous day, walking down St. Catherine Street, she had spotted someone in the shopping crowd who, from the back at least, looked exactly like Guillaume: Same walk, same hair, same suede jacket and faded blue jeans.

It was not Guillaume, although the stranger seemed only too eager to chat when Kate stopped and apologized. This was when she decided that she must try to find Guillaume, never mind her mother's opinions.

So here she was now, with Véronique Anfousse, but the thought of Guillaume, of the empty weeks which had crawled by since she'd last seen him, filled Kate with renewed despair. What to do now? She raised her eyes to the ceiling, fighting the threat of tears.

And then she just sat there until Véronique came back from the kitchen, carrying the steaming teapot with its frayed bamboo handle.

"I'm addicted to this tea," she said at length, "especially now, with these draughty windows." She set the teapot on a pile of books, then settled into a rocking chair, cradling her mug. Neither of them seemed to know what to say, but Kate could not help noticing that Véronique, too, was reading *The Wretched of the Earth*. Well, what of it? Hundreds of Québecers must have read Franz Fanon. The book might not even belong to Véronique but to her brother Marc.

Kate stubbed out her cigarette, contemplating her own paint-stained fingers. The basement and kitchen had just been painted in her parents' home. She sat abstracted, rubbing the stains, trying to formulate a new question nagging in the back of her mind.

"Okay, Véronique," she said at length. "Let's say you don't know where he is. But you must know what this is all about. Why ... why is he avoiding me? Can you tell me this much?" Véronique must have noted Kate's quivering chin, but she seemed determined not to be suckered by pity. She might look fragile, but Véronique Anfousse was not sentimental. She sat looking at Kate steadily, her lips pressed together.

"That you'll have to ask him yourself." Though her tone was not unkind, Kate's skin had become too tight to hold her growing frustration.

"How can I ask him when I don't know where he is!" she let out. She had been brought up in a home where losing one's temper was strictly frowned upon.

"Kate—" A reproachful edge had crept into Véronique's voice. "I have nothing ... absolutely nothing to do with your relationship with Guillaume. I—"

"You have nothing to do with it, but you know what it's all about, don't you? Don't you!" she repeated, losing all control of her voice. Not that Véronique seemed unnerved by this sudden outburst. Her facial muscles flickered, but she held on to her icy composure. She gazed at Kate for a long, charged moment.

"Guillaume's got a lot of thinking to do," she stated after a while. "He's not quite the same guy he was before, you know. He—"

"Fine, okay!" The words came spilling out of Kate's mouth. "So he's all shook up, I understand that! He's written to me, you know!" She paused, licking her cracked lips.

"But what do politics have to do with *me*, with Guillaume and me?"

At this, Véronique shifted in her rocking chair. She re-crossed her legs and offered a tolerant little smile.

"I don't think I can make you understand," she said, speaking resignedly. "But Guillaume gets it now: Politics is what it's all about. It's far more important than music, believe me." She was, of course, alluding to the Youth Orchestra, which all three of them had stopped attending back in October. Kate had gone only once in recent weeks, and then just to speak to Marc and Véronique's cousin. Johanne Anfousse had given Kate the St. Lawrence Boulevard address. Had she been willing to do so because she knew that Guillaume was no longer there?

The possibility occurred to Kate as she sat scanning Véronique's features, groping for clarity. Johanne had also been arrested in mid-October, but only for a couple of days. Kate was beginning to feel there was some sort of Québecois conspiracy here. The thought left her more muddled than ever. Something was happening and she, it seemed, was the only one who didn't know what it was all about.

"I'd better go," she said. She set the mug down and got to her feet, hearing footsteps on the landing below; footsteps and then raucous laughter, followed by a screech of delight as a door opened on the second floor, then promptly slammed shut. Véronique was trailing behind her, her thumbs hooked on her belt. There seemed to be nothing left to say.

Kate had yanked her coat off the pegboard by the entrance and was getting into her boots when Véronique said she wanted to give her something. For a moment, Kate thought she'd changed her mind and was going to let her have Guillaume's new address after all. What she gave her instead was a photocopy of a French poem entitled *l'Octobre*.

"Read it," she said quietly. "It's by Gaston Miron. He was jailed as well."

Kate said nothing. She folded the sheet of paper and slid it into her bag, then turned to go with a perfunctory thank you. "If you speak to him, please ask him to call me, will you?" Tears were welling in her eyes all over again. *"Please?"*

"I have no control over what Guillaume decides to do or not do," Véronique said. "But sure, I'll give him your message ... *if* he calls," she hastened to add with careful emphasis. She wished Kate a good day in French, and then closed the door. Kate had the feeling that she would waste no time getting on the phone to report on her visit. Would she be mocking her efforts behind her back? Would Guillaume listen?

Kate had no idea, but the feeling of deliberate exclusion had her brain throbbing all over again. Was she so overwrought she was becoming paranoid?

II

She was halfway down the long flight of stairs when the door across the top landing was flung open.

"Wait!" a shrill voice commanded at Kate's back. "Wait right where you are, Miss!"

"What?!" Kate had spun around, eyes flying towards the top landing.

A ravaged-looking woman in a quilted blue housecoat was scuttling down, eyes bulging in a pockmarked face, a shock of grey hair flying in all directions. A madwoman, Kate quickly decided. The stranger was sizing her up, taking in her open winter coat and high boots, her suede miniskirt.

"Do you realize what you're doing, do you know what the Bible says about fornication?" On and on, she spat out her venom, while Kate stood transfixed, eyes riveted to the twisted mouth, the large, rotting teeth.

And then, all at once, any control she still possessed abruptly evaporated.

"How dare you talk to me like that!" she let out, staring up with loathing. It was the word "fornication" that had loosened her tongue. "Who do you think you are anyway?" She paused for a moment, then turned her back and took a step down. One step only because the woman was lurching towards her, clutching her sleeve with her claw-like hand, still mouthing her biblical mumbo-jumbo. There was an odd smell about her; something reminiscent of the mothballs in Kate's grandmother's chests. Nausea was tugging at her stomach.

"Fuck off!" she yelled. "He wasn't even there, you stupid old hag!" Trembling, she jerked out of the stranger's grasp, then resumed running down the stairs, bare hands clapped over her ears.

On the street she realized she'd forgotten her gloves at Véronique's. They were good red gloves she'd received as a Christmas gift, but she was not going back right now. She could do without them today. It was early December, a week after James Cross's release, but the winter weather had given way to a day as mild as spring. For several hours, the sun had been melting the crumbling snow banks. Icicle-frosted eaves dripped down as Kate plodded north.

Outside the Metro station, a derelict sat leaning against the wall, belting out a Gilles Vigneault song. He stopped only long enough to ask Kate for spare change. Ordinarily, she would have searched her pockets for a few loose coins, but that day she discovered that misery does not make us more kindly disposed towards others; it makes us mean and angry and spiteful.

The vagrant resumed singing. Kate had no idea where she was going. It was one o'clock. She had a Shakespeare exam that afternoon but right then and there decided she would not write it. What was the point? What was the point of rehashing *King Lear* or *Macbeth*? She longed to head straight home and crawl under the covers, though not before she let her mother know what she thought of her stupid advice.

Her mother was not in the habit of telling her children what they ought to do, but when asked, she did not hesitate to express an honest opinion. She did so very gently, very thoughtfully, somehow making all of them feel there was no point in trying to resist her. Kate had always felt she could tell her mother anything.

All the same, thinking she might find herself subtly pressured, she had said nothing that morning about her decision to search for Guillaume. She was going to the library and then to class, to write an English exam, she had told her mother. She would be back in time for dinner. Her mother wished Kate good luck with Shakespeare. She asked her to pick up some bread and orange juice on the

way back. She was not planning to go out that day; the
new house painter was coming back, she'd said.

III

Obviously, she was not expecting Kate; did not even hear
her come in, for in her churlish mood, Kate did not sing out
"I'm h-o-m-e!" as she usually did on closing the door. Her
mother might not have heard her anyway because of her
beloved Wagner. No one else in the family liked opera, especially not Wagner, so Fiona Abbitson listened to it whenever she was alone, turning up the volume as high as her
children did while playing Neil Diamond or Van Morrison.

So, no, she did not hear Kate come through the front
door. She certainly did not see her. Crossing the shadowy
hallway, Kate glanced mechanically into the living room,
only to be arrested by a heart-stopping tableau; a sordid
scene out of some TV drama, inexplicably being played out
in the cozy familiarity of her own home.

There were two rose-hued settees in the stately room;
two Victorian fainting-couches, one of which Fiona Abbitson was now languidly ensconced on, her eyes shut
tight, passionately locked in a man's arms. For a moment
or two, Kate thought she herself might faint. The man was
not her father; she had never seen her parents embrace like
this. It was unbearably hot in the hallway. Her mother's
greying hair had come loose; her long fingers with their
scarlet nails were blindly digging into the stranger's back.

Later, Kate would not be able to say just how long she
had stood there, hands dangling uselessly at her sides,

while *Tristan und Isolde* played on and on and on, an operatic soundtrack to a scene that would haunt her for years to come.

At length, she wrenched herself away and raced upstairs to the guest room, where she was temporarily lodged while the basement was being painted. Could the stranger in the living room be the house painter? She vaguely remembered something about his being related to some European acquaintance in her mother's choir. She thought of Guillaume's father, also a house painter, but this only compounded her inner chaos.

A few minutes passed before she became aware of the pigeons.

There was a balcony off the guest room and, as it was seldom used, pigeons often roosted on it, cooing at all hours. In winter, her mother often fed them. Whenever the children tried to talk her out of it, she would smile but resist giving in. The pigeons had the right to exist, just like the rest of God's creatures, she might say every now and then. When she spoke like that, the rest of them would roll their eyes and sigh, then hasten to change the subject. It was generally understood that their mother was not only more delicate than their father; she was also a little eccentric and had to be indulged, much as she had always indulged their own childish foibles.

And so the pigeons kept coming back, sometimes building their nest well into the winter, cooing and cooing just outside the windows. The day Kate returned from her futile trip to St. Lawrence, their ceaseless call made her want to crawl right out of her skin. She scrambled off the bed to go for a cigarette; shoo the nasty creatures away.

The moment she opened the balcony door, two plump birds scuffled from the corner and fluttered away, settling on the neighbour's deck. The neighbour, an old widow named Mrs. Harris, had passed away recently and the house was up for sale. No one had bothered to remove the barbecue or the flowerpots from the old pine deck. The Abbitsons' own balcony still had a vinyl table and chairs brought up from the basement for the benefit of some visiting summer guests. Kate's mother was an indifferent housekeeper, but she loathed the smell of cigarettes and made her children smoke outdoors.

Kate had for years been only an occasional smoker, but that afternoon she was desperate for a cigarette. She hadn't eaten anything since breakfast, but there was a Granny Smith apple in her bag, which she thought she would have with her second cigarette. She pulled out one of the white vinyl chairs on the balcony. Then she saw the egg.

Very slowly, as if her eyes were setting it in motion, one of two white eggs was rolling towards the balcony's edge, rolling off and crashing in the driveway below. Kate's hand had snapped up as soon as the egg had left the wooden plank; had reached out and was still hanging in the air when she heard the tiny crash below. The sound left her heart trembling. She thought: You could've stopped it; could've stopped it with a movement of your eyes almost! You hated the pigeons — you did!

All at once, everything fell out of focus. Only one pigeon egg was left, but countless eggs danced before Kate's eyes as she picked up the chair and brought it down. Again and again. Like some frenzied killer battering a victim already dead, she was still hitting with the chair long after the second egg had crashed below; long after the nest's straw was scattered in all directions. When at last she raised her head, the two fat pigeons were eyeing her from the opposite deck, helplessly raising their wings, then bringing them down. Again. Again. And again.

Soon, the anger flared into childish resentment. Why their balcony? Why theirs, when the deck across was abandoned; when no one had lived in that house for months?

But of course it was her mother's food. Kate knew that, but the knowledge did nothing to subdue her heart. The pigeons continued to huddle close to each other. Kate sank into the chair for a hasty smoke, then went back to the guest room and stood watching through the curtains, waiting to see what would happen. Something had to happen, she knew. Was she merely trying to distract herself from thoughts of her mother, of Guillaume?

The pigeons returned to the balcony. They hopped from corner to corner, their heads bobbing. Kate tried to tell herself that this bewildered look was natural to pigeons. She reasoned it was no different from removing the egg a chicken had laid. Not very different.

The pigeons went on hopping all over the balcony, heart-wrenching in their apparent distress. Only when they had covered every square inch several times did the pigeons fly away. They disappeared while Kate collapsed on the bed again, staring at the ceiling. Down in the living room, her mother's record was playing on and on while Kate lay breathing deeply, striving for self-control. The thought of her mother, of what was taking place on the living room couch, made her stomach roil. She jumped up and dashed to the window for a breath of air.

The pigeons were back! They had flown away briefly but were now picking whatever straw was left on the balcony, gathering it into the building of a new nest.

Kate's tears were rivers of grief and remorse. She had no idea where Guillaume was and, unlike the pigeons, did not have the wherewithal to start over again. Either she managed to find him; managed to bring him back to her, or ...

Or what?

The question was left to dangle. She became aware that the record was no longer playing downstairs; it must have stopped while she'd stood by the window, briefly distracted by the pigeons. Rushing back across the creaking floorboards, she heard her mother's muffled voice; hers and the stranger's. There was the sound of a quietly closing door and, barely a minute later, her mother appeared.

She stood in the doorway, her eyes dilated, a hand pressed to her shapely neck. Dressed in a T-shirt and black jeans, she glanced at the open window with a little shiver. There was a gauzy white curtain, billowing in the breeze.

"I thought I heard you ... I hadn't realized you were home," she said and her eyelids flickered. Then she fell silent. Outdoors, the pigeons resumed their incessant cooing. Kate's mother did not say another word, but the air in the room was charged with mutual sorrow. After a moment, Fiona Abbitson raised her hands in a brief, beseeching gesture, then wheeled about and left with her usual dignity, her back erect, her dark hair loosened below her shoulders.

And that was all.

It would later be said that this was the day on which Kate's nervous breakdown began. In truth, it had started

184 · IRENA KARAFILLY

the day Guillaume's first letter had been delivered, its handwritten words like scissors trimming the edges of her
heart. For weeks, Kate's mother had made it possible for
her to endure Guillaume's absence; had managed to persuade her that he would gradually pull himself together,
and come back to her when he was good and ready.

Would he, though? For the first time in her life, Kate
felt completely adrift — an orphan abandoned on some
once-radiant shore, watching the sky grow abruptly dark
and inscrutable.

SEVEN

I

ALMOST THREE DECADES have gone by since Véronique Anfousse handed Kate the Gaston Miron poem, but the poem is one of the reasons Kate has decided to cycle over to Westmount Park instead of Beaver Lake, as originally planned. After three weeks away from her Edmonton health club, she feels a little out of shape; not quite up to cycling all the way up the mountain.

There is a small park on the street where the Abbitsons used to live, but Westmount Park, with its vast landscaped grounds and fine play structures, was where Kate and her siblings liked to come throughout their childhood, to play or swim or skate; eventually, to study at the vast library. Kate thinks they are bound to have Gaston Miron's books.

For the moment, though, she is content to sit on the park bench, resting from her ride, photographing children at play. The grounds, with their winding paths, their bridges and trees and duck ponds, captivate at this time of year, flaming with gold and scarlet. It is going on four o'clock and the park, as always on Sunday, is bustling with shrieking children and gossiping parents. Three adolescent girls huddle, giggling, under a weeping willow; a fresh-faced couple strolls by, fingers intertwined. Across from Kate, an elderly woman sits alone on a park bench, her Schnauzer asleep at her feet. She wears sunglasses and a short fur jacket; too much red lipstick on her butterfly-shaped mouth.

Far too warm for fur, Kate thinks. She remembers her own elderly mother complaining of the cold at the height of summer, warning her daughter that she would catch her death, dressed in shorts and T-shirt. In mid-July! Every time it snowed, she would offer Kate her own sable coat, her mouth tightening on being turned down. She was opposed to luxury fur, Kate would in vain try to explain; she was not even wearing her own nutria coat, which she used to like, now hanging uselessly in her cedar closet.

The coat had been a Christmas present from her husband, purchased early in their marriage, when Brad was still pulsing with optimism and good will. Poor Brad. Even on her worst days, Kate could never deny his devotion to his family; his determined efforts to win her over and raise her headstrong son as if he were his own. For years, she secretly held it against her husband that he had not quite succeeded, but was she being fair? Throughout Sean's childhood, Brad had treated the boy with unflagging interest and affection. For a long time, Kate believed he had all but forgotten that Sean was not his natural child. There was a certain stiffness, a slight formality, in his manner, but it was not unlike her own father's attitude towards his three children.

It was only after Sean started to turn his back on his father's interests and values that Kate began to sense Brad's suppressed resentment. All his hard work, all his generosity, and look at the boy! And what did he know about the biological father anyway? Nothing. Kate had told him nothing and he hadn't asked, but Megan was right: By the time Sean had reached his sophomore year, Brad seemed to feel he knew all he needed to know.

The thought is accompanied by a weary breath. Brad has reluctantly consented to spending Christmas in Vancouver, though it means having to rearrange his professional schedule. How Sean will feel about it — the entire family descending on him for a whole week — remains to be seen. Will it make him feel more loved, as Megan seems to believe it might? Kate is not sure, but this may well be her only hope of bringing about some sort of reconciliation. Could she have managed it before if she had been a more thoughtful person? She cannot stop dwelling on Megan's implicit criticism; her earnest attempt to remind Kate of Brad's fundamental decency.

As she rehashes all this yet again, Kate's thoughts meander back to her own mother. When Fiona Abbitson's mental decline became apparent, Brad did not hesitate to suggest that she must be made to come live with them. In Edmonton. Late in the summer of 1989, with Sean working at summer camp, Brad came east to join Kate and Megan in Westmount. He spent his annual vacation helping Kate sell the Wood Avenue house, while she cared for her mother and prepared for the imminent move. Kate's sister, who had years earlier fallen out with their mother, had a whirlwind legal career in Ottawa; Paul was on a European tour and had, in any case, always resisted anything that might interfere with his two lifelong passions: music and tennis.

Kate loved her brother who, in the right mood, might show a certain interest in his family. But any practical demands usually left Paul nervously rubbing his jaw, wringing his fine musician's hands. Even in middle age he was a man who seemed unable to manage without at least one woman to take care of his daily affairs.

So, no, her brother could not be counted on, but Brad rose to the occasion as usual, with no more than a jibe or two at ineffectual artists. By the time he and Megan left for Edmonton—school was about to start and Sean was due to return from camp, Kate had only minor matters to settle on her own. What she dreaded above all was being left alone with her demented mother; that and the necessity of disposing of a lifetime's possessions. Most of the furniture was to be auctioned off but, like a child forced to choose only one doll among many favourites, her mother wanted to take everything with her, all the way to Edmonton. She was by then beyond reason, though her iron will had, if anything, become more unyielding than ever.

There were maternal tears and peevish recriminations; the emerald earrings hidden in the bra, the refusal to take medication, to wear protection against incontinence. They had an experienced caretaker waiting in Edmonton, but in Montreal, there was no one to share the burden until Paul and Dianne came back from one of their trips abroad.

II

A few days after their return, Kate dropped her mother off at her brother's house and took her first evening off, going downtown to see a film with her friend, Isabelle Deslauriers.

Isabelle, who not only had a full-time job but was volunteering at *Parti Québecois* headquarters, had to get up at six the next morning, so they went to the early show. When it ended shortly after nine o'clock, Isabelle headed back to her Outremont condo, while Kate, all alone downtown, found herself recoiling from the thought of going home so soon. She had by then spent several weeks with her ailing mother, every muscle in her body feeling the weight of her private anguish. It was the first day of October. It had been a beautiful day but now the weather seemed to be changing.

She took a walk down lively Crescent Street, trying to muster the courage to enter a noisy pub on her own. The thought of going home so early was like a telegram one has received but is loath to open, having no doubt about its unsettling content. To make matters worse, she had her period, which always made her irritable and restless. What she longed to do was stay downtown for a while, surrounded by youthful voices: the laughter of young men, the scent of women's perfume. She certainly had no intention of picking up a stranger at Winnie's. All she hoped for was a little distraction; something that might help dissolve the lump of sorrow lodged within her chest.

A man came in and sat next to her, smiling amiably. He turned out to be a witty, hard-drinking journalist, on business from Toronto. He lit a pipe, then asked why she was looking so sad. How does one respond to a question like that?

Kate took a slow swallow of her bourbon, swivelling slightly on her bar stool. Fall always made her a little melancholy, she said, trying for a smile. As usual, the truth but not the whole truth. She had been melancholy long before September.

They exchanged appraising looks. After a while, Kate found herself speaking of her demented mother. Why did it seem so much easier to be frank with strangers?

The tall, sandy-haired Torontonian, whose name was Ivan Jacobson, said it was no doubt because strangers' judgements carried so little weight. He went on to quote Aristotle; something about melancholiacs being generally more intelligent than other people.

"Aristotle said that?" Kate smiled into his eyes. Fancy meeting a stranger in a pub who could quote Aristotle. "Did he really say that?"

"So I'm told." He had a lopsided, oddly beguiling, smile. A smile that said he would forgive anyone just about anything, but expected no less from others. He fixed her with a bright, blue gaze. "Do you think it's true?" he asked, drawing on his pipe.

"Our being more intelligent? I like to think so!"

The sound of her own laughter took Kate by surprise. She had a second drink with Ivan. They went on to talk about her recent travels, his job at the *Toronto Star*. All around them was the buzz of carefree banter, the clinking of ice cubes, glasses. Within an hour or so, Kate's drink was well on its way to smoothing the edges of her anxiety. She didn't want to talk about herself anymore. She began to ask questions.

Ivan turned out to be recently divorced. The divorce had been amicable, he said, his tongue working around his mouth. "But ... well, I'll tell you something I've just discovered, shall I?" He raised his Scotch to his lips, scanning her features. "An amicable divorce is a good thing, of course it is. But it's like ... well, it's like having all your teeth extracted, and still having to smile, you know?" A look of amusement twitched his lips, but instantly faded. There were two young children complicating parental good will. Ivan drained his glass in a gulp; he glanced at her left hand. "What about you? Any kids?"

"I have two as well." She toyed with her wedding ring, shifting her thighs on the hard barstool. She was wearing grey leather pants and a persimmon-hued turtleneck; the pub was too warm. Her daughter wanted to be a ballerina, she said; her son a famous writer. She rolled her eyes at these childish ambitions. "Why do you suppose so many people long for fame?"

"Well, I can only speak for myself." Ivan looked up from his glass, his eyes twinkling. He personally would have liked to be famous so he could thumb his nose at a snooty classmate who didn't invite him to his birthday party. "You think I'm kidding? I'm not!"

Kate laughed out loud. Encouraged, Ivan went on to confess that he, too, had once dreamt of being a writer. Another Philip Roth. At twenty-one, he could clearly see himself at it: signing books, getting fan mail.

"The works ... but, alas, not the work." Ivan chuckled, looking boyishly self-deprecating. He seemed to be in his early thirties; Kate was a few years older. But his age hardly mattered; she had no designs on him. None, though she was becoming conscious of a loosening in her chest; a surge of a light, almost forgotten, pleasure. Another hour passed.

"Another drink?" Ivan asked at length.

"Well—" She glanced at herself in the long bar mirror:

her cheeks were distinctly flushed. "No, I think I'd better be going," she said, glancing at her watch. "I am driving home."

They got up to leave together.

When they stepped outside and found the night splattered with rain, Kate offered to drop Ivan off on her way to Westmount; she was driving her mother's car. Ivan was staying at the Chateau Versailles, easily within walking distance, but neither of them had thought to bring an umbrella. Ivan took Kate's elbow and they ran to her mother's old Subaru, under a furious, tar-coloured sky. At the hotel, he invited her up for a nightcap. It was by then past midnight. The moon shone feebly through the drifting clouds. Kate took her time answering. She sat thinking of her mother's gloomy rooms, the sour odour invading every corner.

"I think what I need is coffee," she said, peering out through the splattered windshield. The rain was coming down in sheets now, pelting the deserted sidewalk. "God, look at it. It's a deluge!"

"I hope it stops by morning," Ivan said. "My mother got me a huge wind-proof umbrella for my birthday. I wish I'd remembered to take it."

"My daughter insists on borrowing my umbrellas." Kate smiled. "And she keeps losing them." She had unbuckled her belt but was still staring at the rain, not moving a muscle. "I hate driving in heavy rain," she said, speaking more or less to herself.

"Well, you could come up and wait it out," Ivan said, one corner of his mouth ever so slightly raised. "I'll be happy to order coffee."

Kate thought about it some more.

"Well ... okay. Why not?" she finally said.

She ended up spending the night at the Versailles Hotel. A night through which the wind whistled and bellowed, sporting with the hissing rain, and through which she and Ivan did nothing but talk. They talked about his marriage. They talked about hers. Would they have made love if she didn't happen to be menstruating?

Kate thought they probably would have, but who could tell? It might have turned out that, as with the abortion she'd once contemplated, she would have balked at the last minute.

In some fifteen years of marriage, it was the first time Kate had ever spent the night with a man other than her husband. It might or might not have been the first time that Brad Thuringer had hired a private detective to report on his wife's movements. But this Kate would learn only later, after she had returned home.

III

On the northern edge of Westmount Park, the old woman in the fur jacket rises from the bench and tugs on her dog's leash until the grey Schnauzer rouses himself and starts trotting alongside her. Kate is itching to take a photograph but is unwilling to violate the stranger's privacy. A photograph is without mercy. It is, of course, why people are so often reluctant to be photographed. What they find hard to tolerate is the knowledge that any stranger can steal — can mindlessly possess — their private image, judging them forever without their having any control over what others do, or say, or think.

So, there will be no photo of the fading old woman and her Schnauzer snapped against the gorgeous fall background. They seem to be heading towards the retirement home behind the library; the very place where Paul and Dianne thought Fiona should move to, after Dwight Abbitson's premature demise. Kate's mother refused to leave her Wood Avenue home; refused, even, to discuss the matter with her daughter-in-law, whom she had never much liked. A butterfly with steel wings was how she described Dianne, though not in the early days; not until Alzheimer's began to unleash her genteel tongue.

Now, watching the fur-clad stranger walk away with her dog, Kate feels a fresh stab of pain. She remembers the terrible winter day when she walked in on her mother; her still-young mother and the Slovenian painter. Or was he a Slovak? Anyway, she can't help musing on how differently her entire life might have unfolded had she gone ahead and written her Shakespeare exam as she was meant to do that winter afternoon.

It is not in the Stars to hold our Destiny but in ourselves.

Kate reminds herself of Shakespeare's cautionary words, though she no longer remembers the play in which she had read them. To this day she doesn't know whether her mother ever saw the house painter again. What she does know is this: Had she not walked in on the two of them, she probably wouldn't have married Brad on finding herself pregnant. What would she have done? She might have come home and told her mother that she was, as they said in those days, "in the family way." Her mother would have urged her to marry Brad only if she loved him. Of this Kate is sure. If she said she didn't, her mother would have most likely arranged for her to go stay with her own sister in Boston; give birth there, and then put the child up for adoption.

But in the months following the incident with the painter, Kate's relationship with her mother had become tense and murky. It was not that she couldn't forgive her mother, but rather that Fiona Abbitson seemed unable to forgive herself; or even talk about what had happened. On at least one occasion, the two of them alone in the kitchen, Kate thought that they might finally get through their polite impasse. About to go to bed, her mother seemed on the verge of speaking her mind but finally didn't. Kate guessed she couldn't formulate an explanation that would exculpate her in her own mind, though many years later, new facts would come to light which Kate had never even suspected. But that night, her mother remained silent; they both remained polite and aloof, neither willing to venture into stormy waters.

This is one of the deepest regrets Kate has had to live with; has managed to do so only by learning to steer her thoughts in other directions. After the old woman and her silly dog have disappeared from view, she rises from the park bench, gets hold of Megan's bike, and heads towards the library.

What if, she thinks as she locks the bike to the bicycle rack, what if there really were such a thing as backward-flowing time? Let's say God spoke to her on some sleepless night, offering her this extraordinary backward-flowing option. Would she be brave enough to take advantage of it? And if she did, if she took full advantage, would her life really turn out to be any happier than it is today?

Kate doesn't know the answer; she honestly doesn't. What she finally decides as she steps into the recently renovated library is that the present is quite complicated enough. To change, or even contemplate changing, the contours of one's past, is not only painful, it is mind-boggling!

The changes to the 1899 library instantly banish Kate's philosophical musings. It is a magnificent building, fully restored to its former Victorian splendour. Kate remembers an old mezzanine, which has been knocked down, as have various dividers and partitions. She is dazzled by the newly exposed windows, the coffered ceilings, the exquisitely stencilled walls. The restored library offers a sense of elegant spaciousness, its rooms divided by marbleized columns, the sun streaming in through the high leaded windows. She asks for the poetry section and soon finds herself sitting in a green leather chair, her brand-new reading glasses on her nose, a bilingual edition of Gaston Miron resting between her hands.

She finally reads the poem.

IV

L'Octobre is one of Gaston Miron's most celebrated poems, and Kate reads both French and English versions, pausing to think, compare. It is a famously patriotic poem depicting Québec as Mother Courage; a poem in which the travails of the past give way to a future of national pride and resurrected dreams. The day Véronique had given it to her, Kate barely glanced at the sheet of paper before tearing it up and tossing it into the garbage bin. She never thought to look

for the poem before today. But, yes, she thinks she understands the passion that had inspired Miron's words much
better now than she could have done in the early 70s. She
also thinks the poem's last two lines sound much better in
French than they do in English: *l'avenir dégagé, l'avenir engagé.*

Despite her sympathy for French-Canadians' political
aspirations, Kate admits to having felt nothing but relief
when the *Parti Québecois* failed to win the last referendum.
She would have hated having to enter a foreign country
whenever she visited Montreal. How she loves this city!
The longer she stays here, the more she wishes she could
settle here permanently. Perhaps with Megan here and
Sean in Vancouver, Brad would consider moving back to
Québec? She doubts she could ever bring herself to offer an
ultimatum. She knows that both her family and her husband have always thought her a little unstable, and perhaps
she is.

The future free, the future committed.

Well, this is what it all boils down to, doesn't it? Kate
muses as she cycles away from Westmount park. In some
ways, the problem has been made much easier by Megan's
independence. The only person she might have to worry
about would be Brad himself. And oh yes, she would
surely worry! Whenever she thinks of her husband, all
alone in their empty Edmonton home, the weight of her
sympathy brings tears to her eyes. So, does she love him,
as she insisted to Megan? Does she?

Oh, not as she would have loved Guillaume, she thinks
with a weary sigh. As she *believes* she would have loved him.

Kate is old enough to know that the course of any
marriage is no more predictable than fall weather. But she

is still young enough, still vain enough, to wonder whom Guillaume ended up marrying. If he is not married, she thinks, he must at least be living with someone.

Not for the first time, Kate tries to imagine this unknown woman. She wonders how they spend their evenings, their weekends. If she really wanted to, she could try to find out by questioning Isabelle. Isabelle must know someone she could ask. But what would the point be? a judicious voice repeats inwardly. What she told Antonia is true: she would be much too afraid to meet Guillaume. And yet, she remains intermittently curious. Who wouldn't be?

Which is perhaps why, when she returns to her daughter's apartment and finds a note saying that Megan has run out to get a library book, Kate reaches for the telephone, and this time lets herself go so far as to dial Guillaume Beauregard's number on Old Orchard Avenue. All she wants is to hear his voice once again, or at least the voice of the woman he is married to. If he is indeed married.

After four rings, a woman does answer; a pleasant-sounding francophone with a slightly breathless voice whom Kate, for some reason, imagines as a statuesque pianist, as tall and fair as Guillaume himself.

"*Allo*," the woman at the other end says. And then again: "*Allo? Allo?*"

Finally, with an impatient exhalation of breath, the stranger replaces the receiver. Kate hangs up as well. Of course, she would have done so anyway, even if Guillaume himself had been the one to answer.

PART III

If we open a quarrel between past and present,
we find that we have lost the future.

—WINSTON CHURCHILL

ONE

I

*D*ecember 11, 1970

Dear Katherine,

This is a letter I've been trying to write for many days now, a letter I know I should have sent days ago. If I didn't, it was only because I desperately wanted to first sort out my own feelings; to be absolutely sure of all the complicated things I was about to say to you. I was so afraid of needlessly hurting you through my own confusion!

I've been thinking hard, very hard, about the past as well as the future, Katherine. No matter how long I mull things over, though, there seems to be no way around the pain this letter is going to cause you. I say this even though I still care for you, very, very deeply. But the truth is I can no longer imagine a future with you. Maybe I was wrong all along to imagine one. I know I wanted to. I refused to listen to my brother's diatribes, the heated discussions among my own classmates. I shut my mind against the thoughts and feelings I had after the Labour Day weekend I spent with your family at the cottage. Remember that long weekend?

*I told myself it was all just my imagination:
your wonderful mother's careful kindness, the way
your father kept steering the conversation away
from anything to do with Québec politics. They
did their best, I appreciate that they did. Lately,
though, I've been asking myself how your father
would feel about a son-in-law with whom he
wouldn't feel free to discuss politics at the dinner
table. A son-in-law who doesn't know the first
thing about stocks and bonds and real estate, who
can't play golf or tennis, who can't even swim! I've
tried to tell myself that it doesn't matter, but I
honestly can't see myself ever feeling comfortable in
your milieu, my dear. I thought I could, I sincerely
hoped so, but recent events have finally convinced
me that I was wrong; that I must join the struggle
to improve ordinary Québecers' lot, instead of
focusing on my own grandiose ambitions.*

*Katherine, have you by any chance seen The
Battle of Algiers? If you haven't, I ask you to see
it because I feel—I hope—that it will help you
understand what I've been going through since the
October Crisis. I'm not the person I was before my
arrest. I feel as if years have gone by since we were
together, and that even if I saw you, we couldn't
possibly look at life through the same window
ever again.*

*It was great to be with you; I have no wish to
ever deny it, but neither can I deny the advantages
I would stand to reap in marrying you. I thought
what all your relatives would likely be saying behind*

your back; about poor Kate, who got herself hitched to the wrong kind of guy. Oh, maybe if I'd become another Pablo Casals, they would have all come around, but that isn't likely to ever happen, is it?

I never told you this, Katherine, but all my hard work, the ambition that everyone was always praising me for, had a lot to do with my need to prove myself to your kind of people. I used to lie awake nights, worrying about what would happen if I turned out not to have the brilliant career I was dreaming of. How many of us do after all?

And then, after the recent crisis, it all became even more complicated. You have to understand that, from the moment I arrived at Parthenais until today, I've been surrounded by people with strong political views; people I've had to listen to and who slowly gained my grudging respect. The other day, after we saw The Battle of Algiers, we stayed up all night talking about our days in jail, about the way this terrible experience has radicalised ordinary guys like myself.

Several times now, I've found myself trying to imagine having dinner with your parents during the recent crisis. It's not hard to imagine the reaction of your family and their friends. And what would I do among all of you, Katherine? Keep my mouth shut so as not to disturb the cozy harmony of your Sunday dinners?

I thought about this all fall. I was so deeply attached to you I was afraid that if I spent any time with you, all my new insights, all my resolve, might go out the window. This is why I've had to avoid seeing you, why I needed to be alone to think things through. To be sure of what I had to do.

It is now over six weeks since I was released from Parthenais, and I know that I don't belong in Westmount. I've come to feel that to marry you would mean allowing myself to be lured by a life of comfort and privilege. It would mean turning my back on my own people. Oh, I don't know if you can understand any of this, but I hope you will, if not immediately, then perhaps some day.

How difficult all this must be for someone from your background! I know you've always thought of me as apolitical and I guess I was. I resisted involvement by keeping myself focused on my own professional future. After my incarceration, though, all my petty preoccupations, my personal ambitions, have come to seem so selfish! so pretentious! So what if I happened to "make it" as you anglophones like to say; what if my wildest dreams came true and I became every bit as successful as your brother, giving concerts, getting great reviews? What difference does one man's life make when his people's destiny is governed by a political system totally indifferent to their cries? A system that concerns itself with the institutions of American high finance instead of its own downtrodden citizens? The citizens themselves —most Québecers, for sure—don't even begin to understand the powers that govern them. They think they live in a democracy, but it's only a

*democracy of the rich, Katherine! When I think
that once, all of Canada belonged to the French, I
can't help seething inside at how little we have
settled for; at how we have allowed ourselves to
become the cowering servants and boot lickers of
anglophone big shots!*

*And still, most of us choose to keep silent. We
remain silent when Bourassa fails to keep his
promise to reduce our abysmal unemployment rate;
when he kowtows to the Federal bullies, subjecting
us all to the most repressive powers ever invoked in
a democracy! We keep silent because, when all is
said and done, we prefer not to see ourselves as the
victims of others' arrogance and greed. Oh, I admit
I was just as bad as most Québecers. But not
anymore! You may think me heartless, Katherine,
but the question that tortures my soul these days is
this: Are we to go on leading this semi-somnolent
existence; go on living like naive children incapable
of standing up for their rights?*

*I won't let it happen. Or, at least, I am determined
to do whatever is in my power to help my people
wake up and liberate themselves. The last thing I
want is to be like Monsieur Trudeau, enjoying the
good life while bringing down the boot on his own
people! Obviously, not being a politician, I'm not
likely to ever have that kind of power, but the man
I am today feels that to go back to the life I was
leading before my arrest—to go back to you—would
constitute rejection of my own people.*

I see that I'm beginning to repeat myself,

Katherine, but here is something I haven't said yet. Though being incarcerated was probably the worst experience I've ever had, a part of me is actually glad that it happened, because without these twelve days—without the fear, the humiliation, the outrage—I would still be going about my complacent life the way my parents are doing.

The truth is that poverty takes the fight out of you, Kate. It makes people like my parents and sister scurry back to the safety of their family, their home. Our official motto may be 'Je Me Souviens' but Chantal and my parents just want to forget; to put this terrible time behind them and think only of getting a new fridge, a bigger television. Things.

Oh, Katherine, Katherine: please try to understand, and try to forgive all the pain I've caused you. You may find it difficult to believe, but I'm crying as I write this letter. I hope you will believe me when I say that my best—my very best—wishes go with it. I hope you find happiness again some day. As for me, I'll never forget you.

Je t'embrasse,
Guillaume

II

Guillaume's farewell missive reached the Abbitsons' residence on December 13, 1970. It was Saturday, but in those days, Canada Post still provided weekend delivery. The letter, which arrived while Kate was recovering from a stomach flu, had been written one day after her visit to Marc and Véronique's loft. It persuaded Kate that Véronique had indeed been in touch with Guillaume that day; that, despite all her denials, she had known his whereabouts all along.

Was it all over then? Could the universe gaze at her anguish and remain indifferent?

Kate stumbled towards the bathroom and stood retching into the toilet bowl, feverishly toying with the idea of going back to Véronique's loft. She had her gloves as an excuse if she needed one. Even in her agitated state, however, Kate was lucid enough to know that a second visit would be as futile as the first. At some point, her body had begun to shake, as if a small electric current were running through her bones. Outside, light snow was falling; her parents and siblings were upstairs, getting ready for lunch. Kate went back to bed, burrowing under her warm duvet.

It took about an hour, but by the time her sister came down with a lunch tray, Kate's muddled brain had tossed up a new idea. She did not stop to think it through; did not touch the chicken broth or slices of dry toast. Somehow, the lunch prepared by her conscience-stricken mother only seemed to harden her new resolve. The moment Heather was gone, Kate scrambled out of bed and pulled on her clothes, going out without a word through the basement entrance.

It was by then after one o'clock. She sat in the car for a few minutes, hunched over the wheel, waiting for the engine to warm up. Though Guillaume's words were scraping her heart, she had not quite reached the cliffs of despair. She would find him! If it was the last thing she did, she would find him and bring him around!

The snow was turning into a blizzard. Although she knew the neighbourhood in which Guillaume's sister lived, Kate could not recall Chantal's address, or even her married name. With Guillaume there to navigate on that late-summer evening, she'd paid scant attention to the names of the streets they were passing through. So at three p.m. on that stormy December Saturday, she was still driving around in circles, squinting through the snow-splattered windshield, tears streaming down her face. Not only did all the streets in Chantal's neighbourhood look much the same, but the snow was playing havoc with her memory.

She had only one point of reference, which she eventually stopped to verify in a public phone booth's directory: the Bienvenue, where she'd stayed with Guillaume on the night of Chantal's birthday.

Starting from the shabby *pension*, Kate gradually found her way back to the laundromat, the pool hall, the corner pharmacy. Like much of the city at this time of year, the streets were decorated with ribbons of light, the occasional Santa Claus or twinkling Christmas tree. Halfway down the block she was crawling through, three children in red and blue snowsuits played in the fresh snow, their mittened hands shaping a large fortress. A man in a black *tuque* stood twining Christmas lights around a snow-blanketed spruce.

Kate came to a halt a few feet away from the muffled stranger. She sat with the engine running for a moment or two. She rolled down her window. Feeling like a fool, she finally brought herself to call out, her warm breath wafting into the frosty air.

"Would you happen to know a couple named Chantal and Claude?" She tossed out the question in French, leaning out the window, mopping her eyes as the stranger plodded his way towards her VW. "A young couple," she said, "she's blond, he's dark, with two little children?"

"*Désolé.*" The Frenchman shrugged, a cigarette dangling from the corner of his mouth. He did not know any Chantal or Claude, but thought she should ask at the *dépanneur* around the corner. "They know everyone in this *quartier.*"

"*Merci. Merci bien, Monsieur.*"

The *dépanneur* looked familiar, but these convenience stores were much the same all over the city. Kate crept along, searching for a parking spot amid the snow-marooned cars. Sighting a vacant space, she was about to pull in when her eyes landed on a defunct store with a papered window and a red-and-black A LOUER sign. A vacant shoe store.

She stared at the rental sign, her pulse quickening. She was sure she had passed this empty shop before. Clambering out of her car, she plodded for half a block, slowing down before a familiar door. A dark green door with a hand-crocheted curtain in its square window. The most ordinary of doors leading to a walkup; to the only person in the whole city who might be able to help her. The gods, she thought, had taken pity on her. She could feel fresh hope surge into her chest, lifting her sagging heart.

And yet, the dread was not entirely vanquished. It made her pause for a moment before she pressed the bell, an inner voice urging her to turn around and flee from a probable disappointment. But then she rallied herself. Guillaume might be confused, he might be overwrought and misguided, but his tortured words had left no doubt about the strength of his feelings for her.

For the first time since her childhood, Kate found herself praying.

III

Chantal Thibodeau seemed to share both Kate's faith and her unwillingness to relinquish hope. The two best things that ever happened to Guillaume, she was saying, were having Alex Lehotay for a childhood friend, and, later, meeting Kate at the Youth Orchestra. She thought Guillaume had everything going for him; he was the only one in the family who seemed to have what she called *a real future.*

"And now he's about to blow it all on politics? *Tabernacle!*"

Chantal, sitting next to Kate, shifted on the living room sofa, lighting a cigarette. She thought politics was best left to those with no talent to squander. Michel might also be gifted, but he'd always been a hothead; anyway, he'd never had Guillaume's brains or his self-discipline.

"*Une tête brulée,*" she said, exhaling a puff of smoke. "First he gets himself involved in all this political shit, then gets Guillaume sucked in as well!"

The statement was accompanied by a long, furious release of smoke. If they didn't watch out, both Guillaume and Michel could end up back where they'd come from, counting the days from one pay day to the next. "Mark my words ... just like me and Claude." There was no mention of their youngest brother. Jacques, the junkie, was considered a hopeless case.

They went on to talk about the October arrests.

The War Measures Act, Chantal said, had only hardened people's resolve to fight the status quo. She plucked a tissue out of a ceramic box and leaned forward to wipe her son's chocolate-smeared face. Jean-Paul had come in from the kitchen, cupping Smarties in one tiny fist, and gummy worms in the other. He was four years old. He stood leaning against his mother, giggling when she made to snap up some of his candy.

"I'm so glad you came." Chantal drew her son up to her knees, stubbing out her cigarette. "I hope you manage to bring him to his senses ... before he lands himself back in jail."

Michel was out on bail, awaiting trial; Guillaume was living on Mount Royal Avenue, in some sort of commune not far from the mountain. Chantal herself had gone to visit her brother there, but had failed to persuade him to keep his nose out of politics.

"Maybe he'll listen to you," she said. She did not sound very hopeful, possibly because she knew how pig-headed Guillaume could be. "I worry about his studies, his music, you know?"

She fell silent, releasing Jean-Paul, who was squirming to get off her knees. The smell of tomato sauce wafted out of the kitchen.

"Go see what the baby's doing," Chantal told her son.

"He's sleeping!" Jean-Paul lisped, but went anyway, throwing his head back and dangling a rubbery red-and-green worm into his open mouth.

Chantal and Kate exchanged rueful smiles. From the street came the steady rattle of a passing snow plough. Kate stirred, glancing at her watch. The day was starting to fade. She asked Chantal who was living in the Selkirk Avenue apartment now.

"I don't know. Someone from Trois Rivières," Chantal said, shrugging.

Guillaume had sublet his apartment so he could save on rent money. His room on Mount Royal cost a quarter what he'd been paying on Selkirk Avenue.

"That's good, it's good to save on rent, but only if he can practise with all those people coming and going." Chantal peered into Kate's eyes as if she might possess all the answers. "Do you think he can?"

"I don't know. I honestly don't," Kate said, opting for silence. Not only was she afraid to say anything that might make Chantal change her mind about letting her have Guillaume's address, she was also somewhat distracted by her resemblance to her brother: the same mane of honey-coloured hair, the steady, penetrating green gaze; even the occasional stammer, followed by the familiar little scowl, the pursing of the mouth—even that was pure Guillaume. The resemblance sent a ripple of pain through Kate's chest.

Claude was standing in the doorway, offering a beer.

"No, thank you." Kate turned slightly, glancing out the window. The snow seemed to be slackening. "I think I should probably get going," she said after a moment. "I'd like to try and catch him before he goes out for the evening. It's Saturday."

Guillaume's sister nodded. "I'm really glad you managed to find us."

"Me too." Kate heaved herself up to her feet, the cooking smells from the kitchen reminding her of her empty stomach. Claude was preparing a pot of spaghetti sauce. From the direction of the bedrooms came the sound of a fussing baby. Chantal turned and called out to her husband.

Finally, she went to fetch the Mount Royal commune's address. She kissed Kate on both cheeks and stood with hands resting on her shoulders, gazing into her eyes. "He'll listen to you," she stated with conviction. "If he doesn't, drag him by the ears, if you have to, okay?"

She stepped aside, absently ruffling her son's dark curls. The child had followed his father, who had come out to shake hands with Kate, the baby drooling against his shoulder.

"Drag him by the ears!" Jean-Paul echoed. They all laughed. Despite her initial sympathy for Chantal's situation, Kate thought the young family looked content with their lot.

"*Bonne chance!*" Chantal said. She kissed Kate on both cheeks, her eyes moist with tears.

IV

It was pitch dark by the time Kate arrived at Mount Royal Avenue, parking halfway down on Esplanade. The wind had subsided at some point and, by evening, the snow was coming down in a languid dance of swirling wet flakes, settling on nude tree branches, on the looming mountain with its glittering cross. It was a beautiful evening, fragrant with the scent of fresh snow, of burning firewood.

The huge cross atop the mountain was illuminated year round, but as she trudged past the festively-decorated houses on Esplanade, Kate's mind scurried away from the possibility of having to endure the holiday season without Guillaume. The thought made her skin feel too tight for her body. What if she failed? She stepped off the sidewalk, making way for a creeping snow plough. What if she failed to bring him around?

The snow ploughs were roaring all over the city, clearing snow off buried sidewalks and leaving it piled up in huge powdery banks to await the municipal dump trucks. Here and there, the cleared snow exposed patches of black ice, yet to be sprinkled with salt and gravel. Kate loved a fresh snowfall, but ice and slush were what you had to put up with through much of a Montreal winter.

Mount Royal Avenue was a long ramshackle street with steep stairwells and thrift shops garishly decorated for Christmas. Every block seemed to have a second-hand clothing or music store, as well as its share of vagrants. Pawnshops and junk shops abounded, selling everything from chipped chamber pots to painted vanity tables. If you wanted to get high in those days, Mount Royal Avenue was one of the obvious streets to come to.

The bearded man clearing the snow off Guillaume's commune's stairwell seemed a little spaced out as well, blinking and tugging at his beard as Kate stumbled by. She guessed him to be the janitor, but why was he looking at her so curiously, like someone awakened from the deepest sleep?

The tall girl who opened the door to Guillaume's commune had eyes as sharp as black pebbles; slanted eyes with dark arching eyebrows that gave her face an expression of such remarkable haughtiness she might have been a bored princess instead of an impoverished Québecoise answering the doorbell at a possibly inconvenient hour. It was dinnertime.

"*Oui?*" She had the high cheekbones of some Indian ancestor, a tiny beauty mark drawing the eye to a large, sculpted mouth. Inwardly, almost instantly, Kate dubbed her The Iroquois Princess. She'd always felt a little intimidated by women who carried themselves with such blatant female arrogance.

"Is Guillaume in by any chance?" she asked. "Guillaume Beauregard?"

The girl looked Kate over for a moment, *de haut en bas*. "Who are you?" she said. She had straight black hair reaching halfway down her back. They both spoke in French. "Is he expecting you?"

"Well no, not exactly." Kate did her best to smile, then glanced over her shoulder, hearing the janitor shout something below. It was not aimed at her. He had abandoned clearing the stairwell and, shovel in hand, was bouncing across the road, towards some passing acquaintance.

"In that case—" The Iroquois Princess looked ready to close the door. "I—"

"Wait! Wait a minute. Please!"

Striving for a calm, authoritative air, Kate gave her name to Guillaume's roommate, with a look on which, she dimly felt, everything hung at that moment. She asked the gatekeeper to please let Guillaume know she'd like to see him for a few minutes. She would wait outside. "I've been looking for him all afternoon."

"That's too bad," the Iroquois Princess said. "Guillaume isn't home."

They stood eyeing each other for a long, fraught moment.

"Are you sure?" Kate asked, her stomach rumbling. "Maybe—"

"Am I *what?*" The plucked eyebrows shot up, black and disdainful. "Of course, I'm sure!" She stood hugging herself, speaking in a low, husky voice. "He doesn't want to see you anyway—I'm sure of that!"

The statement was accompanied by a faint smile hinting at private access to some restricted realm. She had, when she opened the door, appeared eager to be rid of Kate; now she seemed to be almost enjoying herself. Her last words had been uttered with palpable satisfaction. They made blood rush up to Kate's head.

"You may be right, but I'd really like to hear him say so himself, okay? Would you—"

"*Quelle bête!*" said the Iroquois Princess. She let out a sound of histrionic impatience. "Look, would it help if I said it in English?" Her tone hardened. "He don't want to see you no more, okay?"

The words went careening through Kate's head, the tortured grammar compounding her emotional turmoil. She tried to bring her rage under control; to summon forth an appearance of unflappable confidence.

She did her best, but the knowledge that, at any moment, that door would be slammed in her face seemed to split her brain. If Guillaume was not home, why had his roommate asked whether he was expecting her?

"You're lying," she heard herself say with sudden authority. She moved forward, hoping to push her way past the gatekeeper. "You just—"

But the Iroquois Princess's mild amusement evaporated as quickly as it had come.

"Did you just call me a liar?" She stepped onto the landing and pointed down the long stairwell, her eyes skewering Kate. "Get out of here! Right now, or—"

"I will not get out!" Kate spat back, every muscle straining against the unexpected hurdle. "Bitch!" she shrieked, lunging towards the entrance. "I've never met such a fuck-ing arrogant bitch. Who do you think you are?"

"You're calling me a bitch?" The francophone girl took another step forward and, this time, gave Kate a little push, right in the middle of her chest.

It was the last thing Kate would later be able to recall with any certainty; the aggressive move, then the sudden explosion in the pit of her stomach as her arm flew up, trying to ... what? Defend herself, shove the other girl out of her way, slap her face?

She would never know.

There must have been a scuffle. Eventually, inter-viewed by the police, Kate could not bring herself to deny that she might have indeed pushed the Iroquois Princess, whose name turned out to be Sylvie Laplante. She *thought* Sylvie had lost her footing and fallen over backwards, slid-ing down the icy steps. To be honest, though, she really wasn't sure. Sylvie Laplante had suffered a concussion, as well as a broken leg. By the time the ambulance arrived on the scene, she was lying unconscious at the bottom of the stairwell, her black hair fanned out against the snow, blood oozing out of one ferociously scratched cheek.

Kate had passed out as well, dimly aware of shouts, the crunch of boots on fresh snow. The smell of snow; the smell of blood on her fingertips. The distant wailing of sirens.

There was a police cruiser, as well as an ambulance. She regained consciousness on the way to the Montreal Gen-eral Hospital, not knowing that Guillaume's roommate would eventually recover. She thought she might have killed her, and the knowledge was like a razor slashing through her veins.

The police had telephoned her mother, who hastened

to come down to Emergency, her face the colour of dish-water. Kate's father was trying to locate his brother, the Ottawa judge, though later, when Sylvie Laplante was discharged from hospital, Guillaume himself would per-suade her to drop the charges.

But all this was still in the future. For the moment, Kate's only relief lay in being allowed to leave the hospital; to go home with her solicitous mother, like any innocent patient briefly treated in Emergency, released to the near-est kin.

Oh, but she did not feel innocent; would never feel quite innocent again. In the years that followed, the first snowfall of the season would invariably ambush her with the memory of that blinding winter of 1970, when she fought to keep the wolves off in their distant lairs. Away from her own spurned flesh, her savage, useless bones.

V

The nightmare was now well and truly in progress. Back home in Westmount, having pressed her to down a couple of Valiums, Kate's mother kept murmuring to her not to worry about a thing. Everything would soon be set to rights, she promised. She put Kate to bed as one might a child, then sat stroking her hair with her soft, fragrant hand.

"Sleep now. Sleep, sweetheart. Sleep."

The scent of her mother's hand was the last thing to penetrate Kate's drowsy consciousness. The Valium worked until just after three a.m., a menacing hour that found her sitting bolt upright in bed, heart pounding against ribcage.

The house was silent with sleep, the only sounds being the humming of radiators, the soft whistling of the furnace next to her parents' garage. She had come to the kitchen to get a glass of water. Her mouth felt parched, her chest hollowed out. A part of her was still in the throes of medicated sleep. The snow went on falling.

She took a can of Coke out of the fridge and stood sipping at the kitchen window, knowledge of the previous day's events throbbing in her veins. She kept trying to ward off the wave of searing images; to stop the raw wound expanding within her chest. She lingered at the window, dressed in her flannel nightgown and furry moccasins, listening to the hiss of falling snow, the howling of a dog somewhere in the distance.

Only she wasn't sure the howl had not come out of her own churning gut. Nor did she care. What did any of it matter now? Every time she blinked, she saw Sylvie Laplante lying in a heap, as still as a corpse. She saw Guillaume, too, though fragmented; a collection of stylized erotic images tumbling in her head: Guillaume's lips pressed against her own belly, her thigh, his vein-corded hand lingering over her breast, as casual, as inevitable, as if it were an extension of his own body.

There was nothing left to do. Kate sank into a kitchen chair and put her head down on her arms. She was more or less past thought, but snatches of memory kept flickering through her mind, like the bright pieces of a broken kaleidoscope. The time she'd cut her leg, shaving it for Guillaume's hand, and the leg bled and bled. The time she woke up from a bad dream in his bed, shrieking about black owls. Pointless but desperate images of fighting cocks and ruffled feathers, of shadowy handcuffed figures swaying behind curtained windows, and cats shrieking in dark, icy alleys. At some point, she dozed off for a while but, a little before dawn, found herself jolted into sharp awareness.

It was all over.

The knowledge assailed her all over again. There was a shattering sensation, as if the vital organs held together within her skin had inexplicably become dislodged and were, one by one, starting to collapse. She felt the weight of both her heart and her full bladder.

She got up and went to the bathroom. She used the toilet, then stood at the bathroom sink for a while, staring into the medicine cabinet mirror. She saw a familiar stranger with bloodless lips and frog-like eyes, her skin the colour of dough. She was overcome by the rush of pity one might feel for a hapless relative; someone in dire straits, calling out for help. When she found the bottle of Valium in the medicine cabinet, a sense of intense relief, of unexpected reprieve, washed over Kate, sweeping away all thoughts of the dawning day.

Weeks later, talking to her sister-in-law—talking quite lucidly, she thought, despite heavy sedation, Kate would tell Dianne that reaching for the Valium that night had not felt like an act of desperation; not really. Searching her mind for an analogy, she said it felt the way she imagined a starving child might feel, standing hopelessly at a fragrant bakery door, then suddenly finding it ajar; open just wide enough to lend easy access to the rolls and cakes and sugar doughnuts, forbidden yet miraculously available, and sweet beyond imagining.

Kate ended up sharing all this with Dianne just before

Christmas, though she suspected that neither her sister-in-law nor anyone else was likely to understand what she was trying to say. She couldn't have shot herself, or cut her wrists, or jumped off the Jacques Cartier bridge into the cold St. Lawrence River. But yes, she insisted, the Valium had tasted quite wonderful that night. A gift of divine mercy expunging the taste of ashes.

TWO

I

It is the first day of October, 1998. Dianne Abbitson, Kate's sister-in-law, sits reading Guillaume's farewell letter, while Kate drinks her café latte, gazing through the coffee shop window at the whirl of activity outside.

Like so much that she remembers from her youth, Montreal's Atwater Market has been upgraded since she and Brad left the city in the early 1970s. Today's farmers seem to be vying with each other in the artful arrangement of their fresh produce: baskets of blackberries and eel-like eggplants; pyramids of shiny apples, mountains of spiky artichokes. The old indoor market, with its tacky shops, has been turned into an upscale mall, with gourmet boutiques, sausage counters, French *fromageries*.

But some things haven't changed at all. The market still has outdoor stalls selling plants and flowers; also, though Halloween is still almost a month away, colossal piles of fat, freshly picked pumpkins.

Kate remembers stopping here with her mother every Halloween; remembers, too, coming with Guillaume one glorious spring day, giggling to find herself presented with a bunch of exquisite daffodils. When she lowered her face to smell them, the flowers left a touch of pollen on the tip

of her nose, a soft yellow spot which Guillaume hastened
to kiss. And then kiss again.

This is one of the most cherished memories Kate has
of the young Guillaume, a man given to romantic gestures.
She herself is given to flirting with the past, but there are
times when she has difficulty visualising Guillaume. It is
not that she has forgotten what he looked like—she could
describe him in the most minute detail: the vaccine scar on
his upper left arm, the tiny birthmark near his armpit. But
that's just it: she can recall all the details but her mind, at
times, seems reluctant to pull the fragments into a sharply
defined portrait. The more she thinks of Guillaume, the
more elusive the full-blown image becomes.

The first time Kate experienced the difficulty was
soon after Guillaume's old letter had surfaced, just before
she met Antonia Offe. Is it possible that the impulse to revisit Selkirk Avenue had sprung from a subconscious fear
of having the past slip away from her the way it gradually
had from her mother? Her treasured past, which she holds
onto like some illicit lover's gift, hidden away from both
husband and children?

She turns to study Dianne, whose eyes are sliding
across the handwritten letter, left to right, left to right. She
and Paul have just returned from their Sicilian holiday. Kate
is to have dinner with them later today; she has come shopping with Dianne in the hope of getting personal advice.

Her sister-in-law is one of the few people familiar with
the last chapter of the Guillaume saga; the last chapter and
also the epilogue. She has heard all about it because, after
her nervous breakdown, Kate refused to discuss her problems with anyone other than Dianne, who was not even a

licensed therapist at the time. Dwight Abbitson had engaged some of the city's most prominent psychiatrists, but
Kate had clammed up in their distinguished presence,
harbouring her pain the way her father's sister was said to
have harboured her stillborn child, refusing to give him up
to the obstetrical nurses.

To this day, it's not clear to Kate why she had opened
up to her brother's fiancée. Because she was a woman? Because she was not being paid for her tender solicitude? Because she had met, and had liked, Guillaume?

Dianne is not the kind of woman Kate would normally
choose for an intimate friend. When her mother spoke of her
daughter-in-law as a butterfly with steel wings, Kate thought
that she'd got it right. All of 5'3" and as perky as a cheer-
leader, Dianne has a wry, carefully outlined mouth, a hel-
met of strawberry-blond hair, and a frequent, unexpectedly
endearing, myopic squint. She can't tolerate contact lenses,
and will not wear glasses, except while driving or listening
to a patient. A man watching Dianne squint over an Yves St.
Laurent dress rack or a Hermes scarf, would never suspect
the steely resolve behind those myopic blue eyes. Did Paul?

Kate's brother was nothing if not used to strong
women. But whereas their mother had a quiet, bemused,
disposition, Dianne is a brisk, purposeful little person, with
a passion for labelling and alphabetizing everything in her
domestic domain. One summer, when she and Paul visited
Edmonton, Kate spent days cleaning and reorganizing
every closet and cupboard in her own suburban home.

In some ways, Dianne resembles Kate's old friend, Eva
Walny; like her, she seems to find satisfaction in helping
others fix their deeply flawed lives. Kate respects Dianne's

insights. Somehow, after talking to her sister-in-law, she is usually able to see her own situation with greater clarity; as if a benevolent gust had blown through her dusty mental chambers, sweeping away barely-visible cobwebs.

It is mid-afternoon at the Atwater Market. Lost in reminiscence, Kate sits picking up muffin crumbs with the tip of her moist finger, waiting for Dianne to finish reading. She has a mental vision of her young self jumping up to hide the letter on hearing her sister approach the basement with that day's lunch tray. She recalls, too, the day when she tried to find it, but by then so much had happened, she was so heavily medicated, that she wasn't at all sure she had kept the letter, much less where she might have hidden it. For years, she hears herself tell Dianne, she thought her mother must have burnt it.

"She packed all my college things when I came back from Europe ... after I decided to marry Brad," she says when at last Dianne looks up from the letter. "I'd told her to throw everything out but ... well, she must have hoped Brad would talk me into going back to school. She kept all my books, my papers ... everything." Kate hangs her head like a wayward schoolgirl. Why is she babbling like this? "I think Plato was absolutely right. Love is a grave mental disease," she says instead, eliciting a sad chuckle.

She never did attend graduate school, but she thinks now that her parents were right, encouraging her to resume her studies after her breakdown; right, also, to urge her to go to Europe for a change of scene. Had it not been for the foolishness on the train to Paris, she might well have come home as they'd hoped, and picked up the pieces of her shattered life.

This is not the first time Kate has found herself be-latedly sympathizing with her distraught parents. What surprises her now is the thought that Guillaume, too, might have been right.

"At the time," she tells Dianne, "all I could think was: 'That's the most ridiculous thing I've ever heard!' I thought he must have been brainwashed by his new Separatist buddies—you know, like Charles Manson's gang." The Manson trial had been going on at the time, but after all these years, Dianne only chuckles.

"I remember," she says. "You seemed to feel that you had to rescue him from their clutches."

"I did!" Kate almost smiles. "Oh, I wish I could remem-ber half the things I told you. Have I ever thanked you for rescuing *me*?"

"Hm. Now that you mention it, I'm not sure!" Dianne mock-frowns across the table, then leans over to pat Kate's hand. "It's quite all right, my dear."

Dianne is only a little older than Kate; she turned fifty about two years ago, while Kate was away in Fiji. The last time they saw each other was five years ago, when they both happened to be in New York.

"I'm going to be fifty next month," Kate says. "I can't believe it: Fifty!" She pauses, then goes on to tell Dianne about a recent afternoon, when she stopped to buy makeup at Holt Renfrew. Waiting to be served, she glanced up and met her own reflection in the cosmetics mirror, standing next to a lovely young woman trying on a new shade of lipstick. "All at once I thought: Oh, my God, this stupid face is almost half a century old! How did I let that happen?"

"It's not stupid at all." Dianne shakes her head, openly

scanning Kate's features. "In fact, it's a pretty good face to have after half a century. You haven't really changed all that much, you know."

"Well, neither have you." Kate smiles into her sister-in-law's carefully made-up eyes. "I guess we must be doing something right, eh?"

Dianne laughs. "Lots of raw vegetables, lots of sleep, and as much sex as time will allow!"

Paul is often away on tour; Dianne's own professional commitments don't always permit her to accompany him. She and Kate are close, but not so close that Kate feels free to ask why they never had children. Now and then, she has wondered how a childless woman can seem so content with her life. Her own strong feeling for family is one thing she has always had in common with Brad. Is she just one of those women who expect too much from marriage? From life?

Dianne checks her watch, then jumps up: she has to make a phone call, and then use the washroom.

"Okay." Kate offers to stay and watch their things: four shopping bags bulging with Dianne's groceries, purchased after four weeks away from home. Megan has her first Montreal date this evening, but Kate's mind just now is less on her daughter than on her distant husband. She imagines Brad, coming home from work with his briefcase and daily paper, eating his solitary dinner in the den, in front of the television. When she spoke to him yesterday evening, he sounded distinctly lonely in Edmonton, perhaps a little de-pressed?

Well, a woman can hardly afford to dwell on her hus-band's emotional state while contemplating the possibility of leaving him, can she?

II

Dianne is taking her time. Kate sits staring out the window, her thoughts meandering to the day she had first heard about the private detective. On the face of it, her current dilemma has nothing to do with what happened during that dreadful fall of 1989. The Montreal detective had been hired just before they sold her family's Wood Avenue home. As far as Kate knows, it was the first time Brad had her followed, but he had, by his own admission, had his doubts about her for several years.

Of course, Kate didn't know any of this at the time; not until after she had brought her mother to live with them in Edmonton. Barely two weeks later, the whole sordid tale unravelled, all because of a cancelled children's play in downtown Edmonton.

It was Sunday and her mother's hired caretaker had the day off. Brad was home, watching sports, so Kate had set her mother down for a nap, then drove Megan downtown as promised, to see a much-anticipated production of *Cinderella*. Neither of them was in the best of moods. Megan was suffering from an as-yet-undiagnosed allergy; Fiona had been cranky all morning. Kate hated leaving her mother with Brad, who also seemed to be feeling under the weather that weekend. The weather itself had abruptly turned. By the time they left the house, the weak afternoon sun had been swallowed up by clouds and rain was hurtling across the windshield. They arrived at the theatre, only to learn that the play had been postponed: the child playing Cinderella had come down with mumps!

Oh, some days you were better off just staying in bed,

Kate remembers thinking. Megan kept sobbing, refusing to be consoled, until Kate offered to take her to Dairy Queen. She bought her a banana split, then drove back home in the downpour, while her nine-year-old daughter sat strapped in the back seat, quietly nibbling on her treat. It was not yet four p.m. but the sky was almost as dark as midnight, split every now and then by a savage rip of lightning.

Kate parked her Audi in the family garage. They entered through the basement, meekly greeted by their fat cocker spaniel. The dog cowered and whined, terrified by the thunder. Megan dawdled behind, cuddling the dog, while Kate hurried upstairs, running through the dim house to ensure that the windows were all securely fastened. She was glad to see her mother sleeping peacefully; Brad must have dozed off in front of the television. There was another crash of thunder as she approached the den. She reached it, but froze on the threshold, her heart turning over.

Brad was sitting hunched in the shadows, his face buried in his hands, sobbing like a disconsolate child.

Kate had never seen Brad cry before. The television was on and, what with the thunderstorm, he hadn't heard them come in. She knew nothing as yet about the Montreal detective's report and so had no idea why Brad was weeping. He was not immediately aware of her presence, but the sight of him made a wave of pity wash over her. She was about to rush over and comfort her husband when Megan came bounding up the stairs. Another minute and she would be there, witness to her father's private grief.

Kate drew back abruptly. She closed the door behind her, a finger on her lips.

"Shhh ... daddy's having a nap," she whispered.

It would be several hours before Brad showed her the detective's file; the damning photographs which had captured her entering the Chateau Versailles with Ivan Jacobson, then coming out alone in the early morning. She did not bother to tell her husband that nothing had happened in that hotel room; made no effort to persuade him that all she and Ivan had done was talk. Perhaps she wanted to punish Brad that night? Wanted him to suffer?

She walked away from her husband, feeling at once culpable and deeply resentful, refusing to speak to him for the next two weeks. She had no idea what the future held, but what had actually happened or not happened at the Chateau Versailles seemed just then almost beside the point.

III

The day after she learnt about the private detective, Kate considered calling her sister-in-law long distance. She thought about it for several days, but in the end decided against it. Why?

Partly because Brad is Dianne's second cousin, but mostly, Kate thinks, because she was loath to confess that she'd been caught picking up a stranger in a Montreal pub; could not bear the thought of her sister-in-law doubting her word about what had taken place at the Chateau Versailles. If Dianne did doubt it, if she thought Kate had in fact been unfaithful to Brad, would they still be friends?

Kate watches Dianne saunter back from the washroom, daintily stifling a yawn. Dianne squints in her direction; then, as she comes closer, her face lights up, as if in relief at having safely found her way back to her own table.

Kate waits for her to settle back in her chair.

"There's something I think I should tell you," she says in a decisive voice. Her left eyelid is twitching again, but she goes right on. "I know this will come as a shock to you —I think it will anyway—but ... oh, hell, I might as well come right out with it: I'm thinking of leaving Brad."

There, she has said it now! Kate looks up, gratified by the spark of interest in her sister-in-law's eyes; interest, but certainly not shock.

"Oh?"

That's all Dianne says. She gives Kate a long, probing look, then beckons for more coffee, while Kate sits staring out the window, nervously rubbing her wedding ring. It looks like rain again.

"I keep wishing I could stay here, in Montreal. I don't really want to go back to Edmonton," she says. Her sister-in-law is looking at her with impassive interest; not a muscle moves in her sun-bronzed face.

"Why? Has anything happened?"

Kate pauses, weighing the question.

"Yes. No. It's been happening for years," she says, glancing about with hopeless eyes. The coffee shop is all but empty, but she recalls the evening she had dinner with Antonia Offe, crying in public, in a crowded Chinese restaurant. She wouldn't want to risk a repeat of that scene.

She sits shredding her napkin for a while, then tells Dianne about her new friend, Antonia, and her belief that marriage requires a special talent.

"So, I've been thinking," she says. "I've been asking myself: Are Brad and I really incompatible, or is there some kind of flaw in my own makeup? I mean, is it possible that I just lack this particular talent?" Kate scans Dianne's face, as if expecting her sister-in-law to come up with a definitive answer.

"I don't know about talent," Dianne says. "But ... well, maybe that's just another way of saying you must really want the relationship to work." She stops, appraising Kate's face. "Do you think you ever cared all that much? Cared enough to work at it?"

Now, that is a question worth considering.

"Oh, I don't know," Kate says at last. Personally, she is not convinced that work belongs anywhere in this discussion. It may be a rather naive notion, but she still believes that marriage to the right person need not entail so much work. Maybe if ...

Dianne shifts forward, gazing at Kate intently. She knows that Kate married Brad in good faith, she says. "You tried very hard to put the past behind you. I know you did. But—" She hesitates, but presses right on. "Did you ... do you think you ever came to terms with it ... with the way things turned out with Guillaume?"

The question makes Kate sit up in her chair. "What can I say?" She stares into the distance. "You always ask such difficult questions."

"So?"

"I don't know the answer."

"What do you think?"

"Did I come to terms with losing Guillaume? I guess not, judging by how I still obsess about him after all these years."

Kate says this musingly, her eyes following a passing

shopper puffing on a fragrant pipe. She gave up smoking several years ago, after one of her pipe-smoking colleagues had died of lung cancer. She still has occasional cravings; has a strong one right now. But what her mind settles on is not her Edmonton colleague but Ivan Jacobson, smoking his pipe at Winnie's, smiling at her through a haze of smoke. She knows that there is no avoiding a discussion of this embarrassing subject; not if she truly wants Dianne to help her figure out what she ought to do.

"Do you think I may be a little cracked?" she asks.

"Oh, my dear! If you only knew how many menopausal women ask me the same question!" Dianne lets out a despondent sigh. "We're all a little cracked if you look close enough."

Kate is silent, breathing deeply, conscious of something like relief, even gratitude. She is also conscious of Dianne studying her from across the table, her eyes hazy with thought.

"How did it feel to be there again, by the way?" she asks after a long moment. "In Guillaume's apartment."

"Oh, unbelievable! Truly mind-boggling," Kate says, slipping into silence. She would like to answer Dianne's question, but just now there seem to be too many layers between her and the truth. It's not what she wants to talk about; not yet anyway. What she needs is Dianne's help in figuring out what it is she wants from her future. The truth is that Brad has been on her mind at least as much as Guillaume; that she is still as confused about him as she was on the day she first crossed Antonia's threshold.

But does Antonia have anything to do with it? Does Guillaume's letter?

Kate's mind is still buzzing with questions when Dianne turns away, reaching for her handbag.

"Let's go, shall we?" she says, not unkindly. "It's going to rain and anyway, I don't think you're quite ready to talk."

"Oh—" Kate stirs, listening to the landlocked seagulls shrieking outside. There is a definite ache at the back of her throat, but also a muddled desire to unburden herself, once and for all. "There *is* something that happened, but not recently ... something you might actually prefer not to know about," she says, staring into her café latte.

"Try me," Dianne says. As simple as that: "Try me."

So, at last, Kate goes ahead and tells her sister-in-law about the night spent at the Chateau Versailles; and then the day she found out about the detective. She speaks of her fear, when she first contemplated leaving her husband, that he would end up getting custody of Megan. He prob-ably would not have wanted to keep Sean; would have, she suspects, even refused to pay child support. She could have managed financially, but never without Megan. Anyway, how would she have explained it all to her son?

"How do you tell a teenager that his father—the only father he's ever known—suddenly doesn't want to have anything to do with him?" she asks. "I ... I felt—"

Kate's voice wobbles; she stops and puts her hand to her eyes. "I felt sick just thinking about it ... telling Sean about his real father. How could I possibly do this? To a fifteen-year-old?"

Dianne listens calmly, without expression. "So that's why you stayed?"

"I think so, but ... oh, everything's so complicated. I don't know what it is I feel anymore, you know? Things have not been right between us for years. Not since I found out about being followed." She pauses, asking herself whether 'things' had ever been right between them. She does not voice the thought.

"I eventually told Brad what had actually happened, and it was ... oh, just awful! Pathetic! I could see he was trying to understand—he *wanted* to believe me—but I'm not sure ... I don't think he really did, you know? And I ... I still couldn't forgive him. I was so angry, for months afterwards. At the same time I felt, I secretly felt, that maybe Brad was right, hiring that detective. After all, I probably *would* have slept with Ivan if it didn't happen to be the wrong time of month."

Dianne's face remains neutral. "You think?"

"Yes! Oh, don't look at me like that, Dianne. I'm trying to be honest! Does it really count, my being technically innocent?" Kate pauses for a moment, then makes a small hopeless gesture. "Oh, I don't know anything anymore!"

"So how do you know that you didn't go up with this Ivan only because you knew you wouldn't sleep with him—given your hang-up about menstrual blood?"

"How do I know? I don't know! That's what I mean ... that's exactly the problem! How can we ever be sure what's true and what's just a convenient rationalization?"

Dianne studies her for a moment. "You're so ... scrupulous," she says at length. "There are few people as honest with themselves as you try to be. Very few, believe me."

Kate blushes: a compliment from Dianne! What she doesn't say is that, though they decided to stay together, Brad became aloof after that terrible weekend; as if he'd finally given up trying to win her over.

"I've been crying quite a lot since I got here," she says instead, averting her eyes. Rain is starting to spit on the sidewalk, tentatively as yet, as if testing its own powers.

"Do you think you're still in love with Guillaume?" Dianne asks.

"Oh! Well, not with Guillaume, exactly. Not really with him as an actual person, I guess, but ... I don't know how to put it." Kate bows her head, pausing to blow her nose. "I'm not sure I understand what's happening to me ... something is happening though."

Dianne says nothing.

"You see, I don't trust my own feelings anymore," Kate says. "My thoughts seem so ... contradictory, you know?"

Dianne drinks her coffee.

For a moment, Kate sits fiddling with her crumpled tissue, then goes on to talk about the old woman on the Westmount park bench, her dog asleep beside her. "I think we—this old woman and I—were the only ones alone in the park that day. And ... well, I found myself imagining what it would be like to be that woman: my children gone, Brad probably married to someone else, while I ... I would just keep growing older and ... more and more eccentric." Tears are sliding down Kate's cheeks as she says all this. "Like my mother," she says at length. Forces herself to say.

Dianne presses Kate's fingers, gazing at her with wordless sympathy. "Oh, Kate," she says, a dent between her eyebrows. "Your mother was deeply depressed; you know that. She lost the will to live after your father died."

"Maybe," Kate allows. "It would certainly make sense if ... if they'd been happy together, but—"

"They weren't?" Dianne's eyebrows are two arcs of dainty surprise.

"No. Not for a long time." Kate doesn't say that her mother too had once considered leaving her husband but lacked the courage to break up the family. It is something she herself learnt only a few years ago, after her mother's brain had begun to betray her. Maybe this is what her mother was really depressed about, Kate says to herself. The failure to take charge of her own life?

She has no way of knowing whether her mother had been more, or less, happy with her life than most women, but it doesn't feel right to be discussing her secrets with Dianne. She glances out at the tattered sky, the now steady drizzle.

"We should go," she says. "Before this turns into a serious downpour."

Dianne turns to glance at the window. She consults her watch again, then levers herself from her chair and picks up the shopping bags. It is late afternoon by now and, despite the weather, the market is getting crowded. A strong wind has begun blowing from the north, whipping up the farmers' canvas awnings. Dianne places her bags on the sidewalk. She gives a theatrical little shudder as she stops to button her coat.

Fortunately, the car is not parked far. They are halfway to Dianne's brand new BMW when a stray cat darts out from behind the dumpsters—a scrawny black-and-white tabby scooting between two fruit stalls, reminding Kate that she'd meant to ask her daughter's superintendent whether pets are allowed in the building.

Kate's eyes are still following the stray tabby when her

restive mind tosses up the vision of a blind cat she encountered in Athens, many years ago. Her memories of Greece are full of wretched animals; mangy dogs and battered cats with bitten ears and festering wounds, struggling to survive off tourists' scraps and restaurant leftovers. But what comes back to her now is how that sightless cat had paused, sniffing, outside a busy *taverna*, trembling with apprehension. She and Brad had just enjoyed a huge seafood lunch; they were on their way out when Kate noticed the ginger-striped stray approach the open entrance. It was a radiant spring afternoon. The *taverna* was in the Acropolis area and had a large, shady terrace overhung with vine, packed with jolly diners. But the stray cat was sluggish with hunger and blind with mucus. And both the smell of grilled fish and sound of waiters' boots came from the same direction.

THREE

THERE ARE NO photographs from that turbulent Christmas of 1970. Kate's family did not go to Boston that year and, in any case, no one would have dreamt of approaching her with a camera in those last days of December. It was the worst holiday any of them had ever known; a grim, chaotic season whose memory Kate has for years done her best to bury. They say that time heals all wounds, but she thinks this is not really true. All time does, she believes, is make scars invisible to the casual eye. In a certain kind of person, what it sometimes does is transmute the pain into a work of art.

For a long time, the pain was akin to what a gravely wounded soldier might feel after a long battle, regaining consciousness to discover that one of his legs had been amputated. Every now and then, Kate would experience a deep unexpected ache—something she privately thought of as phantom pain—often brought on by wholly unrelated events.

One year, travelling in Mexico on a winter assignment, she came upon a young woman begging with her two children on a busy seaside promenade. The beggar's infant was asleep, but the older child, three or four years old, was standing like a sentry next to his entreating mother, his dark eyes pools of hunger and mute accusation.

It was early evening. The promenade was crowded with well-fed, bejewelled, tourists out for a stroll, a cocktail. A few of them stopped to buy an ice cream cone from a wagon parked under a shady tree. Giving the woman a few pesos was easy, but the child's eyes sent an arrow of pain through Kate: her daughter was just about the same age as the Mexican urchin; both Megan and Kate's brother, Paul, were passionate about ice cream.

"Wait for me," she said to her colleagues. "I'll be right back."

She went to the wagon and bought strawberry ice cream — her daughter's favourite — then bent down and held out the sugar cone to the half-naked child, seeing his eyes widen. The boy snatched the cone from her hand and began licking it furiously, running circles around his mother's voluminous skirts.

The beggar woman tried to make her son stop. She reached out and slapped at his bare legs, but the boy would not stand still. It was about six or six-thirty but the sun still had teeth, as someone in Kate's travel group said. The boy went on running as if possessed. Kate's colleagues stood watching, transfixed.

Kate was watching more intently than any of them. Sometimes, taking a good photograph is all about where you happen to be standing. Hoping to capture this extraordinary display of frenzied joy, Kate had grabbed her camera and was clicking the shutter just as the pink scoop of frozen cream slid off its crisp cone; slid off and landed on the grimy pavement, at the child's bare feet.

"Oh, no!" Kate lowered her camera. Photography being as full of surprises as life itself, she had caught not the
intended rapture, but the exquisite moment of its vanishing: the bewilderment and grief on the child's face; the
chaotic awareness of irrevocable loss. The boy thrust his
tongue out, yearning for the quickly-thawing treat. Another moment and he was down on his knees, bent over
the squalid sidewalk in order to lick the mound of melting
pink cream.

"No, don't! Don't!" Kate had lunged forward and was
still clutching the child's arm. "Come, I'll buy you another
one," she said, assuring the mother she would be right
back. Her friends would stay and wait for them right there,
on the sidewalk. She was unspeakably happy to be able to
end both the woman's shrill reprimands and the little boy's
wails; to walk over to the ice cream wagon, and stand in
line, with a small child's hand in hers, waiting to buy a
new ice cream cone.

By the time all this took place, years had passed since
Kate had lost Guillaume, but the Mexican child's crumpled
face brought it all back in one dizzying spell: the impotent
tears, the piercing sense of loss. In the few seconds it took
to click a camera shutter, the world had withdrawn its
promised sweetness. How well she remembered the feeling! It was, perhaps, an odd mental connection, but seeing
laughter return to the street urchin's face had made her
feel like a good fairy come to the rescue.

Kate has not thought of the Mexican child for years,
but she thinks of him now as she sits on a park bench in
Québec City, watching her aging brother enjoy an ice
cream cone in the picturesque Old Town. Paul had been

such an angelic-looking boy, dreamy and pampered, yet no less greedy than the beggar's child in Acapulco. The grownup Paul still enjoys cakes and pastries, but his passion for ice cream has turned into something of a gustatory obsession. One of the first things Paul does on arriving in any new town, in any country, is to find out where the best ice cream is being sold, and head there as soon as his professional obligations permit.

It is Saturday afternoon, the day after the McGill Chamber Orchestra's concert. Kate and her brother have been strolling through the town's historic centre, alone for the first time in years. Dianne is home in Montreal, preparing for a return to work; Megan has gone back to the hotel, to finish a term paper due on Monday morning. She went off in a huff, looking disgusted with both her mother and her uncle because they had ordered a rabbit dish for lunch. Paul has managed to get tickets for the Denis Brott cello recital this evening; has promised to drive back to Montreal on Sunday morning, in plenty of time for Antonia's party.

For now, they linger in the Palais de Glace, where Paul slowly consumes his nutty macadamia ice cream, as absorbed in his sensual pleasure as any four year old. Odd, perhaps, that Kate should feel so maternal towards her brother; he is older after all. Yet something about Paul tends to elicit such sentiments. He might be in his early fifties, but it's easy to think of him as a grown altar boy, even if his ethereal looks have begun to fade. Kate notes that, though her brother's eyes are as strikingly blue as ever, his fair hair is thinning, his tender little mouth grown a little prissy. He is still fit, yet somehow fragile-looking, like a graceful, fine-boned boy on the threshold to puberty.

It is colder in Québec City than it was in Montreal and, though the morning rain has stopped, the air is sharp with the breath of lurking winter. Every now and then, a cold gust of wind sweeps up from the river; brittle leaves keep blowing across the narrow streets in hissing, colourful swarms.

Having had his ice cream fix, Paul seems content to show Kate Québec's restored Lower Town, pausing to look at quaint shops and gallery windows, waiting patiently while she stops to snap an occasional photograph. On the steps of Québec's oldest church, Paul pauses to blow his nose and Kate is assailed by the thought of Brad who, every night, at precisely eleven p.m., sits on the edge of their king-size bed and loudly blows his nose. Brad has been doing this ever since they got married but now, after twenty-six years of sharing a bedroom, the mental vision clenches Kate's throat.

"I suppose Dianne's told you I've been thinking of leaving Brad?"

Kate says this without preamble, standing on the very spot where Samuel de Champlain founded the fur-trading centre that has over the years become Québec City. Her brother has been patient, not asking any personal questions, waiting for her to broach the subject.

"Yes. She has." Paul thrusts his handkerchief back into his pocket. He gives his sister a quick sidelong glance. "What's it all about, Kate?"

"Well, that's what I'm trying to figure out. I seem to be having some sort of mid-life crisis ... I don't know." She sighs and resumes walking alongside Paul, her eyes on the cobblestones. A flurry sends a shower of rain hissing down through the branches of a horse chestnut tree. Kate wishes she could answer her brother's question, but two days after her tête-à-tête with Dianne, she is no less confused than she was last week. One thing she knows: It is utterly childish to feel such deep antipathy for the way your husband blows his nose. Couldn't she have asked him to do it in the bathroom if it bothered her all that much? Is it possible that human beings have a secret need to nurture their pet aversions?

Kate thinks of her parents. In the early stages of Alzheimer's, her mother disclosed how maddening she used to find her husband's random parsimoniousness; incomprehensible, it seemed to her, because he thought nothing of spending lavishly on his own pleasures, or even occasional gifts for his family. And yet, any time she bought a new rug or a dress, and despite the fact that she had an inheritance of her own, her husband would grow sulky, his face set in a mask of ill-suppressed displeasure.

All this Fiona Abbitson had gradually learnt to deal with, but what made her want to jump out of her skin, she would eventually tell Kate, was Dwight's habit of complaining that she was using more dishwashing detergent than strictly necessary. And another thing: He never failed to stop in stores, to count the small change he received after buying an expensive tennis racquet, or a fine bottle of wine.

Kate ponders all this in Québec City and, as if reading her mind, Paul turns to look at her, tugging at his earlobe.

"Dianne said you also hinted at something about Mom and Dad's relationship ... something about their not being happy with each other." He kicks aside a banana peel lying in his path. "Is there something I don't know, Kate?"

Kate stops to weigh her words. There was a time, right

after her mother's death, when she longed to speak to her brother. Paul, alas, had to leave right after the funeral and Kate was never one for discussing anything of importance over the telephone. Also, once the initial impulse had passed, she began to feel a sisterly need to protect her brother; or at least preserve his idealized view of their mother. Being the only boy in a family of sisters and female cousins, showing from an early age a strong musical talent, Paul had once been deeply attached to his mother; had, perhaps, been her favourite. Even today, Kate suspects, he might be shaken to learn of the sordid affair with the house painter.

She decides to spare her brother.

She spares him not only the details of her own unexpected arrival the terrible day of her skipped Shakespeare exam, but also her mother's eventual disclosure of their father's sexual impotence while he was still in his midforties. Pulling up her hood, she tells Paul only about their father's compulsive gambling and drinking, a problem her mother had managed to conceal until Alzheimer's began to invade her brain. This was how Kate came to learn that her father had at some point begun buying stocks on margin; that in 1987, when the stock market crashed, he, like so many others, ended up losing the bulk of his investments.

Kate remembers her brother and sister's astonishment on learning just how meagre their parents' assets had become over the years. She told them about the financial losses brought on by the crash, but said nothing about their father's gambling. And, now that he knows, Paul shakes his head with an air at once sorrowful and bemused.

"No wonder he had a massive heart attack ... all that booze and stress."

As he says this, Paul's interest in taking Kate around town seems to evaporate. He wants to sit down somewhere warm and have a good cup of coffee, he says. It is by now past four o'clock; the kind of chilly October afternoon that brings an obscure ache to the chest. As he leads the way down a crooked little street towards his favourite cafe, another flurry raises a swarm of dead leaves off the cobblestones, blowing them up against their shins.

Kate has not visited Québec City for some three decades, but she is content to pass the time in this cozy French café, seated by a blazing fire. Unlike their sister, she and Paul are confirmed sybarites. Heather, by contrast, has always been the sort of person whose blood is stirred mostly by professional competition. This was no doubt why she was so obviously favoured by their hard-nosed father.

They talk about their father, comparing personal notes. Dwight Abbitson died in December, 1987, seventeen years, almost to the day, after Kate had attempted to take her own life. He was barely sixty-five. Eventually, her mother would tell Kate how she had for a long time feared that he, too, might be suicidal.

Kate does not share this thought with her brother. She talks instead about Pauline Julien, who committed suicide on Thursday, the very day Kate and Dianne went shopping at the Atwater Market. Although she had barely known Julien, the news hit Kate with the force of a fist striking an already-vulnerable belly. To think the death took place while she sat with her sister-in-law, hashing over relatively minor dilemmas. The singer had been suffering from a rare degenerative brain disease. It was a tragic death. For Kate, moreover, it seemed to mark the end of an era.

"Have you ever run into Guillaume Beauregard?" she

asks Paul after a long pause. "Do you know if he's playing with any orchestra?"

Paul shrugs, shooting Kate a quick, appraising glance. He has neither seen nor heard of Guillaume, he says. He could ask around, he adds after a moment. Denis Brott, whose recital they are planning to attend this evening, would probably know.

"No," Kate says firmly. "Please don't. It was just a thought."

"Okay." Paul dabs at his nose with a handkerchief. Dianne must have told him about Kate's sudden obsession with the past, but he makes no allusion to it. Kate wishes he would. She keeps hoping that someone, something, might shed light on both her past and her present, and help her find her way back to normal.

"Funny to think that Guillaume actually made me want to die, then turned out to be the one who saved my life."

"It's not my idea of funny," Paul says, his eyebrows sliding towards each other. "If you ask me, you —"

"Well, I don't mean *funny,* of course ... you know what I mean." Kate pauses, fidgeting with her wedding ring. She had always sensed that, although he liked Guillaume, her brother had strong reservations about her relationship, if only because he dreaded the possibility of having to occasionally rub shoulders with Guillaume's family. This, at least, was Kate's guess, but all she says now is: "I wouldn't be here talking to you today, would I, if he hadn't cared enough to phone when he did?"

"I guess." Paul shrugs. He stuffs his handkerchief back into his pocket, then resumes sipping his coffee, while Kate slides into private reverie.

Guillaume, of course, had no way of knowing about

the overdose she'd taken. He had been visiting friends during Kate's run-in with Sylvie Laplante; it was well past midnight when he finally heard the news. Early the following morning, possibly overcome by remorse, he telephoned her home. He wanted to make sure that she was all right, he said to her mother.

Fiona Abbitson suggested he should speak to Kate himself. She asked Guillaume to hold on, then hurried downstairs to wake her daughter.

Kate did not respond; not even on being told that Guillaume was on the phone. Unable to rouse her daughter, Fiona ran back upstairs and told Guillaume she must hang up and call an ambulance. Within minutes, Kate's inert body was being placed on a stretcher, transported in a shrilling ambulance back to the emergency ward she had left less than twelve hours earlier.

Today, Kate has a blurred memory of Guillaume standing at her hospital bedside; of his reaching out to gently take her hand. But then he seemed to vanish. For years, she believed Guillaume's presence had been a drug-induced apparition, but he had indeed come to visit her at the hospital; had called a second time after she'd been released, only to have her father slam down the receiver.

Kate learnt this only after her mother's neurons began to get tangled. She is surprised to know that her brother had never heard about their father's uncharacteristic rudeness. Listening to Kate, Paul shakes his head and lets out a prolonged sigh, as is his wont whenever family problems threaten his peace of mind.

"He could be such an insensitive bastard," he says, speaking of their father. "So obtuse at times."

Kate is silent for a long moment, contemplating the leaping flames in the fireplace.

"It's just as well he was dead by the time I learnt all this," she says and achieves a smile. "I might have been tempted to shoot him."

Paul does not smile back. He sits sipping his coffee in silence, watching Kate get up to go to the washroom.

It is dark by the time they head towards the funicular that will take them up to their Upper Town hotel. The evening is sharply damp as they enter the outdoor elevator, watching the riverside town's lights twinkle below the funicular's glass walls. Paul says that the fashionable streets of the Petit Champlain district they have just left behind had once been an impoverished neighbourhood; American tourists in the Upper Town used to throw coins to the scrambling French kids below.

"Really? I didn't know that."

Kate guesses that her brother's mind has tossed up this historical morsel because they have just passed a blanket-wrapped panhandler begging for spare change outside the funicular's entrance. He looked to be a rather dishevelled sixty, but, in the light of the street lamp, Kate couldn't help but make out the traces of beauty in the man's ravaged features: the bony face, the aquiline nose, the large, haunted eyes.

She recalls something she'd read in the papers, many years ago. Unsure of the details, she asks whether Paul ever heard about the Westmount banker who ended up as a downtown panhandler.

"Really? I don't think so," says Paul. "A *banker?*" He gives her a sceptical look, steering her towards the boardwalk.

"Yes," Kate says. "Maybe a financier—something to do with money. It was in the papers."

"What happened? Did he lose everything in the crash?"

"No. I don't think so."

She thinks about it some more, breathing in the briny smell of the river. She believes it had started after the banker's wife had left him for another man and he began to drink. His wife's lawyer saw to it that she got the house as well as a handsome financial settlement. Were there children in the picture? There must have been. Kate steps off the road as a brightly festooned *calèche* comes towards them, the horse's hooves clip-clopping on the dark cobble-stones.

"I think his drinking got to be a real problem," she says. "He ended up losing his job and ... well, after that, it was all the way downhill." Kate looks up, exchanging glances with the *calèche* driver. "That's all I remember."

"Unbelievable! The stories you always manage to dig up," he says, sounding at once wistful and affectionate. He doesn't ask what has made Kate recall this particular story; in fact, she suspects he knows. Her feelings towards her father may have been ambivalent at best, but as she muses on his lamentable end, there is a brief, unsettling moment in which she envisions her father reclining by the funicular's entrance, his arm reaching out from within the dark blanket, his haunted eyes begging her for forgiveness.

FOUR

⚮

TWENTY-FOUR HOURS after hearing Denis Brott's recital in Québec City, Gabriel Fauré's *Elegy Opus 24* is still echoing in the back of Kate's head, the cello refrain repeating itself like some plaintive, persistent question. Kate can't put the question into words, but the French composer's work seems to her like the perfect musical accompaniment to the season. Something about its poignant, drawn-out rhythms, perhaps, or the melancholy interplay between piano and cello.

It is Sunday evening and Kate is in the back of a Montreal taxi, on her way to Antonia's birthday party. She had originally planned to walk all the way to Selkirk, but decided to call a cab because the streets are said to be hazardous this evening. The dropping temperature and freezing rain have left trees and lamp posts heavily sheathed in ice. All afternoon, groaning branches have been snapping off, the splintering ice showering onto sidewalks like slivers of shattered crystal.

It is not an ideal night for a party, but Kate is enthralled by the view from the back of the cab. All along Sherbrooke Street, the maple trees glitter in the light of street lamps. The roads are certainly slippery, but how picturesque the icicles look, hanging from eaves and gables, like illustrations in some Grimm Brothers fairy tale. For Antonia's sake, Kate hopes that the weather will not keep guests from venturing out this evening. She's been looking forward to the party. Not only has she managed to get Antonia's photograph developed and framed, but in her Québec City wanderings, she came across a poster which instantly made her think of Elizabeth Berg, and which she hastened to buy for the old woman.

The poster is a blown-up photograph of a Tunisian entryway with studded blue portals and white steps, on the bottom of which three cats huddle in the sun, staring into the camera with drowsy feline disdain. Kate liked the whitewashed entrance, and thought that Elizabeth would probably adore the three winsome cats. She left Megan's apartment a little early so as to drop the gift off on her way to the party. It is going on eight o'clock. She has asked the driver to let her off in front of Elizabeth's house.

When Elizabeth sees Kate standing on her lit-up porch, she insists on inviting her in for a drink. No one arrives at parties on time anyway, she points out, fiddling with one of her plastic combs. It so happens she was just about to have her nightly glass of port and would love the company.

And so Kate removes her shoes and enters the foyer, recoiling from the sharp feline smell. There are cats everywhere: on needlepoint cushions and fireside throw rugs; on chairs and shelves and chests and table tops. Cats blinking and swishing their tails, cats curled up in sleep, cats energetically licking themselves, or each other's fur.

"Goodness! How many of them do you have these days, Miss Elizabeth?"

The old woman cackles, sweeping the room with her faded eyes. "Thirteen at the moment. Would you like to have one from the new litter? I can live happily with nine or ten," she says, spreading a clean blanket on the sofa for Kate to sit on. "Any more and I start feeling like one of those poor French Canadian wives who wouldn't use contraceptives in the old days because the priests forbade it."

Kate smiles at this, wondering whether her hostess ever had occasion to worry about contraception. Judging by family photographs, Elizabeth was once a lovely young woman. She spent years working as an interpreter in the Immigration Department, where she must have met her share of eligible men. Yet, for one reason or another, she never married. Long ago, Kate recalls, there had been a fiancé back in Germany. Yes, it's all coming back to her as she studies the sepia photographs on display, listening to the vaguely familiar narrative.

Elizabeth's mother had been Jewish; her father, a Heidelberg linguist, made the decision to emigrate soon after Hitler passed his infamous racial laws. Elizabeth was in her early twenties at the time, engaged to marry a brilliant chemical engineer.

She obviously has no recollection of having already shared any of this with Kate. Filling two glasses with ruby-hued port, she lowers her heavy bulk into an armchair and sits massaging her thigh.

There is no photograph of the fiancé, who had been dead-set against leaving Nazi Germany. Kate recalls Elizabeth telling her years ago it was just as well they did not marry as planned; her Helmut had turned out to be among the chemical engineers responsible for developing Zyklon, the gas that would eventually kill most of her mother's family.

Despite this grim legacy, and though a good part of her life has been spent caring for ailing parents, there is no trace of bitterness or self-pity about Elizabeth. She is unabashedly eccentric, yet everything about her speaks of an undiminished capacity for squeezing pleasure out of circumstance.

Sitting in what Elizabeth still calls "the parlour," Kate finds herself musing on the universally held belief that a woman must have, if not children, then at least a man to give her life meaning. One of her own friends, an unmarried Edmonton woman in her early forties, has recently confessed that she still finds herself getting dressed for large parties with a strong sense of girlish anticipation. Though she has absolutely no desire to marry, Kate's lawyer friend can't quite shake the deeply-rooted notion that her life is somehow a failure because she has never married.

Elizabeth, on the other hand, has contrived to give her life both structure and purpose, to say nothing of daily pleasure. She is as delighted by Kate's unexpected gift as she is by all the little routines and rewards she pursues daily, with seemingly unflagging zeal. In her late eighties, she spends her days looking after her home and garden, her cats and her flourishing orchids. She knits socks and scarves for her siblings' children and grandchildren, puts up fruit preserves, reads German and English novels. She reads mostly in the evening, she says, when all her chores are done, sitting by the fire each evening with her glass of port.

As she speaks of all this, Elizabeth's eyes come to rest

on a paperback copy of Rosamund Pilcher's *The Shell Seekers*, which lies open on a cat-scratched chair, next to the fireplace. Pilcher turns out to be one of Elizabeth's favourite authors.

"There are so many depressing books on the market today. Why do you suppose people like to read them?" she asks in her wheezing voice.

"I don't know," Kate says. "I suppose they can relate to that kind of reality."

"*Pffff!*" Elizabeth makes a dismissive gesture. "Reality is what you choose to make it," she states with all the authority of a lecturing metaphysician. She has a sister-in-law who has everything a woman could possibly want but still finds something to complain about every single day. If it's not her arthritis, it's her back; if not her back, then her legs. "I tell her, I say: 'You can't expect to reach old age without some kind of pain, eh?' The important thing is to treat all aches and pains as challenges; challenges instead of—how do you say that in English—afflictions!"

"Oh, I'm sure you're right." Kate smiles at the old woman: her pale, withered skin, the pasty folds of her sagging neck, her unsightly moles. Though Kate's response is nothing if not sincere, Elizabeth seems to feel she has not quite managed to put her point across.

"If you think about it," she says. "If you stop and think —well, every age has its own special challenges, no?" She regards Kate with her cloudy brown eyes, but doesn't bother to wait for an answer. "I too may be more cranky than I used to be ... sure I am! But ... well, there are still so many things to be grateful for, don't you think?"

"Yes." Kate stares into her wineglass, feeling mildly

rebuked. "There certainly are." She smiles. One of the cats has jumped into her lap with a little plaintive meow.

"So, you haven't told me! Would you like to take one of the kittens?" Elizabeth asks. "Maybe for your daughter?"

"I'm still thinking about it," Kate says. Although she has no doubt that Megan would be thrilled to have a kitten, and though the apartment building's management does permit it, she has yet to decide whether keeping a cat would be advisable, given Megan's frenetic schedule, her travel plans for the coming year. She would have to find someone to care for it in her absence. And is it really worth it?

Elizabeth clears her sinuses. "Tell me about yourself then. I've been doing all the talking, as usual." She chuckles, fiddling with a threaded needle she had attached to the collar of her blouse. She is wearing a rather school-girlish white blouse and a frayed red cardigan over a dark skirt sprinkled with little white birds. "I suppose you must have a family?"

"Yes." Kate shifts her legs on the flowery sofa. "I do."

She tells Elizabeth about her husband and two children, and then about her photography. One of Elizabeth's brothers became a studio photographer on arriving from Germany, so she assumes this is what Kate's job entails. Kate has to explain the kind of photographs she actually takes. Sipping her port, she tells Elizabeth about the collection she is currently working on — the one about artists — but says nothing of the new book idea that came to her only yesterday, soon after she and Paul had encountered the panhandler in Québec City.

She doesn't like to speak of new projects; is still a little bemused by the fact that it took so long for her latest idea to hatch in her head. By now, she knows the book will probably be titled STRAYS; she also knows it will be a collection devoted to the vagrants she has been encountering everywhere: from the bag lady outside the Guy Metro to the blanket-wrapped panhandler lolling next to Québec City's funicular. And others like them. She wishes she had her camera with her so she could photograph Elizabeth Berg. Not that Elizabeth belongs in the envisioned collection. She not only has a cozy home, but also a life almost as rich as that of most people Kate knows. What she wants is to have a photograph of Elizabeth to keep on her desk, as a daily reminder of something she thinks she is prone to forget.

Ever since she had her first camera stolen in Italy, Kate doesn't bring her camera to large parties. As she finishes her port and prepares to leave for Antonia's, she tells Elizabeth she would very much like to stop in again and take a photograph of her.

"Me! Ach, I'm an old woman!" Elizabeth exclaims with a dismissive wave. She smiles her gap-toothed smile, then looks up with dawning shrewdness. Something about her expression tells Kate that a suspicion has crept into Elizabeth's mind. Does she think that the Tunisian poster was offered as some sort of bribe?

Yes, perhaps she does. Stopping in the foyer, Kate can see her trying to work out why anyone would be interested in taking her photograph. She wishes she never asked.

"Miss Elizabeth ..." Kate reaches out and takes the old woman's hand in her own. She looks straight into the shrivelled face, trying to make it clear that she has no intention of publishing the photograph, or making any commercial use of it whatsoever. All she wants is a souvenir of their meeting. "After all, you gave a good home to my Pablo." She smiles. "You took care of him for years, didn't you?"

"Mm." Elizabeth wags her head but is not quite ready to relinquish her doubts. She looks and looks at Kate. Suddenly, her face offers the hint of a new idea. As Kate stands buttoning her coat, Elizabeth gives her a curious smile suggestive of a shared conspiracy.

"All right, my dear." She pats Kate's arm. "I'll let you do it," she says, "but only if you take one of the kittens." The old woman gives one of her hoarse cackles. She still doesn't understand what it's all about, but is clearly pleased with her own cunning. "Your daughter can come and choose her favourite. They are all very, very pretty."

Kate hesitates, then picks up her umbrella, smiling back at the old woman.

"Okay, it's a deal!"

FIVE

I

Antonia is in the kitchen, fiddling with a large tray of baked *hors d'oeuvres* when Kate arrives, stopping to exchange greetings. Two National Theatre School students have been hired to help prepare and serve, but Antonia wants to make sure the buffet is exactly as she would have it.

"Call me a control freak, but I hired a professional caterer last time I had a party. And, I'm telling you, nothing turned out as it was supposed to. Not a single dish!"

Antonia says all this, then pours Kate a glass of Chardonnay. She adds a sprig of parsley to the silver platter, hands the platter to one of her young assistants, then hangs her oven mitts in their place by the stove. Only then does she pick up Kate's carefully wrapped present, which she raises to her ear and shakes, like a child trying to guess the contents of a Christmas gift. She instructs Kate to put it under the spiral staircase, along with the other boxes. She'll be opening presents at midnight, the precise time of her birth.

This at least is what she says to Kate, and, for all Kate knows, it is true. But it is also, she senses, the sort of innocent fabrication Antonia might produce for no better reason than its dramatic appeal.

"I'll be out as soon as I've got everything under control here," she says, taking a sip from her wineglass. "Oh, by the way," she adds as Kate is leaving the kitchen. "Yves is somewhere out there. See if you can find him."

"Yves—?" Kate stops in her tracks. "Yves Letourneau?"

"Who else? Didn't you say you were thinking of photographing him?"

"Yes—"

"So, go and find him, my dear!" Antonia pauses, offering a quick, mischievous smile from behind the sink. "See if you can recognize him."

"Well ... okay. I'll try," Kate says. "Let's see if he recognizes me!"

She makes her way through the dining area, where the buffet is to be served. Despite the weather, Antonia's living room is packed with well-dressed and perfumed guests huddling in small, animated groups. Every now and then, one of them twists around to pick an *hors d'oeuvre* from the charming young students Antonia has managed to round up. The guests themselves seem to be of all ages, all races, and speaking at least three languages. Antonia did not invite her ex after all, but there is a fair number of theatre people, as well as family members, old friends, a couple of neighbours. Antonia even invited her osteopath, in gratitude for having been cured of a chronic backache.

Kate has no idea who the osteopath might be, but she soon spots a man she recognizes from photographs she has seen in the Centaur Theatre lounge. Terence Pace, the theatre's managing director, is a large Englishman with straight, wheat-coloured hair and a frizzy rust-hued beard. He stands at the centre of a small group, puffing on his pipe, his head partially tilted, like a man slightly hard of hearing. A woman in tight silver pants and earrings down to her shoulders stops to whisper something in his ear, making Pace roar with laughter.

Holding on to her wineglass and squeezing through what she takes to be the theatre crowd, Kate soon identifies the director's pipe tobacco as the probable source of the scent lingering in Antonia's car. As Terence Pace is over twenty years younger than Antonia, she quickly dismisses the possibility of a romantic liaison. Antonia must have given Pace a lift, she surmises, smiling a little at her own conjectures.

But Terence Pace seems to think the smile is aimed at him. He smiles back, listening to his companions while following Kate's movements with bright, speculative eyes.

Kate's smile quickens. She may be a month shy of her fiftieth birthday, but if Megan is to be believed, she looks exceptionally well tonight in her short burgundy dress. The dress is belted and buttoned from top to bottom; the silk scarf she wears at the neck has a paisley pattern whose colours match both the dress and her slate-grey eyes.

She goes on searching the room for a man bearing a resemblance to Yves Letourneau. She briefly considers a bearded stranger sitting on one of the ivory sofas, but no, this cannot be Yves. The playwright she remembers not only spoke English with a pronounced French accent, but had a different sort of laughter from this man, who is just now absorbed in explaining why he has gone from vegetarian to vegan. He sits with one leg crossed over the other, so that Kate can't help noticing his fine brown-leather shoes, which look to her like the expensive San Marinos her husband likes to wear.

"Oops, excuse me!"

A woman with her back to Kate has carelessly spun around, almost bumping into the wineglass Kate is still clutching in her right hand. Kate smiles blandly and goes to stand by the window, gazing out at the moon-washed street, listening to yet another conversation. She is eavesdropping on this one because the earnest-looking couple and old man appear to be engaged in an interesting discussion about time and free will. She is guessing that the younger man, who is sitting with his chin in his hand, must be Antonia's godson, the philosophy professor.

Since she has failed to find—or at least recognize—Yves Letourneau, and knowing no one else at this glittering party, Kate stands to the side, waiting for a break in the conversation so she can introduce herself to Antonia's godson. She exchanges smiles with the philosopher's wife, who looks rather bored by the men's prolonged argument. Kate gathers that some distinction is being drawn between a philosophical notion of time as an endlessly-flowing process, and the view of physicists who apparently see objects and events in something like succession. Once again, she remembers having come across the theory of backward-flowing time and thinks, with some irritation, of the verbal games that highly-educated people seem willing to dedicate their lives to. Just ask Elizabeth Berg about time, she says to herself; she won't waste a minute of it on the idea of its ever flowing back.

Or is she just vexed because she doesn't like to admit there are some things she can't understand?

Possibly, but the older she gets, the less patience she has for anything that seems to her to obfuscate the obvious. Having decided against waiting to introduce herself to Antonia's godson, she makes her way back across the crowded room. She has by now scanned every face around her and has seen no one who resembles the playwright she used to know. She remembers moreover that she never particularly liked Yves, though she was quite friendly with Suzanne, the schoolteacher he used to live with in the upstairs apartment. She tries to recall what it was she didn't like about Yves, but can think of nothing beyond his tendency to wallow in self-pity. Could she have been simply prejudiced against anyone connected with the theatre?

Oh, possibly, she concedes. Many years ago, a year or so before meeting Yves, she used to date a drama student, whom she had quickly come to mistrust. Although she is capable of enjoying theatre folks' company — enjoys Antonia's, certainly, she can't help feeling that they are all exceedingly fond of drawing attention to themselves; of creating drama just to alleviate a propensity to boredom.

Just now, though, she herself is a little bored; bored and childishly disgruntled at having been left to her own devices. Everyone in the room seems to know someone, and she tends to be a little tongue-tied at large gatherings. She takes a sip of wine, then decides to offer help in the kitchen. She is almost back in the dining area — is facing the spiral staircase — when Terence Pace emerges from the powder room, lips stretched with apparent delight.

"Hi, I'm Terence Pace," he says, stopping to shake Kate's hand next to a large potted palm. "Who are you?"

"Kate. Kate Thuringer." She smiles, takes a sip of wine, then goes on to tell Pace about the Centaur rehearsal she has recently attended. Fortunately, she is able to praise *The Crabapple Season* with perfect sincerity.

"Isn't Antonia wonderful as the grandmother?" she says warmly. "Even her accent sounds authentic!" Years ago Kate had a Greek housekeeper, so she knows whereof she speaks.

"Oh, Antonia's quite brilliant!" Terence Pace says, drawing on his pipe. His gaze flicks to Kate's left hand; to the wedding ring which, just now, she is not toying with. She has a wineglass to fidget with; perhaps even to explain her flushed cheeks. She can feel the heat, even if she is not attracted to Pace; not in the least. At the age of fifty, though, no woman is above being flattered by such overt interest.

This is the thought flitting through Kate's head when her eyes idly travel towards a man coming down the spiral staircase. He is an exceptionally slender man, dressed in blue jeans and an eye-popping vest, all colourful zippers, pockets. He is holding a broken wineglass, frowning a little. The stranger seems to be heading towards the kitchen, but as he reaches the bottom step, Kate casually meets his gaze and sees the clean-shaven face light up in recognition.

"Kate!" exclaims Yves Letourneau, chucking the broken wineglass into the potted palm. He darts to hug her, then stands back with his arms folded for a more thorough look. Terence Pace raises his hand to the back of his neck and holds it there for a moment.

"An old friend," Kate mutters apologetically. She starts to introduce them, but it seems Terence and Yves are already acquainted. Of course they are, thinks Kate, though there seems to be little warmth in their mutual greeting. The theatre director touches Kate's arm lightly, then moves on, leaving her and Yves grinning and exclaiming.

"But look at you!" Yves' eyes keep appraising Kate's

figure, her slightly greying hair. "You're still beautiful!" He stands beaming at her, a thoroughly altered man with a sonorous voice and expansive gestures.

Well, she is at last beginning to enjoy herself. She has had only one glass of port and one of Chardonnay but she feels all at once as giddy as a sought-after debutante. She tells Yves she would have never recognized him had she happened to pass him on the street.

"What happened to all the hair ... to your beard?" she exclaims. "You look so ... so grown up!" She laughs, offering congratulations for all his success.

"Well, I finally got lucky," Yves says, achieving a look of genial modesty.

Acclaim seems to agree with him. Not for the first time, Kate observes that men who were not particularly attractive in their youth often fare better in middle age than their once handsome friends. Gaunt and rake-like in his twenties, Yves Letourneau is now elegantly slender, his skin still smooth, his abundant salt-and-pepper hair cut down to a fashionable length. Gone are the unkempt beard and wild hair, the red-rimmed eyes, the expression of perpetual rancour. Kate recalls how Suzanne used to nurse Yves' hangovers, running his baths, jumping up to fulfill his requests for water, cigarettes, coffee.

"Are you and Suzanne still together?" she asks. She has a sudden vision of herself and Suzanne trying to comfort each other after their boyfriends' arrests. Yves' improved appearance makes it hard to reconcile the old with the new.

It turns out that Yves and Suzanne parted soon after the October Crisis. He has been married for over twenty years to an Acadian woman who is in charge of the drama sector at the Québec Arts Council.

"I met her when I was still a poor struggling playwright living off arts grants." Yves' smile is complacent. He too looks at Kate's left hand.

"What about you? I see you're married?"

"Yes." She drops her gaze, but only for a moment. "I am. We've been living in Edmonton all these years, but ... well, I'm now thinking of moving back to Montreal." She swallows and falls silent.

"I?" Yves gives her a long, searching look.

"Maybe we ... I'm not sure yet. It's complicated," she adds, and drops her gaze. There is a moment's silence. Answering Yves' next question, Kate says she has a nineteen-year-old daughter who has just started at McGill, as well as a twenty-six-year-old son, living on the west coast

"*Incroyable!* To think we could both be grandparents, eh?" Yves shakes his head. He turns out to have three children of his own, one of them Megan's age. "The time is out of joint," he declaims, quoting Hamlet but voicing Kate's own thoughts on the subject.

"I was just listening to two philosophers back there," she says, motioning towards the window. "They were also discussing time. I'm not sure they were able to make much sense of it either." She laughs.

All this takes place across from the pale egg photograph on Antonia's wall; the wall once graced by Michel Beauregard's painting of the straw-hatted woman. Kate knows that, sooner or later, one of them will have to say something about Guillaume. It would be too awkward to keep skirting around the subject. Yves asks whether she ever got around to translating any books.

"No. No, I haven't." She shrugs. "Actually, I'm a photographer."

"A photographer! All you seemed to be interested in when I knew you was music and books. How in the world did you become a photographer?"

"It's a long story."

Antonia has come out of the kitchen, hugging an enormous salad bowl. It isn't that long a story, but Kate is, as usual, reluctant to say anything that might expose her as the sort of woman to whom things just happen; someone without volition. The sort of woman she secretly believes she is.

"Do you still play the flute?"

"As a matter of fact no. I gave that up years ago, but—"

"Another long story?"

"I guess!" Kate grins, declining to have her wineglass refilled. "I still love both music and books. I'm not *that* different from who I used to be."

"Well, I'm sure glad to hear that." Yves tweaks her nose, then places a light arm around her shoulders. "Come. I'd like you to meet my wife ... my wife and two of her Arts Council colleagues."

"Oh, your wife is here?" Kate pauses to place her empty glass on the polished sideboard.

"Upstairs," says Yves, his hand gently steering Kate towards the spiral staircase. "I left them in Antonia's guest room—far from the madding crowd." A silver tooth glints in the back of Yves' mouth. "I think you'll like them."

On her way back to the kitchen, Antonia has paused in her tracks for the briefest moment, exchanging looks with Yves. Glancing over her shoulder, Kate sees her twirl her hand in the air, gazing after the two of them with a small, enigmatic smile. It is a smile Kate is by now familiar with: Antonia's sphinx smile.

II

Yves' wife, Carole, has fleecy hair the colour of pumpkins, and a Julia Roberts smile, full of sparkling teeth and friendly intentions. Though not beautiful, she is the kind of woman people at parties tend to be drawn to, not only because of her bright hair and dazzling smile, but also her air of supreme confidence; the sort of woman, in other words, that Kate has always been a little envious of. Carole Trépanier wears chunky African jewellery, accentuating a rather flamboyant outfit in turquoise, magenta, orange. Kate thinks of a large, exotic, rather curious bird.

Carole is without a doubt the most striking person in Antonia's guest room, yet Kate's interest in her, and in her two male companions, evaporates as she finds herself being introduced to the Arts Council's literary officer, a woman named Nadine St. Onge. This second woman is not as instantly striking as Yves' wife, but Kate is nonetheless extremely struck by her. She would have to be blind not to notice the physical resemblance between herself and this gently smiling stranger.

The francophone woman is a little taller than Kate; her expressive eyes are a light shade of brown, emphasized, like Kate's, by dark, thickish eyebrows. Parted on the side, Nadine's hair flows down to her shoulders but hers too is dark and straight and rather thin, framing a pale, heart-shaped face. She looks far more like Kate's sister than does Heather, her twin. As Kate shakes hands, her eyes hold on to Nadine's for a moment. She sees her own surprise reflected in the Frenchwoman's eyes, but perhaps she imagines it? Imagines the resemblance even? Nadine is at least a decade younger.

A moment passes. Kate moves on to meet the man on Nadine's left, an elderly, stiff-backed Québecois writer, whose book Kate remembers enjoying as a university student. She smiles, sharing this memory with the author, then shifts her gaze to Nadine's husband; a tall, balding man dressed in a pullover and a dark corduroy blazer: the Québec Arts Council's music officer. Kate extends her hand mechanically and is about to offer the usual party greeting. The French words are on the tip of her tongue when something seems to snap in her brain, and everyone around her is suddenly stripped of colour. She turns towards Yves Letourneau like a woman coming out of a deep hypnotic spell. Her face is hot all the way down to bottom of her neck.

"*Bonsoir, Katherine.*" Nadine's bespectacled husband holds out his hand. He lets out a small, amused sound, gazing into Kate's face with his long-lashed, melancholy eyes. "Don't tell me you've forgotten me!" The man addressing her is Nadine St. Onge's husband, but the voice is Guillaume Beauregard's — a deep, melodious voice she would recognize anytime, anywhere, on this planet or any other.

Kate stands paralyzed for a moment whose precise duration she will never know. Breathing in, breathing out.

"No ... no, of course not." At last, she achieves a smile; her voice sounds pleasant and well modulated, but she feels the way she did many years ago while visiting Ottawa's Crazy Kitchen. She is a child in a weird amusement park, but the words that are careening through her brain are adult words; words recently encountered in a Canadian novel she borrowed from her daughter's bookshelf. *May you get what you want, and may it be what you meant.*

Just now, she doesn't know what she wants. She wants the room to stop spinning so she can say something both lucid and appropriate. Everyone, it seems to her, is watching them now, waiting for her to speak, to let go of Guillaume's hand.

She lets go at last. "What a nice surprise," she says with her brightest smile, speaking her very best French.

Guillaume stands smiling back. He says something in response, but Kate is unable to register any of it. She fails to absorb it because a cry of protest has become lodged halfway up her throat. Having let go of Guillaume's palm, she doesn't quite know what to do with her hands. Damp with sweat, they seem to be rising of their own accord, suspended in the air like the hands of a woman about to make some significant point, or maybe raise a camera up to eye level.

Her head goes on pounding. She is transfixed by the eyes behind the amber-framed spectacles. The eyes are still the colour of green olives or dry sage, but it is not their colour that holds Kate's attention. What holds her attention is what time has wrought. She studies the hooded, down-sloping eyelids, the pockets of fatigue underneath the eyes. A little magnified by the thick lenses, Guillaume's haunted eyes make her think of something ... what? The faces of Orthodox icons, perhaps, or El Greco's saints.

She stands smiling stiffly, aware of something Yves is saying; of other guests' bursts of laughter. Only she seems not to be laughing; she and Guillaume, who stands clutching the stem of his wineglass, gazing into her eyes.

Kate looks back at Guillaume in silence, taking in the deep grooves in the flesh bracketing his mouth, the balding crown, the rather mousy hair growing down in long-ish, curling strands. Perhaps it all takes only a moment or two, but she becomes aware of an odd sensation dilating her chest; odd yet familiar, since she invariably experiences it whenever she comes upon something she longs to capture with her camera lens.

Yes, the feeling is one she knows well by now, but it remains as mysterious to her as the deep stirrings brought on by autumn. If she were forced to put it into words, she would say that it feels like something between inspiration and liberation—no, not exactly liberation, but the prospect of it; like an awareness, during the agony of sexual intercourse, of the ultimate, glorious moment of perfect gratification.

But of course no one asks, and she never says it, or anything else, for that matter. Another breath-stopping moment goes by. Kate keeps on staring at the eloquent face before her; staring with an almost professional interest. For although her hands are empty, and though Antonia can be heard ringing her dinner bell, the sound Kate is most acutely aware of is that of an imaginary camera shutter softly going *click*.

And then again, over and over: *click, click, click*.

A great photograph, Eva, is about trying to capture shooting stars.

SIX

I

WHAT IS IT about the aftermath of a party—even a fairly successful party—that makes a small bubble of despair rise from a complacent core and cling to the roof of the mouth like congealing grease?

Kate remembers feeling something of the sort after the party she and Brad had given on the day of their 25th anniversary. Re-living it tonight, after a casual friend's birthday party, is not something she had expected to experience when she accepted Antonia Offe's invitation. On the other hand, everything about this day, this evening, would surely defy any reasonable person's expectations.

These thoughts are spinning through Kate's head as she moves about Antonia's living room. She has stayed behind after everyone had gone home, ostensibly to help with the clean-up. Antonia did her best to persuade Kate to accept Yves' offer of a lift home, pointing out it might not be easy to get a cab in this sort of weather. It was, in fact, because of the bad weather that she'd sent the two National Theatre School students home earlier than had been agreed on. But Kate insisted on helping out and, at length, Antonia capitulated.

"I guess you can always sleep in the guest room if

necessary," she said, then went upstairs to remove her contact lenses and get out of her party clothes.

Kate has no desire to spend the night at Antonia's, whatever the outdoor conditions. She is, just now, much more preoccupied with her own inner weather, which is undeniably stormy and which is not likely to ease up anytime soon; not unless she finds some way of relieving the pressure building up around her heart. Her heart has been beating erratically all evening, assailed by several muddled but pressing questions.

One of the questions is still gnawing at Kate and must be voiced as soon as she can trust herself to sound fair and coherent; to express what she feels without sliding into hysterical accusations. She is just sober enough to remember that drinking too much tends to bring out her dormant aggression.

She goes about stuffing leftovers into the garburator, throwing disposable plates into garbage bags. She hopes Antonia will not claim to be too tired to talk. She can hear her moving upstairs, taking her time. Kate wonders whether this is intended to avoid confrontation, but then there is silence and, eventually, the sound of a flushed toilet.

When Antonia comes back, she is once more wearing her yellow silk kimono. "Well, you've made it look a lot more manageable," she says, glancing about with appraising eyes. "I think I need a cup of coffee."

Kate looks up but offers no reply as she goes about putting the living room to rights. She had almost forgotten Antonia's strange, mismatched eyes. The eyes, she sees now, have lost some of their sparkle; they look more than a little droopy at this late hour, lined with fine red threads.

The network of wrinkles around the eyes appears more pronounced. Well, she is going on seventy, Kate says to herself; it is, by now, well past midnight.

Kate herself is not so much tired as edgy, clumsy. At some point, she lost track of the quantity of wine she had swilled during the buffet dinner. She knows she drank more than she is used to, and ate very little, finding one excuse or another to linger in the kitchen, grappling with her inner riot. Halfway through the buffet dinner, Antonia came into the kitchen for a bottle of wine and found Kate leaning against the sink, staring into an empty glass of water.

"So? What do you think of him?" Antonia asked in a stage whisper, over the hum of voices in the dining area, the explosion of distant laughter. Although they were unlikely to be overheard, the only response Kate could summon was a helpless movement involving her head, arms, shoulders; a gesture that, accompanied by a sigh, was meant to communicate the impossibility of answering the question in a few words, at that particular moment.

"We'll talk later," she whispered back, avoiding Antonia's eyes. She was still fighting the urge to make an excuse and leave the party, an impulse she resisted out of a drunken mulishness. She would not leave without having her say.

At length, Kate went back to the buffet table. She managed a bit of party talk, doing her best not to stare, not to weep, not to ask more than a few polite questions. Finally —finally—the food had been eaten, the presents opened, exclamations exchanged, and kisses bestowed in a flurry of goodbyes. Because of the poor weather, the reports of increasingly icy conditions, Antonia reluctantly agreed to open her presents right after dinner. By midnight, everyone was gone, leaving behind dirty paper plates and plastic wineglasses, and a heap of wrapping paper abandoned on the floor, around the spiral staircase.

Kate busies herself collecting this paper, thwarted by Otto's apparent determination to have the crackling heap stay where it is so he can keep treading through it, disappearing briefly under cover, then clambering back to peer out greenly, letting out an occasional hoarse protest.

Kate herself remains torn between the need to protest, and to flee. Like her childhood self, she wishes she could crawl under some warm blanket, shutting out everything but her own struggling heartbeat.

As this is not an option, she goes on collecting the remaining wineglasses while Antonia cleans the kitchen, putting leftovers away in the fridge, stacking the dishwasher. Next to one of the ivory sofas, Kate finds part of a silver earring; she finds a man's scarf just outside the coat closet, and, on one of the window-seat cushions, two small wine stains forming a red exclamation mark.

She picks up the meowing Otto and stands gazing out the window exactly as she had on her first visit. She looks down at the silent street, the glittering trees, the distant lights in the city below. The freezing rain has finally stopped but the wind keeps on blustering. It has blown off some of the contents of a curbside recycling basket. A newspaper keeps flapping against the trunk of the frozen mountain ash; a tin can rolls back and forth, colliding now and then with an empty bottle.

Kate observes all this with mild interest, overcome by an intense need to weep. The contours of her grief are not as yet clear, but as she turns away from the window, as her eyes come to rest on Antonia's combine painting, the spite in the sculpted faces seems to her more ferocious than ever; it intensifies the nausea tugging at the pit of her stomach. Another moment and she finds herself running towards the powder room, where she heaves and retches, arched over the toilet bowl. She is undeniably drunk. The room spins around her. She feels as if the ground were being swept out from under her feet.

"I'm all right," she says to Antonia, who has come to stand at the powder room door, making solicitous sounds. "Please go away ... I'll be out in just a minute."

As she straightens up, Kate sees a pack of cigarettes lying on top of the toilet tank; a red pack of du Mauriers along with a colourful book of matches from a local Spanish restaurant. Someone had obviously enjoyed a smoke while using the john, and then forgot the cigarettes. Could it have been Guillaume?

The Guillaume Kate knew had indeed smoked du Mauriers when they were both students but, as far as she can recall, he did not seem to be smoking during Antonia's party. For all she knows, he has given up smoking along with his altruistic fervour, his blazing musical ambitions. He was, he told her when they found themselves briefly alone, playing with an amateur chamber orchestra, but most of his time was now spent listening to others play, adjudicating grants to aspiring musicians. That sort of thing.

Guillaume had said all this in French, then laughed deprecatingly, somehow managing to cast an ironic light on his cushy bureaucrat's job, his nine-to-five schedule, his new home in leafy Nôtre-Dame-de-Grace.

He had apparently married late, but by now, he and Nadine have two teen-aged sons, as does Guillaume's younger brother. Making conversation, Kate found out that Michel is now married to a Flemish woman and lives in Belgium, where he is a moderately successful artist; that Jacques died of an overdose years ago, that Chantal got divorced after her kids left home and is now working as a lay nun.

The last bit about Guillaume's sister surprised Kate more than the news of Jacques' premature death.

"A nun!" she sputtered, staring at Guillaume.

"A sort of social worker, really, working with underprivileged kids in the east end."

Guillaume gave a familiar little shrug, gazing at Kate with an expression she couldn't quite fathom. His eyes seemed to be telling her that she was right; that the notion of backward-flowing time was pathetic, ridiculous.

A little later, it would occur to her that, despite their obvious differences, all four Beauregard children had been driven by equally passionate natures; that they had all been searching for something lofty to give their life meaning. For reasons she did not understand, Jacques Beauregard had lost his way, and Guillaume … well, Guillaume had become sensible, responsible, mature. She had sensed it instantly, the moment she recognized him up in Antonia's study, when the whole room had briefly gone black and white. When she experienced the longing to photograph Guillaume's aging face, it was partly from the familiar desire to transmute private pain into art, but also from a fervent need to trace any visible vestiges of the man she had spent so much of her life mourning.

And now here he was, trying to explain his sister's life-altering decision. And here she was, listening to him politely, making a gesture meant to hint at the vagaries of time.

After a while she said: "So Michel has given up his revolutionary activities?"

"Ah yes ... yes," Guillaume answered, chewing on a sushi roll. Somehow, they had come to stand together by the potted palm, plastic plates in their hands, directly in front of the wall where Michel's painting used to hang, all those years ago. Michel, said Guillaume, hates to be reminded of his political past. If she were to corner him at a dinner party, he would more than likely wriggle out by echoing Winston Churchill.

Kate stood blinking up at Guillaume. "Churchill?"

"Oh, you know—" Guillaume switched to English, essaying a British accent. "If you're not a revolutionary at eighteen you have no heart; if you're still one at forty, you have no head." He paused to pop a green olive into his mouth. "That's what he says whenever Chantal teases him." He smiled.

"Actually, that's not exactly what Churchill said—"

Kate was about to re-state the quotation when Nadine joined them, a glass of red wine between her fingers. She seemed as intrigued by Kate as Kate was by her. Had Guillaume told his wife about her? Kate found herself wondering.

But all she did was smile blandly. "Actually, Churchill was talking about Communists, not revolutionaries," she said.

"Did he? Yes, you're probably right." Guillaume chuckled. "Did he say anything about what happens to your memory once you reach a certain age?"

"I'm sure he meant to. He just kept forgetting," Nadine interjected.

They laughed in unison while, across the room, Yves picked up a smoked-salmon *canapé* and stared at them with an inscrutable expression. Kate glowered at him, then went on to voice the observation that, in Edmonton at least, the usual risqué party jokes had at some point given way to Alzheimer's humour.

"That's how you know your crowd's finally getting old," she said.

They all laughed again. Kate felt her face flush but congratulated herself on having managed to make a small contribution to party babble. She did not say that, although she had always been absent-minded, she had not experienced any memory loss whatsoever; that in some ways she almost wished she had. Wouldn't she be a more content woman if she could somehow efface the past and surrender to the present?

Yes, indeed.

The present finds Kate seated in Antonia's powder room, having pounced on the forgotten cigarettes with the glee of a starving vagrant stumbling across a fresh loaf of bread. The pack is nearly full and she has stashed it away in her bag, sitting down to smoke her first cigarette in five years.

She sits on Antonia's toilet, inhaling deeply, deeply, promising herself that she will have one more cigarette on the way home, then throw out the rest, or maybe give it to one of the panhandlers at the Metro station. The knowledge that she has the rest of the pack in her bag; that she'll be able to fall back on it should her jangled nerves fail to find relief, calms her down a bit, though she still feels that Antonia owes her some sort of explanation—maybe even an apology?

She stands up and throws the cigarette stub into the bowl. She flushes the toilet, watching the stub whirl in the churning water, and gradually disappear. She spins to face the door—is ready to go out—but at the last moment stops, turns, collapses onto the closed toilet lid, and buries her face in her hands, surrendering at last to her riotous grief.

II

"You did it deliberately, didn't you?"

The question is voiced after Kate has emerged, red eyed, from Antonia's powder room. Hearing her muffled sobs, Antonia had knocked and knocked on the washroom door, pleading with Kate to come out and talk to her. Speaking through the locked door, she sounded as solicitous as a mother, but Kate is determined not to let this come between her and the questions she has been rehearsing all evening. She is furious with Antonia for having overheard her weeping. When, at long last, she tosses out her bitter accusation, Antonia's expression wavers.

"Did what, exactly?" she asks. "Invite Guillaume to the party?" They are both back in the kitchen now, waiting for the fresh coffee to stop dripping.

"Yes." Kate stares for a moment, relishing her own loathing. "Why did you invite him ... invite both of us?" she demands at length. "You didn't even know Guillaume!"

"You're right. I didn't ... I guess I was curious."

"You were curious!"

"Well, of course I was." Antonia shrugs, reaching into the cupboard for two ceramic mugs. "Who wouldn't be, the way you went on and on about him?"

"You didn't think you should ask my permission?" *Permission* is not the right word, Kate realizes, but her mind is too jumbled for quick self-correction.

"*What?!*" Antonia gives an incredulous little laugh. "It was my party, Kate," she states with a tight little smile. "Anyway, it's not as if I'd actually planned the whole scenario, you know."

"Didn't you?" Kate frowns, accepting a mug of coffee.

"No! I happened to be speaking to Yves the day after you came to the stage rehearsal. He was calling to ask if they could bring a friend from Québec City. Marc Sévigny was coming to stay with them for the weekend and Yves wanted permission to bring him along. I told him Sévigny was welcome, but we—you and I—had just had our long chat in Chinatown and ... well, as I said, I *was* curious. I asked Yves if he was still in touch with Guillaume Beauregard."

Antonia's unruffled speech leaves Kate at a temporary loss for words. She raises her mug to her lips. "And then you just said to bring him along?"

"Yes! I'd left a message for Pauline Julien as well. I had no idea that she was so ill!" Antonia pauses for a sip of coffee. Her mismatched eyes unnerve Kate more than ever now—now that she's been made to feel unduly prickly. If only she could think more clearly.

"Did you tell Yves that you'd met me?" she asks after a moment. She may have had too much to drink, but the truth is she doesn't trust Antonia; never really trusted her, she reminds herself.

"Yes, but—"

"But you didn't tell him I would be at the party, did you?"

"No. He didn't ask." Antonia sets her mug down, briskly retying the belt on her silk kimono. Kate keeps on watching, brooding. She may be overwrought, but she can't let go of her suspicion that Antonia *is* acting. The reference to their dinner in Chinatown has tossed up the childhood story Antonia had told her on the way down; her admission that she had always been something of a prankster. Yet here she is now, sipping her coffee with a look that hovers between weary boredom and a sort of arch irony.

"I'm not sure I believe you," Kate says, as evenly as she can.

"You don't believe what, exactly?"

"I believe you were curious, I believe that part, but … I think you deliberately chose not to tell Yves you'd invited me."

"Why in the world would I do that?" Antonia demands. "You think knowing that you were coming would have stopped Yves from bringing Guillaume?" She lets out an unpleasant little laugh. "You don't know Yves very well, do you, my dear?" She detaches herself from the counter and takes a step towards the entrance. "Would you like to sit down?" she asks in a prim, hostess-y voice.

She stands waiting for an answer, while Kate, conscious of her protesting heart, shakes her head distractedly and goes on leaning against the counter. She is still trying to reconcile what her inner voice tells her with Antonia's efforts to make light of her own conduct. A moment goes by before she speaks again.

"Are you saying that Yves would have actually enjoyed

286 · IRENA KARAFILLY

the thought of my meeting Guillaume?" She looks hard into Antonia's face. "Is that what you're trying to tell me?"

"Oh, you bet he would have!" Antonia laughs. She takes another slow sip of coffee. "For all I know, he even guessed you'd be here after I asked him about Guillaume."

At this, Kate allows herself the tiniest of smiles. "Why? Because he knows you as well as you know him?" she ventures. She remembers that she never cared much for theatre people.

Antonia's hesitation lasts only a moment. She looks back at Kate, her lips forming a wry moue. "Are you trying to pick a fight with me, my dear? On my own birthday?"

"I'm trying to figure out whether you were simply thoughtless or ... kind of diabolical."

"Diabolical! I love it!" Antonia says, laughing. "I've been accused of many things in my life, but that's a new one!"

"Well?"

"Well what?"

"Oh, stop it, for chrissake! Do you think I'm stupid or something?"

"N-o," Antonia says. "I think you're unreasonably upset, though. I also think you're doing your best to take it out on me."

"Damn right I'm upset! But maybe you should stop posturing and ask yourself why?"

"Okay, why?"

"*Why?!*" Kate echoes, then falls abruptly silent. Antonia is jiggling the coffee in her mug and, inexplicably, Kate finds herself transfixed by this hand, with its silver rings, its splash of dark spots. It's a ridiculous thing, being stymied by the liver spots on an elderly woman's hand, but this is what happens. Kate surveys the kitchen, groping for her lost equanimity.

"Are you sure it's really me and not yourself you're mad at?" Antonia asks. "Is it possible you just can't accept that Guillaume ended up married to someone else?"

Kate looks into her coffee mug. There may be some malice behind Antonia's question, but she herself is too fair-minded to deny the possible truth in her suggestion.

"What did you expect?" Antonia goes on. "Did you want him to spend the rest of his life worshipping your memory, for God's sake?"

"No! No, I did not! If I seem discombobulated it's because I think—I'm pretty sure—that you derived some ... some perverse satisfaction from setting us up. That you did it for your own amusement!" She looks up at Antonia with open disgust.

Antonia sighs, closing her eyes for a long moment. "I'm not sure I understand what you mean," she says, showing signs of strain.

"I think you do," Kate insists. "I—"

"*I* think," Antonia says with sudden decisiveness, "it's time we went to bed. Would you like to crash in the guest room, or shall I try to call you a cab?" She places a hand on Kate's arm, trying to steer her out of the narrow kitchen. "I'm sure you'll see everything differently in—"

"Don't patronize me, Antonia!" Kate shakes off Antonia's hand and steps back, her eyes blazing.

"I'm not patronizing you. I just think you could probably use some sleep right now. I know I could," Antonia adds, trying for a smile.

"Oh!" Kate says, a vision of the middle-aged Guillaume

floating across her brain. "You think you're so clever, don't you? You think you can just keep pressing buttons and wait to see what will happen, don't you?"

"Well, it seems I've pressed all the wrong buttons tonight," Antonia says. She is leaning against the stainless steel fridge now, her arms folded in stagey forbearance.

"Maybe you did. Didn't it occur to you that I—not only I, but all three of us—might find your clever *mise-en-scène* more than a little painful?"

"Oh, for God's sake! Why must you be so intense all the time?" Antonia flexes her brow. "Try to lighten up a little, my dear—see the humorous side of a situation!"

This is not the first time Kate has been accused of being too intense, but the knowledge does nothing to placate her nerves. She stands appraising Antonia's face. "You thought it might be *funny?*"

"To tell you the truth, I didn't give it a whole lot of thought. It was just an impulse, maybe even a stupid impulse, but I certainly didn't mean to hurt anyone."

Kate turns around and refills her mug, then stands sipping the hot liquid, pondering Antonia's words. The words do have a ring of truth, she concedes to herself.

"I know I'm not the world's most thoughtful person," Antonia says, "but ... well, to be honest, *had* I stopped to think about it, I might have actually decided it would be good for you."

"Good for me?"

"Yes, indeed! I mean, if that's what was needed to get you to stop obsessing over the past."

"Obsessing," Kate repeats, like a foreigner sounding out an unfamiliar word.

"What, you don't think you were being obsessive? Give me a break, my dear. You're almost fifty and still hung up on an affair you had in ..." She trails off here, having become aware of the fresh tears spilling out of Kate's eyes. "Oh!" She puffs up her withered cheeks, wearily theatrical. "I knew you should have gone home with the others. I knew it!" She raises a hand and runs it through her mass of silver curls.

Kate is silent. She has nothing left to say.

"Okay, tell me why you're crying now," says Antonia in a forbearing tone. "Don't *you* think it was good for you to see him as he is? You ... you've mythologized your Guillaume over the years, my dear. Isn't it just as well that you've seen he's flesh and blood like the rest of us, going bald, getting—"

"Oh!" All at once Kate has had enough. "You don't even know him ... you hardly know me. What qualifies you to judge what's good for—?"

Antonia does not let her finish. "Well ... someone apparently had to," she says calmly, handing Kate a box of Kleenex.

Kate stands blowing her nose, silent tears wetting her cheeks. After a moment, Antonia heaves a sigh, repeating her suggestion that they hit the sack. For the second time, she takes hold of Kate's arm.

"Come," she says lightly; she is about to add something but her touch, accompanied by her supercilious tone, makes something snap inside Kate. One way or another, Antonia has managed to whitewash not only her actions but even her own motives.

"Who do you think you are? God?" she spits out, filled

with a physical aversion at the sensation of Antonia's dry fingers on her own skin. "I'm a grown woman!" She wrenches her arm away, this time so violently that some of the hot liquid comes flying out of the ceramic mug, landing on Antonia's exposed forearm.

"Ahhh!" Antonia cries, her mouth a worm of pain. Scalded, she lets go of Kate's arm, and simultaneously does a surprising thing—or perhaps not so surprising, given her suppressed irritation in the past half hour: She reacts physically to the flash of pain. Her eyes flaring, she raises her right hand and slaps Kate's cheek. And then she stops, her mouth twitching, as Kate reaches out and grabs Antonia's withdrawing wrist.

"You bitch! You horrible, horrible old woman!" she hisses, fresh loathing sweeping her heart. Her head is spinning again. All evening, she'd fought the urge to slap Antonia; had longed to do so in front of her guests, then walk out with her head held high, as proud as an avenged queen in some ancient stage play.

But the grim drama taking place in Antonia's kitchen has unfolded without any witnesses, without any script. About to storm out of the kitchen, out of the hateful condo, Kate realizes that the post-party drama has suddenly gone horribly awry. Antonia, who has been left momentarily speechless, seems to have gone limp, her features contorting, as if to suppress pain or outrage. Kate observes all this through the blur of her own welling tears. Blinking, she sees Antonia stagger back a little, looking stunned. A kind of shudder seems to run through her bony frame, and then, before Kate can reach her, she crumples down, thudding onto the floor.

"Call ... call an ambulance," she croaks.

Kate freezes for the briefest moment, feeling something explode in the pit of her stomach. There is a roar in her ears as she stumbles out to call an ambulance.

An ambulance! She punches 9-1-1 but gets a recorded message instructing her to hold on.

She holds on, then hangs up and calls information, trying to get an emergency number, only to be told that all emergency calls are now channelled through 9-1-1. She should hold on until someone answers.

She calls 9-1-1 again. She dials, and holds on, flooded with rising horror. It occurs to her that the telephone lines must be jammed because of road accidents caused by the freezing rain. She hangs up once more and dials the number on the Diamond Taxi sticker glued to Antonia's telephone.

There is no answer. She suspects none of the cab companies will bother answering tonight.

It comes to her then that the Montreal General Hospital is just up the street, on the corner of Côte-des-Neiges and Pine. Perhaps she should run down and try to flag down a taxi, or just some passing driver who might be willing to stop and transport Antonia to the hospital. Surely someone would stop?

She begins to pray.

She prays as she heads for the door, her blood throbbing, her mouth filled with panic. She gallops downstairs, but running to the corner is out of the question. Even simple walking requires the utmost caution; it demands that she firmly plant one foot on the ice-coated sidewalk before bringing the other foot forward. The temperature has dropped, freezing everything in sight, but the municipal trucks have yet to arrive with their salt and gravel. She is wearing her pointy party shoes, with their elegant little heels. She is not wearing a coat or scarf; did not even think of grabbing them in passing, but now registers the winter chill assaulting her cringing body. She is dimly aware of the colourless moon drifting through tattered clouds, the crystalline glitter of trees, of icicles hanging from eaves and wires.

She arrives at the corner, hearing a siren wail somewhere in the distance. A snapped tree branch lies on the icy sidewalk. A stray cat yowls in a nearby alley.

There are no taxis. There is, in fact, little traffic on this normally bustling road. The few cars still out on the street are crawling downhill with the sluggishness of tanks retreating from a battlefield. None of them stops for her, though she stands on a brightly lit corner, frantically waving her arms, shouting at the top of her voice. She remembers there is a police station only three blocks down, but the hill leading to it is now a treacherous, ice-blanketed slope, possibly negotiable on a pair of skates.

Kate is still trying to hail one of the passing cars when she realizes that the drivers in the descending vehicles might have trouble stopping at that particular juncture. They seem, moreover, distracted by a smashed car abandoned on the east side of the street. The spot where she stands, on the corner of Selkirk Avenue, is the point at which the steep Côte-des-Neiges Road forks into Guy and St. Matthew streets, the former running one way north, the latter one way south. There is a traffic island in the middle of the sloping road, and, very gingerly, her temples pounding, Kate starts to inch her way towards this island. She thinks she might have a better chance of getting help from the ascending traffic.

A few minutes fly by. Reaching the icy island, Kate spots a Radio Canada cruiser crawling up from Sherbrooke Street. She tries to flag it down, but has arrived at the curb a moment too late.

Too late.

The two words rattle through her brain as she begins to sob, casting desperate glances up and down the deserted sidewalks. Though the night's chill has by now penetrated her marrow, every one of her pores seems to be seeping sweat. The media car has halted farther up on Côte-des-Neiges Road. Has the driver spotted her after all?

For a moment, Kate thinks he must have. She sees a man climb out of the passenger seat and pause, a little unsteady, on the distant sidewalk, photographing the wrecked car below. He shoots it from several angles, oblivious to Kate's frenzied efforts to capture his attention.

And then, all at once, he looks up from his camera and seems to register her presence. He may or may not have heard her shouts, but watches her for a moment, standing alone on the frozen traffic island, her arms wildly flailing, her dark hair blowing across her face. The wind has been steadily rising. The stranger hesitates. When he finally starts down the street towards her, Kate closes her eyes in sheer relief and stands hugging herself, running her hands up and down her arms.

All this takes barely a minute, but when she opens her eyes again, Kate realizes that the reporter is photographing *her*, even as he keeps inching down in her direction. Her body is now shaking from head to foot. She has a sudden vision of herself as the solitary figure in Edvard Munch's *The Scream*. Across the street, an ice-thickened wire snaps and comes crashing down, sending splinters of frozen rain flying onto the sidewalk.

The reporter acknowledges her with a quick gesture, so Kate motions towards Selkirk and takes a few cautious steps forward. She pauses then, glancing back over her shoulder, but all she sees is the reporter's darkly-clad back. He has his cell phone out and is directing his driver to turn around and come down again. But Kate has no way of knowing this. She thinks he must have changed his mind; that it's too slippery and he has decided to head back to the safety of the parked cruiser.

She starts waving again, shouting hoarsely, until the reporter turns to face her. He signals once more but, almost at once, raises his camera. He has, it seems, decided to snap her again, from this new vantage point. Before he can do so, however, the reporter slips on the ice and comes tumbling down on the traffic island. He lands right on his butt and, despite the growing tightness in her chest, Kate experiences a moment of pure glee. If she had her own camera now, she would pay him back, sitting there on the frozen grass with that dazed look on his face!

The reporter is no youngster. As he scrambles to his feet, it becomes apparent that the fall has done something to his leg. He limps a little as he resumes plodding down, carefully examining his camera, no doubt checking for possible damage.

God, how she hates him—hates him! She can afford to, now that she knows help is on the way. The media cruiser has come around and is slowing down as Kate ventures to cross the slippery road, gesturing straight ahead. Her teeth chattering, she shouts out that there is an emergency; an elderly woman has had a stroke or a heart attack just around the corner. She needs to be taken to Emergency.

The Radio Canada driver has found a parking spot on Selkirk. The reporter clambers out and waits for his colleague to come around so they can lean on each other. It is one of those rare nights when a street looks utterly deserted, as if all its inhabitants have fled some obscure calamity. Kate has by now arrived at Antonia's entrance. The sidewalk is a sheet of ice glittering in the moonlight. She is too far to understand what the two media men are saying, but she hears them laugh as they make their way, and the sound sends a violent impulse through her frozen bones.

The fall has split the back of the reporter's pants. As the men approach, she hears something about occupational hazards; hears them cackle as they reach the sidewalk. The reporter is a heavyset man wearing an expression fixed between scepticism and cockiness. Kate does not thank him. She meets his probing eyes but does not say a word. Shivering from head to foot, she spins and leads the way upstairs. The reporter must have somehow managed to get through to the hospital on his cell phone; an ambulance arrives just as Kate has stopped at Antonia's kitchen.

They all step aside, watching grimly as the two medics lift Antonia's inert body from the tiled floor and place her on a gurney. It is all done more or less in silence, with remarkable speed. Kate sees Antonia's cat peek from under the dining table, then vanish back into the shadows.

Ready to head downstairs, the medics are tightening

the gurney's straps when Antonia opens her eyes and looks about, blinking like a startled owl.

"Oh!" she says and closes her eyes again with a heavy sigh. And then, more softly, "Oh, no."

The reporter records the moment, shuffling behind the medics as they carry the gurney down the long flight of stairs. Rooted to the threshold, Kate weighs her options, wiggling her stiffened toes. She has no choice now but to wait for morning so she can lock up and find a neighbour with whom to leave Antonia's keys. It is, in any case, still too icy to venture out in search of a cab. Every now and then, there is the slithering sound of a passing car, but for the most part, all night life seems to have come to a halt.

Antonia keeps her home well heated but, unable to stop her shivering, Kate wriggles into her coat and winds her scarf around her exposed neck. She stands by the bay window, looking down as the gurney is briskly slid into the back of the ambulance. She is still trembling but cannot bring herself to stop watching. The doors are shut with a muffled bang. The medics jump in while the reporter and driver shuffle back towards the parked cruiser.

The older man still walks with a slight limp. Just before he gets into the car, he turns to glance at Antonia's entrance, aims his camera, and takes a final shot of Kate outlined in the bay window. Kate shrinks back but it is too late. The reporter grins, raising a triumphant thumb as the ambulance takes off, its siren piercing the quiet of the night.

It begins to rain again. Alone in the dimly-lit room, Kate collapses onto the window seat and is still there, head cradled between her hands, when Otto emerges from his hiding place and leaps into her lap. The cat purrs and purrs but fails to offer comfort. The very walls in Antonia's living room seem to gaze down with silent reproach. It occurs to Kate she should call her daughter but it is by now going on three a.m. and Megan is sure to be sleeping. Kate has no choice but to wait, though she is finally ready to keep the promise she made to her daughter during the recent bout with the flu. It is two hours earlier in Edmonton; Brad, too, is likely to be in bed. Kate keeps blowing her nose, tissue after tissue. She wants to speak to her husband. She doesn't want to wake him. If only she, too, could sleep!

She can neither sleep nor sort out her mental muddle. She goes on hugging Otto, watching the rain pummel the frozen sidewalks, the closely parked cars, like a row of some forlorn creatures cowering under the onslaught. Somewhere on Sherbrooke Street, another siren blares, but soon the sound dies down and there is nothing to be heard except the cat's purr and radiator's hum, and, beyond the shivering window, the steady lashing of the rain. There is something punitive about this relentless downpour, or so it seems to Kate as she sits staring out the spotted window, hand absently stroking the cat's warm fur. She will never be warm enough again. She will never come back to Selkirk Avenue. Something within her has begun to ebb away and will not be arrested.

Once more Kate thinks of calling her husband, then begins to weep all over again, sending an incoherent prayer to a God she does not believe in. The storm gains momentum, pelting the frozen street, while the rest of the city —the entire blurred universe—seems to hold its breath, as if waiting for some divine power to wash everything away and make it new again.

Acknowledgements

Being only an amateur photographer, I am grateful for the work of several thoughtful professionals, some of whose insights I have shamelessly stolen for my fictional character. My thanks to Ansel Adams, Susan Sontag, Henri Cartier-Bresson, Roland Barthes, Katie Roiphe, Nan Goldin, Kowtham Kumar K, Robert Goddard, and Guy Le Querrec.

For their interest and early encouragement, I am indebted to Clark Blaise, the late Nina Bawden, Stephen Vizinczey, Bill Weintraub, Sheila Crossey, Anne Henderson, Jane Juska, and Barbara Lewis, without whose support this book might still be languishing in a drawer. I have been fortunate enough to have feedback from several other readers, whose comments have made *The House On Selkirk Avenue* a better novel. I am grateful to Sheila Fischman and Don Winkler, Michael Mirolla, and, last but not least, Kenneth Radu of DC Books.

Finally, many thanks to Robin Spry whose NFB film *ACTION: The October Crisis of 1970* helped me flesh out the historical chapters; and to my daughter, Ranya Karafilly, for her unflagging support and beautiful book jacket.